"SULU, EVASIVE," SNAPPED KIRK.

He watched the Klingon ship *Hakkarl* heel wildly across the screen as the *Enterprise* hit a savage combination break of yaw, roll and pitch all at the same time. It worked. *Hakkarl*'s incoming fire seared under and through where they had been less than a second before.

But any satisfaction generated by that evasion was squashed by the way the Klingon snapped around in pursuit.

Whatever impossible maneuver Sulu attempted, *Hakkarl* matched and exceeded.

Spock looked up from a monitor with a grave expression on his face. "Captain," he said. "There has been a critical overload in the shields, total failure will occur in fifty-seven seconds, unless we are given respite from this constant battering."

In other words, Kirk thought, *do something. Or we're all dead.*

Look for STAR TREK Fiction from Pocket Books

Star Trek: The Original Series

Final Frontier

Strangers from the Sky

Enterprise

Star Trek IV:
  The Voyage Home

Star Trek V:
  The Final Frontier

Spock's World

#1 *Star Trek:*
  The Motion Picture

#2 *The Entropy Effect*

#3 *The Klingon Gambit*

#4 *The Covenant of the Crown*

#5 *The Prometheus Design*

#6 *The Abode of Life*

#7 *Star Trek II:*
  The Wrath of Khan

#8 *Black Fire*

#9 *Triangle*

#10 *Web of the Romulans*

#11 *Yesterday's Son*

#12 *Mutiny on the Enterprise*

#13 *The Wounded Sky*

#14 *The Trellisane Confrontation*

#15 *Corona*

#16 *The Final Reflection*

#17 *Star Trek III:*
  The Search for Spock

#18 *My Enemy, My Ally*

#19 *The Tears of the Singers*

#20 *The Vulcan Academy Murders*

#21 *Uhura's Song*

#22 *Shadow Lord*

#23 *Ishmael*

#24 *Killing Time*

#25 *Dwellers in the Crucible*

#26 *Pawns and Symbols*

#27 *Mindshadow*

#28 *Crisis on Centaurus*

#29 *Dreadnought!*

#30 *Demons*

#31 *Battlestations!*

#32 *Chain of Attack*

#33 *Deep Domain*

#34 *Dreams of the Raven*

#35 *The Romulan Way*

#36 *How Much for Just the Planet?*

#37 *Bloodthirst*

#38 *The IDIC Epidemic*

#39 *Time for Yesterday*

#40 *Timetrap*

#41 *The Three-Minute Universe*

#42 *Memory Prime*

#43 *The Final Nexus*

#44 *Vulcan's Glory*

#45 *Double, Double*

#46 *The Cry of the Onlies*

#47 *The Kobayashi Maru*

#48 *Rules of Engagement*

Star Trek: The Next Generation

Encounter at Farpoint

#1 *Ghost Ship*

#2 *The Peacekeepers*

#3 *The Children of Hamlin*

#4 *Survivors*

#5 *Strike Zone*

#6 *Power Hungry*

#7 *Masks*

#8 *The Captain's Honor*

#9 *A Call to Darkness*

#10 *A Rock and a Hard Place*

STAR TREK®

RULES OF ENGAGEMENT

PETER MORWOOD

POCKET BOOKS

New York   London   Toronto   Sydney   Tokyo   Singapore

An *Original* Publication of POCKET BOOKS

POCKET BOOKS, a division of Simon & Schuster Inc.
1230 Avenue of the Americas, New York, NY 10020

This book is published by Pocket Books, a division of
Simon & Schuster Inc., under exclusive license from
Paramount Pictures.

ISBN: 0-671-66129-9

First Pocket Books printing February 1990

10 9 8 7 6 5 4 3 2 1

POCKET and colophon are registered trademarks of
Simon & Schuster Inc.

Printed in the U.S.A.

This book is dedicated to
The Miami Cruisers
and
The Toronto Celebrants
and to walk-on players everywhere

Historian's Note

This adventure takes place sometime between the events chronicled in *Star Trek: The Motion Picture* and those related in *Star Trek II: The Wrath of Khan*. Readers may wish to consult those two movies, as well as the television episode "Errand of Mercy," as referents.

Chapter One

To: Morrow, Randolph H., Admiral, Chief of Staff (Operations), Starfleet Command. From: James T. Kirk, Captain, NCC-1701 U.S.S. *Enterprise,* inbound Star Base 12. Subject: Border zone 3-39, with special attention to Organian influence, if any. Body: Sir, I am pleased to report at the end of this present tour of duty that the *Enterprise* has completed a full exploratory patrol of the above sector without incident. I can advise Starfleet that although we were scanned by Klingon vessels on three (3) occasions [3/72-5.3, -5.83, -5.91 refer], at no time was any overt or covert hostile maneuver or activity directed at this ship and that as a consequence of this atypical Klingon reluctance to undertake offensive action, this sector may presently be regarded as one of the Organian Treaty Zones, with all policing and protection appertaining thereto. With regard to the information received by Fleet Command (ref: dispatch SFC/P/ 2624301 dated SD 2107.16) it is my opinion that the Organian Peace Treaty is being honorably maintained. End.

Captain's personal log, stardate 2213.5:
It appears that, whether through Organian or some other influence, such as Klingon Imperial policy, this particular area of the frontier corridor is at peace. The *Enterprise* is on a heading away from sector 3-39 and on course for Star

Base 12, where her crew will be able to clear some of their accumulated shore leave and enjoy the period of R&R to which they are entitled. This may involve pulling rank, but in this instance I regard such an act as being in a good cause. This last mission has turned out to be both nerve-wracking and boring. However, there are more relaxing places to be bored than the Klingon Neutral Zone. Unfortunately, there is no way to tell how actively the Organians will enforce their treaty without an actual outbreak of hostilities. No comment needed about that. End entry.

THE WORDING of both dispatch and log entry seemed fine, but James T. Kirk looked carefully at both for one final time before committing one to a transmission chip and the other to secure storage. This mission had initially been a simple one involving astrography charting and stellar analysis. However, proximity to the Neutral Zone had given the mission a flavor of espionage, which made Kirk distinctly uncomfortable. He had felt the same way and for the same reason on several occasions in the past; the long-ago mission into Romulan space to "acquire" a cloaking device was one instance that kept coming back to mind. It had been necessary and even vital to restore the balance of power, but espionage and intelligence missions invariably left a bad taste in his mouth afterward, and that one's flavor had been particularly nasty. A bit like the past three months along the patrol corridor of debated space that separated the Federation from the Klingon Empire. Astrography, maybe; but the Klingons never took kindly to exploration in what they regarded as their own backyard. They called it spying and reacted accordingly. And since there were no recorded instances of Organian enforcement of their treaty restrictions in this sector, there was always that niggling suspicion that maybe they didn't enforce, at least not here, and when the Klingons found out about it . . .

Well, apparently the Organians did enforce the treaty. Or the Klingons hadn't found out that they didn't, which wasn't quite the same thing. At least nobody had tried to blow anyone else to plasma. One more mission successfully concluded. Home, James, and don't spare the horses. Kirk smiled thinly at the notion. Home, in this instance, would be Star Base 12, and the horses were crystalline dilithium. At least James remained more or less the same. He stood up, pulled on his tunic, and then, as the desk-mount communicator chirped, made a sound that might have been a little grunt and sat down again. "Screen on," he said.

"All finished, Jim?" Dr. McCoy grinned at him and Jim repeated the little grunt, knowing what was coming next. *"One grunt for yes and two grunts for no."* The chief medical officer was evidently in a fine mood, no different from any other member of the crew, now that the Klingons and the boredom and the possibility of unpleasantness were being left farther behind with every second that passed. One bit of unpleasantness, however, remained to be dealt with.

"Yes, Bones, I'm all through. Just the rest of the paperwork to deal with, and then—"

"Then, Captain, I'll expect you in sickbay in ten minutes for that full checkup you've been avoiding. You're already two weeks overdue, and you're holding up our schedule down here."

James T. Kirk rolled his eyes, but with McCoy watching from the screen with that knowing little smile on his face, it was beneath Kirk's dignity to rummage for any more excuses. "Make it fifteen minutes?"

"Fifteen. McCoy out."

The screen went blank, and Kirk let out the groan he had been repressing. Flag rank, years in the center seat, multiple decorations, commendations, and mentions in dispatches and he *still* hated medical examinations with the passion that others reserved for toothaches and taxes. Jim grinned a tight little grin that any dentist would have recognized, never mind Fleet medics with specializations in psychiatry, and looked at the desktop with its controlled clutter of pad screens and report-data chips. Just this once he wished there was some real paperwork—on actual paper that could be scrunched up and flung vigorously into a real metal wastebasket with a real and very satisfying thunk. He hadn't been able to spare the time to do anything but captain the ship and oversee the crew members who were collating the mass of data that always accumulated when a Federation vessel ventured anywhere near hostile space, and his inactivity showed. Especially around his waist. McCoy would have words with him about that.

Kirk moved a few things, straightened edges, shifted items from one place to another—but he didn't clear the desk. He had come to regard that as unlucky. An omen, perhaps, of an extended shore leave—like the last one, two and a half years behind a desk console as chief of Starfleet Operations—or a reminder of Fleet Admiral Nogura's ruthlessly clear desktop. His last serious visit to Nogura's office had lasted no longer than the three minutes he had anticipated. That had been long enough for him get his ship back. Keeping it, and staying fit enough to keep it, was his business now.

"Heart, respiration, blood pressure, reflexes—they're all fine, Jim. Of course, you're a little over-

4

weight, but you don't need me to tell you that. Too much time sitting in the captain's chair and not enough watching out for the captain's health." McCoy glanced a final time at the readouts, then switched off the analysis unit. "You're off duty, I presume?"

"Since an hour ago. I'm working on my own time."

"Me, too. Bringing my schedule up to date." Bones grinned and opened the drinks cabinet that—with his own brand of sympathy or sarcasm, as required—was as much a tool of his profession as any number of anabolic protoplasers. "'Take a little wine, for your stomach's sake and your other infirmities.' Not so often, in your case, but when they arrive they're beauties and you hate them."

"I don't like to be sick."

"Quite so. Romulan ale?"

"Kill or cure, eh? I thought you mentioned wine, not illegal substances."

"I merely quoted an authority for my prescription. And this is purely medicinal. Here you are."

Jim sat down at McCoy's desk and eyed the glass warily as he took it. Its contents were the same rich, clear blue as a gem-quality sapphire and looked beguilingly innocent. He knew about Romulan ale and how deceptive that innocent look could be. There were any number of drinks that seemed as harmless as distilled water . . . though none of them, he reflected wryly as the blue ruin scorched its way down his throat, were quite as murderous.

"Feeling better?"

"'Better' is not how I'd put it, but yes. I think." Jim got to his feet, put the glass down very gently, as if it might explode, and picked up his uniform tunic. "I'll be in Rec One. I want to see how the crew's doing, now that we don't have Klingons breathing down our necks."

"Sensible idea. I could make a good diagnostic psychiatrist out of you, Jim."

"I've already got a job, Bones. Don't bother." He pulled on his tunic and glanced back at McCoy as he walked out the door. "I'm a starship captain, remember?"

Rec Deck One was in its usual state—noisy and full of off-duty crew members enjoying their first truly tension-free time off since mission's end. Kirk paused just inside the doorway, unnoticed as yet, and cast a near-paternal eye over his crew. It was a feeling that came over him now and again, more and more often as he grew older and the new crew members became younger with every fresh posting from the Academy. There were those, of course, who were unable to provoke the captain's fatherly interest simply by their fresh-faced youth. It was difficult, for instance, to look at a Sulamid ensign or an Eyren or Lieutenant Naraht and say which particular section qualified as the "face," much less whether its complexion might be called fresh. Craggy, perhaps, in Naraht's case. Now, *there* was one crew member who could manage a stony poker face with no effort at all.

Of course there was a game of poker going on. Three, in fact. And four games of chess, including one of the interestingly explosive 4D variety that was reaching a flashily apocalyptic endgame even as he watched. The cheerful computer-generated phut-flash of pieces annihilating one another didn't completely drown out someone's voice saying "Check"—another popping flash of light as punctuation—"and mate," with the sort of enormous satisfaction that usually accompanied credits changing hands. Heedless of such nominally intellectual pursuits, the usual mixed bag of people had gathered in the largest conversation pit and were indulging in a noisy sing-along that included all of the keys of Z and several contrapuntal *a cappella* variations. They were always at least a semitone off pitch as they chased their theme up and down what had to be a sliding scale. The lyrics—which, given the circumstances, were not surprisingly something scurrilous about Klingons—were of a piece with the melody—only worse.

That sort of reaction was almost a standard response to the end of a duty tour near any of the Neutral Zones, with the butt of the humor shifting from Romulan to Klingon as occasion demanded. The same response was manifested in the games played in both the main and the repeater holo tanks. Before and during the mission, Jim had seen games based on the historic dramas of a dozen cultures; computer generated artwork ranging from Terran Post-Impressionist to Vercingetorig architectural design, which also had a certain Post-Impressionist look to it; and some of the more humorous games held in the *Enterprise* data-storage facilities. But now that the mission was over . . .

He didn't need to move from where he was lounging quietly by the door to know what was being played this time. The sounds of cheering, jeering, explosions, and music told him all he needed to know.

This particular game had started life as a sober, serious and very businesslike Andorian-designed simulator program for helm training on their little atmosphere-capable customs cutters. Its cartographically correct land- and starscape subsystems had formed a pleasant evening's relaxation for anyone aboard the *Enterprise* who wanted to be in full control of a small ship every once in a while. And then somebody—Kirk suspected the Sulu-Chekov team—had put a word in Harb Tanzer's ear and come up with

7

another optional subsystem that had nothing to do with landscapes.

Instead of In-Flight Training, Tri-D Simulation #22715.33—its earlier dryly descriptive title—the game had become as screechily noisy as any of the old-style video arcade games and was now known only as Space Cadet. It was as realistic as careful programming could make it, even though the design criteria for every ship it featured had been stretched to, and once or twice beyond, all the presently accepted limits. Sulu had done the same thing once before, with his notorious and never beaten 3.0 version of Simulated Sublight Maneuvers for Deep-Exploration Starships. But recently he had cross-linked the two games and started to tweak all of the Klingon and Romulan ship capabilities toward optimum for each vessel's class, and as a result, Space Cadet was fast becoming known as the Most Evil Game in the Known Universe.

There were five Klingon ships in the tank right now; they were engaged in confused, confusing, and spectacularly messy combat against a Federation fleet of twelve. All seventeen vessels were performing exactly as their full-size counterparts would have done. For the sake of fairness the enemy ships wore only the plain gray-blue of the Klingon Navy rather than the jazzy yellow and black warp nacelles sported by Sulu's enhanced designs. Beyond that, realism took a holiday, for instead of shipboard quiet or the absolute silence of space, the holo cube provided—at players' discretion, naturally—thrilling music, gunfire, and an abundance of main-drive sound effects.

"Yes, Captain, they're at it again. Coffee?" Harb Tanzer had a cup in each hand. He held one out to Jim without taking his eyes off the performance of the twelve crewmembers who "flew" against far from the worst that the master games computer could throw at them.

"Thanks, Mr. Tanzer." Jim took the coffee gratefully; with luck, its caffeine would do something to offset the effects of Romulan ale on an empty stomach. "Looks as if you're being kept busy down here."

The chief of recreation wiggled the flat of his free hand in a yes-no-maybe gesture. "The Rec facilities are busy, but I've had an easy time of it. Most of them know exactly how they want to spend their time without needing me to tell them how. Like that, for instance."

Lieutenant Athende from Maintenance executed a neat firing pass, producing the first big jump in the game's score tally. The maneuver was greeted with cheers and a quick and dirty rendition of a fanfare. Coiling four of its tentacles in a gesture of pleased excitement, the Sulamid twiddled its console pad with three of the remaining tentacles and sent its ship into a flashy victory roll. One of the Klingon vessels responded like a shark in bloodied water; it whipped around in a turn tight enough to set off inertia-compensation warnings aboard any ship flown, then fired a bracketing salvo of disrupter bolts from its forward batteries. Athende forgot all about being pleased with itself and began concentrating again on staying un-blown-up.

The Klingon's brother-ships reacted to Athende's first strike by following their consort into a right-echelon formation that brought all of their forward weapons to bear on the Sulamid's ship. "Uh-oh," said Jim under his breath as the Klingons locked into firing position, then laughed aloud as Athende directed its ship into a simultaneous pitch and yaw that not only took it out of the direct line of fire but left the rightmost Klingon vessel on a collision course with one of its own consorts. As the entire Klingon formation broke every which way, the halo tank's voder cried "Hurrah!" in a tone that could only be described as sarcastic, then produced another of those brassy fanfares that sounded like a jazz trumpet full of molasses.

"The music was your idea, I presume?" said Jim as the horrid echoes died away.

Harb smiled. "The simulator was fine, but I thought the game version lacked something."

"Like razzing the players when they score a point?"

"Captain, just wait till someone loses. Oh, it can produce more subtle music if that's what they want. This bunch doesn't."

Right then there was a small but impressive explosion from the games tank, where two of the other Federation pilots had plainly not been watching where they were going and had rammed first each other and then the second Klingon cruiser at a game speed of $.73c$. This time the voder played the first ten notes of Haydn's Funeral March at four times proper speed and finished with a flatulent chuckle.

Jim cleared his throat and looked at Harb, whose face was carefully devoid of expression except where the laugh lines around his eyes made their telltale crinkles. "Lieutenant Tanzer," said the captain, sounding like a man who was choosing his words with care, "you are, without a doubt, sick."

"Why, thank you, sir. I'll keep up the good work." He might have said more, but right then there was another fairly rude noise, this time not from the games tank. It came from the ambient-sound system of the holography stage. "Good," said Harb, sounding relieved. "He's got it working at last."

"Uh, Lieutenant, is this something I should be warned about?"

"No, sir, it's just more of Mr. Freeman's image-processing work. You remember the archived two-

D material that he started rechanneling a while back?"

"He's still at it? I was under the impression it was up and running. What's the problem?"

"Well . . ." Harb took a reviving swallow of his coffee. "Jerry told me the image-enhancement and data-reprocessing chips have had a little trouble at the base scan level. They refuse to read anything but standard-format tapes."

"So? Everybody in the Federation uses standard tapes nowadays."

"Everybody in the Federation, aye," said Harb enigmatically. He didn't explain further, but Jim suspected that he was about to get all the answers he wanted.

The holo stage made another noise, remarkably like that of a man clearing his throat. Or, more accurately, like Lieutenant Jerry Freeman clearing his throat. He was standing in front of the holo's main control console holding its all-call mike in one hand and a tape cartridge in the other. Almost everyone on the rec deck was looking in his direction, and even the Space Cadet game had been set on pause. Jim couldn't help noticing that the crew members who had noticed his presence were dividing their attention more or less equally between Mr. Freeman and the captain—as if they were expecting something interesting to happen in both directions. "Friends, gentlebeings, and audience," said Jerry, smiling like man satisfied with a job well done, "you've been very patient. You've waited, and now here it is: *may'Duj BortaS!*"

Even though he had been expecting a surprise of some sort, Jim knew that his face probably twitched most satisfyingly at the news that a Klingon space opera was about to have its Federation premier on *his* rec deck—and at the sound of high-phase

Tlhinganaase being spoken on board the *Enterprise* again. It had always meant trouble in the past, or at the very least an unwanted ripple in shipboard routine. He smiled, the humor of the expression perhaps a bit thinner than Lieutenant Freeman's efforts deserved; but right then Jim wasn't thinking about Freeman or about rescanned sterry tapes.

We were in Star Base 12's area the last time, too, he thought, *before most of this crew had even entered the Academy. Certainly before any of them knew of Klingons as anything but "the enemy"—cardboard cutouts marked "villain." It was a long time ago, but now it seems like yesterday. I wonder how many of these children read* The Final Reflection *before they joined Starfleet?*

Certainly a great many of them had read it since and then, not content with fiction, had raided the ship's library for anything else that they could find on the subject of the Klingons and their empire. According to library records, a lot of the reading had taken place while the *Enterprise* was in the Klingon patrol corridor. Jim had noticed the increased turnover in data and hard copy printouts and had been sufficiently concerned to pay a visit both to Rec One and to sickbay. Recreation was a subdepartment of Medicine, and Harb Tanzer reported directly to Dr. McCoy on anything concerning the crew's leisure activities that might in his opinion indicate something amiss about their physical or mental health. There were attitudes and states of mind concerning, and held by, the nominally fictional characters—both Klingon and Terran—in *The Final Reflection* that could have had an unfavorable effect on morale. If that had happened, Jim wanted to find out sooner rather than later. The two conversations—one could scarcely refer to anything so informal as a staff meeting—had laid his apprehensions to rest, and with the peaceful conclusion of the mission he had thought no more about them. Until now.

"Battle Cruiser Vengeance? Coincidence, do you think?" he said very softly, for Harb's ears only.

"Half and half. I'd say that the patrol mission had something to do with it, but those old tapes have been available as xenosociological material for years. Ever since the Federation ambassador to the Empire brought them back from the Klingon homeworld when he was recalled. Nobody ever bothered to look at them until Mr. Freeman decided to run them through his conversion program." Harb's amused expression changed, growing just a bit more serious. "Captain, I don't know of any restrictions covering nonclassified material from nonaligned sources."

"Such as Klingon space operas?"

"Especially Klingon space operas. Have you any objections to it being run? I mean, would you like an advance viewing to check it for . . ."

"Propaganda? Threats to morale? Improper conduct? I don't think I need to worry." Harb looked relieved, probably more for Jerry Freeman's sake than for any other reason. Jim had seen the lieutenant's face when he realized that the captain was attending his premiere, a mixture of pleasure at the compliment and apprehension that it wasn't a compliment at all but a prelude to his being hauled over the coals. That nervous little pause was enough to make Jim raise his voice a bit, just enough to be overheard. "Mr. Tanzer, I doubt that a space opera—even a Klingon space opera—is likely to harm the physical or mental welfare of *this* crew." Then, much louder, "Well, let's see it, Lieutenant. Have you arranged for popcorn?"

It was a poor attempt at a joke—Jim had just finished a long day—and the laughter that greeted it was out of all proportion. Relief of tension, he thought. Good grief, did he scare the new recruits that much?

"You're a genuine galactic hero as well as a captain, sir. What you think matters," Harb said.

Jim looked around sharply and blinked at the rec chief. "Harb, you've been taking mind-reading lessons again."

"Just putting two and two together, sir. And if you really want it, two of the smaller processors have already been programmed to provide popcorn."

Harsh metallic music blared from the ambient-sound system, making people jump. Jim—who had started only very slightly—listened with his head cocked to one side, fascinated by this new experience. There had been all those encounters in the past, when he had met Klingons, spoken to them, fought with them; but this was the first time he had ever heard their music. Presumably this was the main title introduction, because he had only just become used to the alien scale and tuning when a chorus of fierce voices burst into song. Somehow Jim had never imagined Klingons singing, but if he had, this was without a doubt how they would have sounded.

"HIchmey tuj, Som chuStaH . . ." It was about hot guns and a noisy hull. The song crashed to a conclusion in a brazen atonal scream of trumpets and a rattle of percussion. There was a silence—nothing from the holo stage, nothing from the audience, neither applause nor comment nor even the sound of breathing. Everybody in Rec One seemed shocked speechless. Then a single voice spoke up from the back of the huge room.

"Hey, Jerry! You didn't say this was a kids' show! I wanna see the toys!"

Even Jim laughed; it had been a long time since Earth's children's-entertainment channels had presented programming whose first and often only purpose was to sell a line of toy products. Spin-offs, they were called. But through his laughter Jim felt a touch of unease as he watched a Klingon warship going into action on the holo stage. *Enterprise* had been on the receiving end of firepower from that sinister crank-winged vessel too many times for her commander to regard such a battle cruiser with anything like equanimity, and the prospect of his crew of largely untried youngsters seeing that same ship as no more than part of an entertainment disturbed him. Especially when it was cutting up one of the old Constitution-class starships, as it was now doing on the holo stage. *Enterprise* had been a Constitution class vessel before her refit. Despite the reassurances from Bones that the morale of the crew was unaffected, the laughter struck him as just a touch unhealthy.

And then he heard that same laughter again and shifted his concentration back to the translated dialogue. It had never occurred to him that Klingons might have had a gift for comedy, and indeed there was no indication that there was anything intentionally humorous in what the crew was watching. It was just that the whole thing was so deadly serious that after a while it became impossible to take seriously. Klingon officers snarled Battle Language at their subordinates, line members conspired against their enemies and one another, commanders moved fleet elements as they might move pieces on a *klin zha* board, and ships blew up other ships in what might have passed for combat maneuvers in an effects studio—but fell a bit short of reality on the Rec Deck of a Federation starship. And all was done without a smile, without a laugh, without a single joke to lighten the oppressive mood of determined glory-seeking.

They aren't like *this,* thought Kirk. *Kor wasn't, at least not much, and Koloth certainly wasn't. So what's the matter with this show? Doesn't the Empire dare to show that its military might have a sense of humor? Or do they regard humor as subversive?* He shrugged, not understanding.

Spock might, indeed probably would, have given a logical, rational and lengthy explanation of it all, but Spock was in his quarters, either fast asleep or in a recuperative trance after far too long on duty. During the last three days on patrol, a sensory-scan ghost had suggested that *Enterprise* was being shadowed by something with higher power-output readings than the average chunk of space debris. Debris didn't usually run at matching warp speeds, either. Of course nothing had come of it, and Spock had finally isolated the problem as a repeater echo in one of the long-range scanner chips. That discovery had taken Kirk's first officer sixty-seven hours without a break by shipboard chrono, because—logically, of course—the long-range units couldn't be taken off line in potentially hostile space and Spock had therefore run diagnostics on each separate chip by one-at-a-time backup substitution. It was the sort of thing that Spock liked to do. No, not liked—considered the only thing to do, after a process of thought as ruthlessly diagnostic as the mechanicals he had brought to bear on the recalcitrant chips.

A Klingon of the Imperial race stood on the shattered bridge of a Romulan Warbird, flanked by his personal guards, and gazed at the members of the Rom vessel's crew as they knelt on one knee to acknowledge his victory and their defeat. *"SoH'Iv?"* one of the Romulans asked. "Who are you?" The Klingon captain put his hands on his hips and glanced about him at sparking consoles and smoke-blackened bulkheads. He smiled that toothy Klingon smile that has nothing to do with humor.

"HoD Qotlh jIH," he said. *"Qotlh BortaS. je*

Dujvam tevwIj maj." Harsh music swelled triumphantly as the image froze. Then both sound and picture faded slowly away.

"This ship is my prize," eh? thought Kirk. He'd never been in a situation like that, where he could claim a ship as plunder—Starfleet just didn't do things like that. All the same, it did have a certain ring to it. "I am Captain Kirk. Kirk of the *Enterprise.* And this ship is . . ." No. It didn't work. Jim showed his teeth in a smile that was unconsciously very Klingon. Maybe in that grim Mirror universe, but not in this one. Thank God.

"Are there many more of those tapes, Mr. Freeman?" he asked as the lieutenant leaned over to twiddle furiously at the holo console. Freeman straightened up with a jerk, not having noticed Jim's quiet approach across the busy Rec Room. A tape cartridge started to slither, and he stopped it with a flat slap of one hand.

"Uh, about ten, sir. They're all in Xeno."

"Mr. Tanzer told me. That's an impressive bit of work, if Xeno base tapes are of the same quality as the batch I saw last year. Rigellian, they were."

"Thank you, sir." Freeman cleared his throat, a little uncomfortable with the compliment in front of so many of the crew, and took refuge behind the tape he had saved from falling. "Sir, about the rest of these . . . Now that you've seen one, do you have any objections to my recoding the others for ship's channels?"

Jim shook his head. "None at all, Mr. Freeman. I'll have it so noted when I log in tomorrow morning. In the meantime, good night, all."

"Thank you, sir. And good night."

There were the usual murmured salutations as Jim made his way back toward the turbolift entrance, thinking pleasant thoughts about being horizontal in the warm dark of his own quarters with his eyes shut, and responding to the ripple of "good night, Captain's" almost automatically. Harb's coffee had balanced McCoy's Romulan ale just nicely enough for his own overworked system to announce how tired it was and how very much it would like him to go to bed *soon*, please. He was almost into the lift and on his way to E deck when the annunciator beside the door spoke his name in Uhura's voice: *"Bridge to Captain Kirk."*

For the barest instant Jim closed his eyes tight, knowing from experience and the tone of his communication chief's voice that it was going to be the only chance he would have for quite a while.

"Kirk here," he said. "Rec One."

"Captain, I'm sorry to break into your off-duty period, but Repeater Station Three has a Captain's Personal signal on closed-line scramble holding for clearance by your command ciphers."

"Captain's Personal?" echoed Jim, all sleepiness gone. It wasn't quite the highest level of Starfleet coding, but it was high enough. "Give me the code groups, please." His voice was quite steady. Jim had always wondered what his reaction would be to a CP dispatch, and he was pleased to notice that it was at least creditable.

"Codes follow." Uhura read off a series of numbers: 111-69-201956-31.

Priority one emergency. Oh, great. There wasn't a war in the offing, but there had to be something very unpleasant lurking in the body of the message to justify that 111 group.

"I'll take it in my quarters, Uhura. Have Commanders Spock and Scott and Dr. McCoy join me there. Kirk out."

None of the other crew on the rec deck had noticed

the brief exchange or the change in their captain's demeanor, and if they had noticed, they were all Starfleet Academy graduates, officers and gentle-beings who would have regarded the whole thing—quite rightly—as none of their business.

Jim's mind touched on, and flinched from, a dozen possibilities in the second and a half before the turbolift car arrived. V'ger had involved a 111-group coding, but even it hadn't rated a Captain's Personal dispatch—at least not when the alert had begun. And there had been a 111 for that horrible business when the Romulans field-tested their plasma projector and cloaking device. But then—and Kirk was actually smiling by the time the lift car's doors hissed open—the tribble alert had been group 111 as well. Jim was actually smiling by the time the lift car's doors hissed open. *Be prepared for the worst,* he thought, *but always hope for the best, because whatever you ask for, you may get.*

The lift doors shut, and he was on his way.

Chapter Two

"GOOD EVENING, CAPTAIN," said Spock as Jim came around the curve of the corridor and found the Vulcan waiting at the door to his quarters.

"First as always, Mr. Spock," said Jim. Not merely first, but wide awake, wearing immaculate full uniform, and in full possession of his breath.

Of course, Jim wouldn't have expected anything else. All senior officers had their quarters on the same deck, but those of the first officer were in an area of the primary-hull saucer that was diametrically opposite those of the captain; the distant placement was designed to prevent accident or attack from taking out the first two levels of *Enterprise*'s command structure. In addition to being some distance away, the first officer had been asleep or in meditation when Uhura's call came through. But neither of those mitigating factors meant anything to Spock. He managed to be the first to arrive despite them.

"I am early only because I was conveniently situated to respond to your summons, sir, since the radial corridors of this deck—"

"Quite so. And of course running along the said corridors never entered your head."

"Running, sir? No, sir. Such an expenditure of energy appeared superfluous in the present circumstance."

However tired Spock had been when he logged off the bridge, he had plainly taken advantage of his rest time. His carefully pedantic conversation and vocabulary were a sure indication that he was feeling thoroughly full of beans. It was just as well that *somebody* was, thought Jim as he went inside and through to the work area at the back of the inner office. Until he got some sleep Spock would be thinking for both of them.

"We have a problem," he said, gesturing Spock to a chair. "A code-group 111 problem." Jim hated the melodramatic sound of that, and he could feel Spock's eyebrow going up long before he turned from the desk screen and saw it.

"More tribbles? Or merely a Klingon declaration of war?"

"No further data yet. I won't clear the ciphers until"—the door opened—"everyone's here. Mr. Scott, Dr. McCoy, good evening."

"So much for your evening in Rec One, Captain," said Bones. "I take it this is business rather than recreation."

"You presume right. Scotty, is main drive behaving itself?"

"Aye, sir, that it is." Commander Scott's mustache moved as he permitted himself a thin smile. "It wouldna dare be otherwise. I've been down in Engineering, supervising things."

"One hundred and ten percent efficiency, then?"

"Och, no. A hundred suits me fine."

"Good. We may need it." Jim swiveled his chair and fed cipher clearance into the screened terminal on his desk. "Communications, this is the captain. Implement transfer at your discretion. Kirk out."

"Transferring. Transfer completed. Bridge out."

The light of an optical scan flickered briefly, checking Kirk's retina to make certain that he was who he claimed to be. It was unusual and rather unsettling; most incoming dispatches considered his personal codes sufficient authority to clear. "Kirk, James T., Admiral," said the terminal's voder tonelessly. "Identity confirmed. Verification complete."

Jim took a deep breath. *Here it comes.* "Run transmission," he said, and was aware of his officers leaning just a little closer. For their benefit he added, "With audio."

"To: Kirk, James T.," came the transmission, *"Admiral, Cmdr NCC-1701* Enterprise."

That use of his full rank was significant. Jim didn't like it.

"Effective immediately: Shore leave clearance is rescinded for duration of present operation. You are ordered to proceed with all due haste to coordinates 00315/22970 mark 816.83, there to rendezvous with support ships enumerated below. Under your command all vessels will make best speed to planet 4725 Cancri IV, a.k.a. Dekkanar. Enterprise *will provide escort for SPE subsequent to breakdown of diplomatic relations with planetary government. Be advised that this is not an exercise. Signed Nhoma, OX., Commodore, SFC 225 Iraz VI/Hodel. CC: Farey, N., Cpt, Cmdr NCC-2360* Vanguard; *North, G., Cpt, Cmdr, NCC-2382* Sir Richard; *Johnson, T., Col, Cmdr 22 Diplomatic Protection Group; Morrow, R.H., Admrl. CoS (Ops) SFC Earth (Sol III/Terra). Additional data follow.*

"Stop," said Kirk, and touched a panel that polarized the screen. "Audio off." He turned from the terminal to survey the three thoughtful faces gazing at him. One in particular drew his eyes. "Bones? You look as if you have something to say."

"Never mind the recreation," said McCoy as he stared at the screen, "wave good-bye to shore leave as well. And just when I was really starting to look forward to getting back on terra firma."

"Doctor," Spock said quietly, "Star Base Twelve is a deep-space facility. Even allowing for the loosest possible interpretation of the term 'terra firma,' you would be some twelve-point-two-seven-five light-years from anything firm enough to stand on, and it would be a form of frozen methane rather than the 'solid earth' of your statement."

"Spock, I don't know how I'd survive without you."

"Gentlemen." Jim caught Scotty stroking his mustache in an effort to hide the expression lurking behind it; he rapped the desk to restore some decorum to the proceedings. "This is hardly the time. I'm already presuming that all departments are running at a reasonable degree of efficiency," said Jim. "I know that at the end of a patrol things tend to slide a bit. But is this ship capable of returning to active status within the somewhat limited parameters of this signal?"

"All science departments are already at optimum stand-down capability, Captain. Commanders Uhura and Chekov reported like status for Communications and Defense respectively as of yesterday."

"I wasna makin' jokes about Engineering, Captain. She'll give ye right to warp ten if and when ye need it."

"Dr. M'benga's working on the crew's medical roster right now," McCoy said. "There's not a thing wrong with any of the whole four hundred ninety, and the report summary'll be ready for your inspection in a few hours. But speaking as your doctor, if you're planning to stay awake and read them—"

"No, Bones, I'm planning to get some sleep. But not until we've reached some sort of conclusion about this damned signal. I'll take it as read that we can answer

Commodore Nhoma's signal with a confirmation of immediate response. So let's see what we're letting ourselves in for. Audio on. Hardcopy printout to science station. Resume."

Jim's suspicions were more than justified. The mission looked like trouble. After a bloodless coup on 4725 Cancri IV, the new Dekkan government had served deportation orders on the Federation personnel, their families, and the various independent neutrals presently planetside. On the face of it, the mission was no more than the provision of top cover for the peacekeeping unit running a standard SPE—a services-protected evacuation of the sort so beloved by Training Command. Except, of course, that this was for real.

"Captain," said Scotty, "if they havena yet laid claim to the Federation facilities on the surface and in the orbital chain, then all of this is more a matter for the diplomats and the politicals than a starship. The expulsion orders would have shown more forceful wording if it wasna in their plans to renegotiate the terms of Federation occupancy. Doubtless when the dust settles it's just more wealth they'll be after."

Spock laid the sheets of data neatly on the desk in front of him and squared their edges, then steepled his index fingers and tapped them against his lips before saying anything, almost as if he was editing his words before letting them be heard. "Certainly there appears to be a diplomatic element involved in this," he said. "But unfortunately whatever financial adjustments the government may have planned are being overtaken by events. I'm sure that all present will agree that the Phalange for Dekkan Independence—the PDI, as they are more popularly known—is an organization worthy of notice."

"You're darn right I agree! It doesn't matter what highfalutin names they give themselves, they're just the same sort of terrorists who always crawl out of the woodwork when something like this happens!" McCoy flicked a hand irritably at the screen in front of Jim. "And you know what they're trying to do with all this throwing their weight about? They weren't able to make a name for themselves during the coup, so now they have to prove how tough they are so that they'll get some attention when the time for making demands comes around."

"The employment of violence toward political, or nominally political, ends has been regrettably common throughout history," said Spock. His face was somber. "Even on Vulcan. An adequate demonstration of force will invariably gain notice, and from notice comes influence and power."

Jim sat quietly and watched the discussion pass to and fro among his officers, gleaning more understanding from the workings of multiple minds than he ever could from sitting alone, hunched before a security-screened terminal. "I suspect, Mr. Spock, that's why Starfleet's sending us. Specially trained personnel to carry out the evacuation, the *Enterprise* in a high-cover orbit—seems to me intended to attract notice. But nothing else."

He tapped a series of controls on the terminal console, and more data appeared on the screen. "Gentlemen, I am advised that the actions of all Starfleet vessels and personnel are restricted by the full provisions of General Order Twelve, subsection seven-point-one, governing rules of engagement. The most we're allowed to show is the flag. No shields, no screens, and most certainly no weapons. There are also indications that General Order One may be invoked if anybody gets too heavy-handed, and the

Prime Directive in this instance will mean 'get out and stay out.' Which brings me to the Klingons."

"Never rains but it pours," said Bones softly.

Jim glanced at him and smiled crookedly. "Too true. The Klingons—and the Orions. Both of these, ah, nonaligned spheres of influence extend too conveniently close to 4725 Cancri for Starfleet to want to give either unfriendly power the opportunity to expand by virtue of our errors."

"Which either or both may already be contemplating." Spock riffled through his printouts, gazed at one sheet with as close to a scowl as he ever allowed himself to show, then neatened them again, his eyes hooded and unreadable. "Perhaps following an invitation . . ."

"From one o' their own intelligence sources, maybe." Scotty looked up unhappily from the latest screen of data. "Captain, I hadna thought the Firechain ran t' here."

"The Fire-*what?*" McCoy leaned over Scotty's shoulder, frowned at the screen, then threw up his hands in exasperation. "Dammit, Jim, I'm a doctor, not a soldier! Will somebody—*anybody*—cut all the military jargon and tell me what all this is about?"

Jim stretched a bit, easing a crick in his spine. *A pain in the neck,* he thought. *Isn't that always what these signals are about?* He felt tired. "It's about the usual: trouble. Computer, desk terminal, off; main holo screen on. Show all systems in the sectors bounded by these coordinates." He fed in the figures and sector boundaries from the dispatch, then watched as the big projection screen fitted to the rear wall of his office came alive with the stars and data of a standard chart display.

"Show destination." Immediately 4725 Cancri IV glowed blue as it orbited its sun, the holographic image passing unconcernedly through Jim's hand as he reached deep into the display and tracked it with his fingertip. "Access authority as before: command level, classification one three-A three. Reveal and flag Federation long-range surveillance and early-warning installations in the same area: designation: Fire-chain.

Forty-odd red fireflies joined the 3-D swirling of simulated orbits: drone satellites fitted with an adaptation of the Romulan cloaking device, like the one that had been monitoring the ill-fated trio of Klingon cruisers at the beginning of the V'ger incident; false asteroids, and real ones hollowed out to no more than a concealing shell; and one planet that glowed like a jewel on Jim's finger, blue and red by turns.

Dr. McCoy stared for what seemed the longest time at the slowly turning display, then raised his eyes to glance from side to side with an odd mixture of amusement and resignation. "Ah," he said. "Dekkanar is right in the middle of it and so are we."

Jim said nothing, Scotty cleared his throat slightly, and both of them looked at Spock. The Vulcan met and held their eyes for perhaps a second, lifted that one eyebrow fractionally, and compressed his lips in an expression that, on anyone else, would have concealed a rueful smile. "Explanations," he said. "Very well. Captain, if I might use your terminal to access the computer . . . ?"

"Be my guest."

"Computer, this is Commander Spock, science officer. Access authorities remain in force. Classification now two one-B three."

"Identity confirmed. Verification complete."

Jim had noticed a peculiarity before and he heard it again now. It might have been his imagination, but he could have sworn that whenever the voderreproduced voice addressed Spock it sounded less toneless and . . . well, *friendlier*. But of course, that was impossible.

As Spock worked, more charts and data flagging overlaid the first display until it was cluttered with colors and information flashes. Finally he glanced once from the desk repeater to the main screen and back, nodded, and pressed a single tab that returned the basic star map.

"The Dekkanar installations remain mostly what they originally were," he said, "a part of the industrial development and self-help program first instituted thirty-seven standard years ago. However, by virtue of Klingon Imperial expansion in the years between the start of the project and the Peace of Organia, it was, and I quote, 'necessary that, by virtue of its position in Federation space so close to the Klingon sphere of influence, a manned facility for detecting potentially threatening incursions be installed in the 4725 Cancri system.' At the time of construction, no fully auto-mated systems were considered for the task. There is a footnote."

To Jim's surprise, Spock glanced back at the small screen; his first officer didn't normally use, or need, prompts. "It concerns misinterpreted DEWline data by ILLIAC-Four for NORAD and SAC in Stone Mountain—on late twentieth-century Earth," the Vulcan elaborated, plainly disapproving of the pletho-ra of acronyms confusing a perfectly adequate language. Spock lifted both eyebrows, plainly inviting an explanation before he got one from the computer.

"DEW was the original distant early warning sys-tem," said Jim. He smiled wearily. "In the late twentieth century Earth's discovery of nuclear fission was still less than fifty years old, Spock." It must have

been a ticklish time. Either fifty years or indefinite—
that was the life span Vulcans had calculated for a
hominid culture that discovered atomics.

"Thank you, Captain. And the rest?"

Jim winced inwardly, sensing the same reaction
from Scotty and Bones. It was not a piece of Earth's
history that any of them could be proud of. "There
were occasions," he said, picking his words with care,
"when the warning system and the computers linked
to it . . . made mistakes. The mistakes were passed
down line to commanders who didn't want to believe
they were mistakes; the errors then were sent to
missile and strategic bomber bases. Most of the errors
occurred when the warning system picked up off-
course civilian aircraft . . . though there was a persis-
tent rumor that war was almost started by a flock of
migrating geese."

He leaned back in his chair and looked across the
office at nothing in particular. "We came so close so
many times. Every so often the recall didn't come
through until the bombers were in the air. Even now, a
few hundred years later, it's unpleasant to think
about."

"But not unfamiliar," said Spock. "I comprehend
the need for personnel in the Dekkanar facility."

"Dekkani personnel," snapped McCoy.

"Of course, Doctor." Spock's face was expressionless. "It *is* their planet, but they appreciate the Federation support."

"You mean they *did.*"

"Quite," said Spock flatly. "Informing the Dekkani
would be informing them. This planet's proximity to
the Klingon Empire is a two-edged sword."

"Look at the chart, man! One link in a chain of
fifty-odd isn't any great loss!"

"Ah," said Scotty, "look at the size o' the place.

Ye're talkin' about the damned main station. It controls all the analysis from the others." Montgomery Scott was getting agitated: his Edinburgh-educated accent was giving way to the harsher sounds of old Glasgow and the shipyards of the Clyde where he had learned the fundamentals of his trade. "Ye'll no' be gettin' that much gear on any o' those wee orbital drones or screenin' the energy output from detection even if ye could. The laddies from Klingon Intelligence would love t' get their hands on the whole kit an' caboodle, so else we keep everythin' quiet and let the politicals get this all back t' normal—or somebody gets t' beam the whole installation up piecemeal; there's no other way t' deal wi' it."

"And how would this new Dekkan government—or the PDI—react if we tried *that,* without asking permission? Which, of course, they, would refuse," Jim demanded, locking eyes with McCoy. It was all very well for the chief medical officer to appoint himself the conscience of the *Enterprise,* but trying to do the same thing for the whole of Starfleet Command—that was way out of his depth.

All the tension went out of McCoy's body and he settled back in his chair with an audible release of breath. "Yeah. They're not up for listening to reason right now, are they? And they'd be likely to invoke the Prime Directive and then invite the Klingons in just out of spite." He grinned and managed to put a bit of humor into it. "So it's a secret. And it stays a secret."

Jim nodded, managed a little grin of his own. Losing the planetary base would be bad enough; losing the surveillance facilities to the Klingons would be far, far worse.

Because they would love it.

The Empire's diplomatic arm would try to use it as political leverage both through the Organians and in other, nastier ways—and, invited or not, they'd be all over Dekkanar within a day of the Federation's withdrawal. To say nothing of the Romulans, who always regarded Federation difficulties as an opportunity. . . . Much more of this and Jim knew he would start to twitch.

"Let's get the ball rolling, shall we?" he said. "Apologies in advance to everyone just coming off duty, but I'm bringing the ship back up to active status. Thanks, everyone. Dismissed." He tapped the desk communicator. "Attention all hands, this is the captain. Now hear this: shore leave has been postponed. *Enterprise* is returning to active duty for an estimated ten days. All stations and departments will go to alert status immediately. Kirk out."

"That was abrupt," said McCoy from the doorway. Spock and Scotty were already out and away.

"Probably," said Jim, knowing there was nothing probable about it. "It's the way I feel. I was looking forward to a little R-and-R as well, you know."

"I do know. It's a tacky way to wind up the tour, Jim—cleaning up an intelligence mess."

"Somebody has to do it, and we're handy. You hold the dustpan and I'll use the brush, eh?"

"After you get some sleep."

"I need to—"

"Sleep."

"Once I've answered my mail and pointed the ship in the right direction. All right?"

"All right. But I'll stay here for a while, just to make sure."

Jim sighed heavily. "There are times, Bones, when you sound like my mother."

31

"Oh, I'm far worse than that, Captain." McCoy smiled again, took a seat on the edge of Kirk's bunk. "I'm your *doctor!*"

"And what about a ship of your own, Pavel?"

"Well, what about it? I don't even know yet if my transfer is to *Nelson* or *Reliant,* and already you talk about a command! I don't know anything at all!" Pavel Andreievich Chekov, acting science officer, threw up his arms in mock despair. "And if I had a choice, would I not serve on something with a good Russian name, like *Sakharov* or *Ivan Groznyy?*"

"What about *Potemkin?*" said Sulu. "Or *Minsk?*"

"If I wanted to stay with this class of starship, *dorogoy moy,* I would not move from this very one. So."

They had been talking shore leave before the message came in for Captain Kirk; now shore leave and anything connected with it was a prohibited subject, just in case too much assuming of things brought disappointment. Their conversation was all about promotions and transfers and whether the next patrol would be more interesting than the last, because it was certain that it couldn't possibly be duller. There were only the three slightly raised voices on the bridge, those of the old hands; other stations were secured by ensigns and a solitary lieutenant, all of whom were keeping quiet and clear of even friendly arguments between these commanders with the legendary names.

And then the annunciator uttered its two-tone three-note whistle and even the legends went quiet. *"Attention all hands, this is the captain. Now hear this: shore leave has been postponed. . . ."*

Sulu released a long breath that lacked only sound

to be a groan of disappointment. "That's ten I owe you," he whispered to Chekov after the rest of the message was done. "And a drink. Better make it off duty rather than off ship—otherwise you might have to wait awhile."

"Just so long as the drink isn't sake. Wodka, *if* you please." He glanced across at Ensign Penney, who was once again keeping Weapons and Defense ticking over, as she had been doing on and off throughout a mission that had seen no need for them at all. "Maintenance checks, Ensign," he said. "And run a preheat on the phaser banks before checking the warp drive power bleed. Make sure any imbalance will cut in the torpedoes. And if it doesn't, scream. Because *I* will."

Chekov had never liked the way the redesign had interlinked phasers to main drive; damage to one would rob *Enterprise* of the other. And the photon torpedoes, while an admirable backup, were not what he considered an adequate defense all by themselves.

"Klingons, do you think?" he asked nobody in particular. Heads went up for an instant all around the bridge before turning back to their allotted tasks.

"Not this far into Federation space." Sulu sounded confident, almost like a man who was considering how he might win his ten credits back.

"Station K-Seven was farther in," said Chekov softly. "So was Organia."

Uhura flapped one hand at them in a shushing gesture and pressed her transdator tighter into her ear with the other. "Watch your screens," she hissed, head turned well away from the comm pickup. "Further info coming up."

Kirk's voice rang out on the bridge: *"Make the*

following signal to Commodore Nhoma: 'Ref your dispatch: sitrep noted, logged; Enterprise *acting.' Usual codes and salutations. Flag it as a Priority One response, and send the message and reply to all department heads. Any queries or comments may be directed to Mr. Spock."*

Uhura touched controls, paused while the verification lights came up, and nodded. "Executed, sir."

"Thank you, Commander." There was a soft small noise in her transdator that took Uhura a second to recognize as an inadequately stifled yawn. *"Patch all coordinates from Commodore Nhoma's signal through to Helm and Navigation, and have a course laid in directly for those coordinates at warp eight-point-five. I"*—another yawn, more audible than the last one—*"think that's all for now. Good night. Kirk out."*

"Aye, Captain. Good night, sir." Uhura wiggled the transdator from her ear and set it down on the comm console right beside the screen. She read the words burning on that screen, words that the captain's authority had put there, and said several words of AmaNdebele kwaZulu under her breath. Now and again occasions arose for which KiSwahili was inadequate: it was too good-natured a language in which to swear in effectively. *Here we go again,* she thought, and hit the key that put Nhoma's signal on line. "Your station, Mr. Mahase."

The deck underfoot was vibrating with that familiar soft subharmonic moan of acceleration when Uhura finished tidying up and rose to return to the center seat where she nominally held the con. Sulu had laid in the course coordinates almost as fast as they appeared on his board, and *Enterprise* was already curving away from Star Base 12 and back out into the uninhabited darkness near the Neutral Zone.

As she settled back into the captain's chair, Uhura touched controls to bring a star chart up on the main screen. She looked at it for a moment, then shook her head. The star called 4725 Cancri was all alone out there. Oh, there were its seven planets, but the only one of interest was their destination, Dekkanar. The rest . . . either too close or too far out; cinders or snowballs. It was an untidy system; literally so, with an orbiting belt of asteroids and bits of space debris from what had probably been an eighth planet sometime long ago, most of them massive enough to overwhelm the long-range navigational pressors that were, after all, meant only to shunt micrometeors from *Enterprise*'s path. At least the *Enterprise* navigators were too sharp to let the ship get anywhere near the asteroids. Larger obstacles of this sort were normally flung aside by the outermost deflector screens after a sensor detection. At present, however, the use of screens and shields was forbidden under General Order 12, and once the ship moved deeper into the star system, its sensors wouldn't work.

Because 4725 Cancri had yet another trick up its metaphorical sleeve. It was a "dirty" star, a testy, marginally unstable type F2 that threw out vast quantities of ionized radiation at all times, and right now it was at the peak of a sunspot cycle. The star's ionization was as effective as deliberate high-frequency jamming and served quite adequately to scramble shipboard helm sensors. The only way around the problem was either to run those sensors at maximum output or to activate the more powerful systems that were expressly designed to burn through jamming whether it was natural or deliberate. That, of course, was impossible for the same reason that everything else was out of the question right now—General Order 12. High-emission sensors, any of which might be perceived as military hardware, were expressly forbidden by Order 12; under the present rules of engagement, they were considered provocative.

This system had better be well charted, thought Uhura. *Otherwise it's going to be interesting. . . .* She cut in an orbital simulation program, set present parameters and restrictions, and watched while it ran a hands-off approach down through the display. The program achieved a geosynchronous orbital insertion —just—and Uhura winced feelingly. Almost any approach from deep space was interesting, all right. Too damned interesting.

"Looks wonderful." Chekov had been watching the simulation in between setting the science station to rights, not much liking what he saw. "And with *Vanguard* and *Sir Richard* keeping us company right down to orbit. Right into the radio pause. Boga radi—"

"One good thing about all this is that we won't be staying long." Sulu, having finished upgrading checks on Helm and Navigation, keyed his department head acknowledgment into the reader and cleared its message to memory. "I've been on SPE exercises before. The security people beam down to protect the civilians and diplomats until they can be brought out. All we have to do is give cover from up top."

"That easy, huh?" Uhura shook her head. "So why am I not convinced?"

"Because the exercise controllers like to throw in the occasional curve. Like the time limitation, of course, and the other civilians. On one exercise we had sociologists, naturalists, and two families off bird-watching somewhere in the fenland—on a planet that was *all* fenland! We found them, directed squads to pick them up, moved them all to the evacuation points, and beamed them out, but it wasn't what I'd call fun. This, though"—Sulu tapped the reader

36

screen—"will have to be neater. If that signal means what I think, then we go in, pick up the folks, and try to get out again within a couple of days. What I read is 'Don't ruffle any feathers, it'll mess up the talks.'"

"The Dekkani act like spoiled children who want us to give them more candy before they let us play in their yard," said Chekov, sounding annoyed. "When I was very small, that kind of behavior did not earn me candy. It got me smacked." He smiled at a wry and probably painful memory. "Few children tried it twice. A pity that approach never works in politics. It would save a lot of time and trouble."

"Gunboat diplomacy, Pavel?" Sulu shrugged, dismissing the idea. "I think the Klingons use those methods on their subject worlds. I don't recommend it."

"I wasn't suggesting gunboats."

Uhura looked at him and raised her eyebrows. "If what you meant was some sort of orbital smack-programmable launcher," she said, "you're more in need of a rest than I thought."

Chapter Three

TWENTY DRYDOCKS surrounded the orbital shipyard, and nineteen of them buzzed with activity. The twentieth was in darkness. All but its running lights and safety beacons had been shut down, so that the ship hanging within its lattice was no more than a huge shadow. Its gray thermoglaze showed no reflections, but rather seemed to attract and absorb even the meager illumination so as to reveal some semblance of its shape.

A solitary engineering pod moved out from the main yard complex and drifted unhurriedly toward Drydock 20. As the pod drew closer, its protective shrouding retracted so that its upper surface became a clear-view bubble, through which those aboard could inspect what little they could see of the ship. The pod's single passenger glanced without speaking at its pilot, who nodded acknowledgment of the look and tripped a toggle on his command board.

All the lights of Drydock 20 and of the ship inside it came on at once.

The pod passed along one side of the support pylons and out beyond the dock, then rotated slowly to face its entrance. The ship was no longer a gray shadow, but glittered like something carved from obsidian and crystal. Even the most uninformed observer would have known this ship had not been out of drydock. Its shape was subtly different from that of others of its class, and the patina of its thermocoat was still untarnished by light-years of travel; it had not yet felt the touch of phaser bolt or stellar dust or anything harsher than the hands and implements of those who had rebuilt it almost from the keel. As the pod began a flyby approach, its passenger rose from his seat and stood to attention, offering without speech or other movement a salute to the ship that had once been his and was now his again.

Everything about it had been remade; it was as pristine now as it had been when the keel had first been flown years and parsecs long past. The pigmentation of insignia and graphics had been refreshed with newer, brighter colors, picked out by selective spotlights buried in the hull. There were even small areas of brilliance around the primary weapon conduits where someone had taken the time and trouble to polish the bare metal of their efflux nozzles and blast tubes—and polish them with hand tools, for there was no other way to achieve such a mirror finish. As it approached the ship, the pod reduced its speed until finally it was moving past the red-lit bridge and out toward the warp nacelles at little more than walking speed. Passing over one of them, it curved around and then down to pass beneath the ventral surface of the hull, initially so close that from horizon to horizon of the pod's 180-degree view, there was nothing to be seen but an infinity of plated belly.

The pod's passenger watched the massive hull, the hull of *his* ship, flowing leisurely past, and the fingers of one hand gripped the polarization console of the viewport hard enough to make indentations in its padding. The other hand, by contrast, tapped a slow, controlled rhythm on the console's metal frame. When the pilot noticed it, he smiled, then concealed the expression behind a busy tapping of his own on controls that illuminated an autodock display above the command board.

Once clear of the farther side of the hull, a few seconds more maneuvering with the reaction thrusters brought the pod into line with its docking port. There was a soft, solid noise as the multiple latches engaged, a brief hiss as air and pressure equalized in the outer lock, and then silence.

As the protective shrouds slid back into place, the passenger watched them as if he had never seen such a thing before, then walked to the rear of the pod and opened its access hatch. He paused with one hand still on the controls, facing the red-lit corridor of the ship beyond, then turned to look at the pilot, who was busy with shutdown routine. Finally, and after evident consideration, he spoke into the silence. "Thank you."

The pilot was on his feet immediately. "This need not be said."

"I say it. Thank you for the tour of inspection." Captain Kasak sutai-Khornezh of the Klingon Imperial race smiled thinly, deciding to let at least some of his amusement show. "And for the music. Especially for the music. *Tales of the Privateers,* indeed."

"This one considered the circumstances appropriate for music." He touched a control and the flight console ejected a tape. "And all of the themes from *Battle Cruiser Vengeance* are overused."

"Appropriate, *zan* Askel?" said Kasak tonelessly, wondering if the ears of Security were listening. "And what of *propriety?* Privateers are not something mentioned to the one when he assumes command of a new ship."

"The reputation of sutai-Khornezh is such that no

impropriety could be implied or suspected," said Askel formally.

Kasak narrowed his eyes, wondering if his science specialist was daring to hint at something else entirely. Perhaps he was with Imperial Intelligence, Kasak thought. Nothing else could have made him so bold. That one word "reputation" never failed to make Kasak's liver move in his chest while he reviewed the other words that had been uttered with it, searching for the hidden slight. It had been his reaction for so long that it was almost a reflex now, pointless in most cases and certainly where Askel was concerned. Imperial Intelligence or not—and the matter had never been more than idle speculation—the specialist was as close to being a friend as Kasak had ever allowed anyone to become. He dismissed the thought as not of immediate concern, not with a shiny new ship to be inspected.

The ship was *Hakkarl*—"Vanguard." He was named for a piece in the game known as *klin zha*. His registry number was KL-1017, and he had started life in these same orbital yards at Taamar five years ago, as the first of the K't'inga class battle cruisers. Kasak had commanded the ship's proving flight, as he commanded the first flights of all new vessels, and had found himself a fine ship, strong, responsive, and swift. And then, as always, the vessel had been taken away and given to someone else, someone who was considered more politically sound.

As politically sound as the fools who had lost three of *Hakkarl's* brother ships to the energy field that the Federation had called V'ger, no doubt.

And now he was back, refitted, uprated, and a little more besides—and he was Kasak's to command again. For a while. Kasak showed his teeth and stalked aboard his ship.

* * *

It had all gone wrong years ago during Kasak's cadet cruise, even though the voyage had been commanded by no less a captain than Koloth vestai-Lasshar himself.

The incident at Space Station K-7 had turned a relatively simple mission into a fiasco, and a flurry of negative security notations had dogged all members of that ship's crew throughout their careers. Only the cadets had emerged relatively unscathed, and then only those not sufficiently capable to have drawn attention to themselves. Midshipman Vasak, as he had then been known, was not one of that fortunate mundane majority. His name had come up too many times for Imperial Intelligence not to take notice when they were looking for scapegoats to carry the blame for the loss of Sherman's Planet, the capture of one of their deep-cover agents, and the infestation of an entire battle cruiser with the furry vermin *yiHmey*. . . .

All the corridors were shadowy, lit only with the deep red glow that Kasak associated with combat, emergency, and imminent violence. Now *that* was appropriate. What was not appropriate, or even comfortable, was the atmosphere. It was too cool, and painfully dry. Kasak found that he needed to breathe shallowly through his nose to keep the lining of his throat from being dehydrated. He had expected something of the sort, given what had been done to the ship, and equally, he hadn't expected to like it.

Askel caught up with him near one of the turbolifts. "Pod's secure," he said.

"Good." Kasak stopped, pressed for a lift car, and when it arrived lifted his eyebrows at the heater-humidifier and airlock flush clamped to its ceiling just inside the door. "You'll like this," said Askel, following Kasak's gaze to the overhead installations. They began to operate as soon as the car was sealed and on its way, filling it with warmth and moisture at least for the duration of transit.

"Bridge," Kasak said. He found himself wishing that the ride from amidships out to the command pod was not quite so fast, and gave serious consideration to putting the car on hold for a few minutes while their desiccated nostrils got back to something approaching normal. Then he decided not to bother. The others would be waiting on the bridge, and while as captain he could do much as he pleased without reproof, the longer he took getting to the preflight briefing, the longer it would take to wind it up and get back to air that everyone could breathe. At least it was just a briefing, nothing more; there would be no need to waste time in impressing the officers of *this* crew. . . .

In the time after his cadet flight, Vasak had often wondered what had saved him from the fate of the others, be it legal termination on trumped-up charges, suicide by command, or simple disappearance. It was true that he was of the Imperial race; but it was equally true that being such was no real protection. Indeed, on Koloth's ship, crewed largely by human fusions, membership in the Imperial race had served only to point out those of pure blood for special punishment, on the assumption that regardless of how low their rank might have been, they at least should have known better. It might have been his line, whose members were not without influence and had certainly acted in his support and defense—just as soon as it was safe to do so and in exchange for his incurring heavy debts both of cash and obligations.

And his survival might just as easily have been due to the fact that he was too useful to dispose of simply for the completeness of things. Certainly it had been his usefulness ever since that order came through; an order not for termination but for promotion to ensign and the change of name it required, and an immediate posting to active duty in the hot spots along the Romulan frontier.

Ensigns had little enough time to call their own, and still less when under a more stringent level of security surveillance than everyone else, but Kasak had managed to scrape together the few minutes he required before they shipped him out to the waiting frigate. It was there, on Orbital Facility 3, that he had stood at a viewport and looked out at the naked stars that surrounded all who sought glory among them, seen or unseen. It was there that he had chosen to play the Perpetual Game. And there, filled with pride and thinking himself the first of all Klingons to do so, he had vowed to write his own rules for himself. He had learned very quickly that in *komerex zha* there were no other kinds of rules.

Kasak had exercised the usual privilege granted to first-flight commanders, of putting forward a list of names for consideration as department heads, based on his evaluations during previous cruises. This flight was a little different: he had recommended an entire crew. All eight of them.

They came to attention as he stepped out onto the bridge, all the familiar faces, familiar names. They had changed only in age and rank and in the appearance of scars here and there. They looked pleased enough to see him and to have been singled out for this honorable if not necessarily glorious duty. Some looked as quizzical as it was proper to appear before the captain gave his briefing—and all of them were as unhappy with the ship's atmosphere as Kasak was.

"Captain," said Weapons Specialist Katta, when the formal greetings were completed, "what *is* this?"

Kasak looked at her mildly. He knew exactly what

she meant, having perceived all the facets of the question, all the layers of the answer. Not just why they were the only crew on the entire ship, or why the atmosphere was so unpleasant, but why the bridge had neither control boards nor any seating other than the small and uncomfortable inspection pads on which they were now perched.

Katta saw the look, remembered him of old, knew what his first reply was likely to be, and said quickly, "Besides a battle cruiser, that is."

"Kai," Kasak said, mocking softly. He gestured to Askel. "This is a matter for Science to explain. The sooner it's done, the sooner we can move from this bridge to the proper one." That drew curious looks, as he had intended it should. "Specialist Askel?"

Askel nodded. "You will all have noticed the low temperature and humidity levels aboard this ship." There was no reply, since his words were not a question but a statement of fact. "Some or all of you may have guessed the reason. Let me confirm. *Hakkarl* is crewed by computer."

Eyes widened and pupils went narrow. Captain Kasak's chosen crew members were all sufficiently senior to know about the occasion when Starfleet had launched a fully computerized ship—and what the consequences had been.

Askel waited a few seconds, then smiled thinly. "But before you all ask for a transfer to somewhere safe—perhaps unarmed interdiction of the Rom zones—it isn't like the Federation's *khest'n* M-5. We know better than that, and so do they. At least, they know it now." His audience laughed; they would have heard the same sort of joke many times before, but never so aptly timed.

"These"—he slapped his hand against one of the dark metal casings that shrouded every work station on the bridge—"are beam-linked repeater arrays

45

boosted through a Z-eight primary core. Neither the repeaters nor the core act for themselves: *you* will control them, just as you would if you sat here. However, you will not. You and the captain will be *here.*"

The main screen, virtually the only piece of equipment on this cold, dry bridge that had remained unchanged, lit up with a view back from the command pod toward *Hakkarl's* main hull, and this time, despite the crew's discipline, Askel heard gasps of astonishment.

There was a Bird of Prey scout hanging there, maneuvering thrusters at station-keeping, far too close for in-dock traffic separation. *"Tazhat,"* said Askel. "Registry number: KL-1018. He will be Flier to our Vanguard." Tight smiles too full of teeth greeted the joke. "Now attend, and learn. Life-support and artificial gravity functions are sited in *Tazhat,* and in him only."

Askel surveyed the watching faces and smiled thinly but with much satisfaction. "Good. Then I need explain that much less to you. Our captain told me that you were swift." He gave the last word the *klin zha* intonation, but there was no response of humor. Not now; his audience was too intent on all the strata of meaning in their science specialist's words to pay much heed to further jests that might, or might not, leaven his briefing. Askel noted this, and was content. They would remember more for their concentration.

"Without crew, and the needs of crew, *Hakkarl* no longer has the need to hold back, as it were, when in combat. This cruiser, similar though he may be to all others of the K't'inga class, can tolerate accelerations and maneuvers far beyond that of his fellows. Of course, an observer will not know this until it is far, far too late. . . . Also, the main drive has no drain other than thrust and shields and weapons. This is far removed from earlier designs in which perhaps a third of all energy output went to light, heat, gravity, and life support."

Kasak's people glanced at one another, filling in the blanks in what the science specialist had said and thinking what that difference could mean in a battle. Too often, skirmishes with Federation or Romulan vessels had to be broken off because the parties were too evenly matched. This ship, and perhaps—if their cruise was a success—this *class* of ship would make all the difference and maybe break that balance.

"Physical connection is by regenerable monoweb filament," Askel continued. His fingers played across a diagnostic keyboard, filling the main screen with diagrams and graphs and figures. Engineer Aktaz stared at them for the drawing of a breath, then laughed softly underneath that same breath and said nothing that the laugh had not made plain already. Among the others there was greater or lesser comprehension dependent upon training and specialization, but all of the small and intimately acquainted crew were plainly aware that this ship was unlike all others they had flown. It was the next generation—if it worked.

"All connections to the cruiser's weapons systems are nonphysical and powered from the scout. Also, and note this well, the two vessels have separate cloaking devices. Both ships can lie in wait together, and the scout, when cast off, can remain concealed from an enemy as effectively as the fathership can—"

Askel broke off, hearing as he had expected to hear at this point the outrage of honorable Klingons who had just been told that they were expected to hide from the foe instead of striking at him and thus gaining glory. He let the birthing argument die still-born, then surveyed them with all the coldness of one who had heard such outcries in the past and had paid them no heed then, either. "Have you said enough?" he began in that low voice that was feared even more than his rage by two generations of ensigns. Then he fell silent as Captain Kasak sutai-Khornezh took a long step forward.

"My children," Kazak said. All of them, even Askel, were hushed by the honor done them through this form of address. "I understand your anger, your concern, your fear for loss of glory to your lines. Know this: if *Hakkarl* responds only one-half as well as the specialists who built him claim he will, there will be glory overflowing for all of you and, yes, for generations yet unborn. The naked stars themselves will watch you, as will the Emperor himself, and all will say, 'Truly, these are Klingons!' Know this, my children, as you know me and all my past endeavors for the Empire: when we are done with *Hakkarl,* our names will be spoken as is that of the Emperor Kahless of ancient times. We will be Unforgettable."

In another commander the shift in language and tone might have been unconscious, but Askel knew Kasak too well to assume anything he did was accidental. So the shift from high-phase oratory to Battle Language was most certainly premeditated. Askel listened to the cheering and the cries of *"kai kassai!"* and kept what he was thinking in the private place behind his own cold eyes.

He wondered what this enthusiastic crew would say if they became aware of the truth behind their captain's intentions for this fine new ship. What they would say—and, more important, what they would do. That was why he was here—not as science specialist, no matter what Kasak sutai-Khornezh might think, but as an operations master of Imperial Intelligence. Askel's "collusion" with I.I. had been a running joke between the two officers since their days in the Houses, lifetimes ago. Askel had always been the quiet one—too thoughtful for his own good was the usual interpretation. A Klingon who thought too much wasn't considered an especially healthy phenomenon, particularly in a navy career where unthinking obedience to superiors was as much a requirement as arms and legs. The I.I. connection had started out as an insult, but time had worn it down. Only the cream of the jest remained, and that was something Askel was not about to share.

Intelligence had become aware that there was likely to be more to the first voyage of KL-1017 than just the usual shakedown cruise. The source of the information had confirmed a great many suspicions and provided answers to several of those niggling questions without which no intelligence executive would be complete.

The amount of time and money spent by a certain passed-over captain to make sure he would acquire *this* ship, for one thing. That sort of activity in a politically unreliable officer was invariably well worth watching, particularly when his reputation was that of Kasak sutai-Khornezh. He had achieved his present status only through a diligent accumulation of glory along the Rom frontier and had used that status as a lever to further himself politically, cultivating powerful supporters both in his own line and among his superior officers by ensuring that his successes reflected well on them. Askel had been impressed by the subtlety the captain had displayed in this undertaking. It had proven so effective that Kasak's surveillance file contained records of regret expressed by high officials that the Empire could not, because of the black mark in his past, reward so worthy an officer in the manner he deserved. Askel had read that twice and then sat for several seconds staring at the name of the epetai—a Thought Admiral no less—who had spoken those words. Stared, and shaken his head in disbelief.

The most that could be done had been done. Kasak had been honored by being entrusted with first-flight command of every new class of ship to leave the yards. It was a backhanded compliment at best, for it implied that if anything went wrong during a test flight, he would be a lesser loss to the Empire than an officer who was considered fully reliable. There was no—and there never had been—taint of treason about Kasak. Only the understandable discontent following the business with the tribbles had blighted his career. Of course there was always a first time for everything.

Particularly when his expensively cultivated chain of contacts was discovered. There was nothing treasonous about that either; Askel had checked, was personally certain, and that sufficed. The certainties of I.I. operations masters were not questioned by lesser forms of life. The data had crossed his desk at irregular intervals for two years now, and at the very most it seemed that Kasak was making moves to feather his own nest through a little privateering on the side.

And *that* was where the most important questions were asked. If this particular captain never had a vessel of his own except for the initial proving voyages of each ship class, then how, and with what, was he intending to become a privateer at all?

And then suddenly the yards refitted a full-size battle cruiser to run with a maximum crew of eight, and it became all too likely where his ship was coming from.

There was another matter, stranger still, and it was the only reason Operations Master Askel had not simply handed the file over to Imperial Security with a termination order attached. It involved Kasak's connection with a planet in Federation space, a planet presently in the throes of some internal dispute.

The Federation called it Dekkanar.

The next briefing was finished in much less time than those among the crew who knew him would normally have expected. Although *zan* Khitar specialized in communications and was skilled at making tight-beam tachyon packets do things their manufacturers hadn't intended, when it came to the preflight lectures that were customary in the navy, his specialization went out of the nearest lock. Khitar had brought the word "boring" to an art form.

Askel watched the others shift on their inspection pads with every indication of pleased relief, and wondered which of them was doubling for Security. Khitar, maybe: Communications was a good position from which to transmit reports. Or maybe it was too good, too obvious. Or maybe that was what he was meant to think, and Security was running another double bluff. Askel smiled his meaningless smile again. I.I. knew most things, but the learning of some of them was more difficult than the learning of others. It would be typical if he went off on this questionable cruise not knowing who his allies were. There was no love lost between Security and Intelligence, and it was not uncommon for the two bureaus to act against each other through sheer professional spite. There was, thought Askel, probably a better way to run things. Security was too quick with its disruptors, and not quick enough with its questions. It was very difficult to interrogate a corpse.

He glanced back at Captain Kasak, who was listening to something Marag was telling him. Marag—acting security officer, for no other reason than that a Klingon ship, even the tiniest deep-space shuttle, *always* had a security officer.

Marag was another longtime friend of the captain's. They were all *friends* insofar as the title could be applied to subordinates of a commander known to hold himself at a distance from the junior grades. At least they were acquaintances, officers who had served with Kasak in the past and had gained by it. During his many successful commands he had gained the respect of his subordinates as well as that of his equals and superiors, through his reputation for success and, more important, because of his unselfish sharing of glory. There were doubtless some who saw this as weakness, but Askel was not one of them. He saw instead a cunningly woven web of strengths, each individually of small account, but when drawn together into the right place at the right time, a most imposing instrument of persuasion that could draw as tight around an unsuspecting throat as a garrote.

Although there was as yet no name to match the eyes, Kasak sutai-Khornezh was quite well aware that he was being watched. There had not been a first flight yet without at least two covert operatives from Imperial Security, and he saw no reason why this one should be any different. There might even be someone from I.I. along for the ride, to keep an eye on what Security was doing. He refused to be concerned. What he was doing was no act of treason.

His contacts were a source of confidential information, the sort of information that seldom came lower down the line than an admiral's private correspondence. Most of it was useless: Kasak had no interest in House politicking, at least not yet. But sooner or later something of real use was bound to reach his ears. It had; it did; it was a gift of glory from the naked stars themselves. He knew of more than just the internal squabbling on Dekkanar and the expulsion orders served on the Federation diplomatic staff. He knew why. A large part of his private fortune had paid for the situation to arise in the first place, and his present position as first-flight commander would let him take best advantage of it. That the present ship, *Hakkarl,* required so small a crew that he could virtually guarantee himself support was just one more gift from whatever spirit guarded honest captains.

The coup, when it succeeded—for there was never any doubt in Kasak's mind but that it *would* succeed —was his chance to restore to his name and to his line all the honors that had been withheld for so long. There would be a promotion to squadron leader, maybe even to admiral, and perhaps the right to start a House and line of his own. All this, and as much more as he dared to dream, would be his through a simple act of provocation.

There would be ships of the Federation Starfleet in orbit around Dekkanar. That was standard practice. When some world or other threw its diplomats off-planet, the Federation always sent ships to protect them. They were a liverless lot, thought Kasak contemptuously, and a far remove from Klingon diplomats, who were well able to take care of themselves, and who indeed were selected as representatives of the Empire only after they had already proved themselves as warriors. And where there were ships there were weapons and the chance of forcing their use. Just one burst of overreaction, one phaser blast or a solitary photon torpedo directed at a vessel of the Klingon Navy, and the Organians would come interfering. In their usual fashion the *g'day't* glowbugs would condemn the aggressor—and cede the questioned planet to the Empire.

The Klingon Empire, of course, would be ignorant of what had happened, and official hands would be thrown up in official horror that any captain should place a new and untried ship in jeopardy from the warmongers of Starfleet. Neither the emperor nor any of his Thought Admirals could dare to authorize such an undertaking, for fear of the whole plan blowing up in their faces should the Organians probe too deep. And so Kasak had determined to act independently. If he failed—not that the possibility entered his mind, so awash was it with schemes and plotting—then there would be no possible allocation of blame against the Empire or against Kasak's line, while if he succeeded . . . *when* he succeeded, it would not merely be a great stroke to bring him all that he desired; it would be an admirable and cunning move in the game of *komerex zha,* the greatest of all games, giving Kasak sutai-Khornezh good repute and, more than that, casting perpetual doubt on the abilities of those who down the years had judged him unworthy. There was just one single hurdle left to clear: the theft or, at the very least, the unauthorized borrowing, of the ship that he was here to test.

All the briefings were completed. Kasak glanced quickly around the bridge and noted that all of his crew were doing as their captain had been doing these five minutes past—breathing shallowly and not through the nose. Kasak said, "Enough of this meat freezer. I transfer my flag to *Tazhat,* and I do it now."

That was a questionable remark at any time, since he was no admiral and had no flag to transfer anywhere, but his crew stood to attention for an instant to salute him. While none smiled outwardly, since that would have been unseemly, Kasak could sense that this present duty had the full support of his crew. He nodded, the only acknowledgment that was required, and said, "Stations."

As was the custom, the crew went together in the first lift car so that they could make the scout ship's bridge ready for Kasak's arrival. The captain and his first officer rode together in the second car. As the door of their car closed, Kasak and Askel said nothing for a moment, only grinned like children with the pleasure of having warm, moist air to breathe again.

"Who'd be a computer?" said Askel finally.

Kasak smiled thinly and tugged mock points on his ears. "I could never get used to the shape," he said. He laughed, then cut the laugh abruptly to silence. "What's your opinion of the ship?"

"Impressive," Askel said, "but I'll trust it when I see it work, and not before. Designers can say what they please, but they don't go out in the *khest'n* things."

"Good."

"Your opinion?"

"Mine exactly." Kasak leaned forward to boost the controls on the heater-humidifier and inhaled the resulting vapor luxuriously. "That's why I insisted on a crew I could rely on."

"Honored, Captain," said Askel.

"No compliment, 'Kel. Just fact. If I can't trust the ship, I'll have to trust the crew." Kasak stared hard at his exec before he spoke again. "I *can* trust them, can't I?"

"There'll be the usual complement of security watchers," said Askel. "And given the ship's capabilities set against the small number of crew aboard, there's probably at least one I.I. agent among them." He paused. "But then you know about me already, don't you?"

Kasak roared with laughter. It was an amusing concept, and that was why Kasak had laughed. It didn't in the least suggest that he was not suspicious of his first officer, and indeed the ploy was so obvious that its use had already increased his watchfulness. I.I. was not so much his concern, however, as Security. Intelligence officers were, by their very title and despite the usual contradiction that it carried, reasonably smart. Certainly they were more than commonly capable of seeing future developments based on current actions. They concerned themselves with the *why* and the *wherefore,* rather than just the *what* observed by Security.

Put another way: a security operative discovering the planned theft of a ship wouldn't even give Kasak time to explain. An I.I. agent wouldn't need the explanation anyway.

Neither officer was interested in further sight-seeing around the battle cruiser's hull. Instead, as soon as they boarded the travel pod, Askel took the little vehicle up and over *Hakkarl*'s back in a single smooth parabola that brought them into precise alignment with the main docking port on *Tazhat*'s spine. Kasak watched without comment. After his display of good humor in the turbolift, he had decided that it was time he became "moody," that being another facet of his reputation and one the crew might be expecting to see during departure from drydock.

Leaving port in a new ship was never the most comfortable time for either captain or crew. More than one captain had been relieved of a command before it had gotten properly under way because some clumsy helmsman had dented either the ship or the dock facilities on the way out. That the accidents might have been a result of faulty systems did little to remove negative notations from their files. There was probably not even much satisfaction in executing the helmsman on the spot. Kasak's moodiness was only half a performance for the benefit of others. The rest of it was genuine concern.

When he stalked onto the scout ship's bridge, everyone was already heads-down and busy. Birds of Prey were built around a nominal crew capacity of twelve, but that had been before the remotes and repeater arrays at every station. Even then, the clutter and the atmosphere within the scout ship—thick, foggy, and warmer even than normal, thanks to the surplus power already being bled off the battle cruiser beneath them—was far preferable to the spaciousness and the dry, grinding chill of the computerized bridge they had just left.

Kasak sat down in the command station and laid both hands flat against the arms of the chair. No one, not even Askel, met the slow glance with which he raked the bridge, for a head raised meant a station unattended, and the crew knew what *that* might lead to. "Screen," he said.

The images came up at once, a multiple overlay of computer-enhanced windows that showed exterior visuals from several points together: from *Tazhat,* from remotes on the structure of Drydock 20, from *Hakkarl.* It was the next best thing to omnipresence. "Status."

"All systems fully active, Dock Control Clearance confirmed. Interlinks live," said Krynn at the helm. "At your command."

"Action."

"Acting."

Kasak felt a brief thrumming of subharmonic vibration underfoot as Krynn brought the scout ship down through that last few meters of separation, handling its thirty thousand tonnes of mass with the delicacy of a dancer. Again the thrumming, and at last, long after he expected it, a deep soft boom that seemed to make the very air shudder in his ears as *Tazhat* settled on *Hakkarl's* back. There was no sensation of impact, but Krynn sat back from her close-maneuvers board, which was now all blue lights, and said, "Secured."

"Then take us out. Maneuvering thrusters forward, impulse power one-third at your discretion."

"Affirm."

"Course, Captain?" said Navigator Khalen.

Kasak analyzed the question for an instant. Of course the navigator needed to know which way to point the ship, but there was bound to be someone aboard, maybe even Khalen himself, who awaited the reply with rather more than professional interest. "Present heading?" he snapped.

"Two-seven-zero, green, standard."

"Then why ask?" Khalen stuck his head down again, suitably chastened. It was a response that gave away no secrets other than that the captain was for some reason out of temper and requiring the bridge crew to read his mind. That in itself would leave them with enough to think about besides extracurricular duties. Kasak waited for a few minutes while they stewed and then said, "Departure angle on viewer."

The Taamar facility filled the screen, receding only slowly as *Hakkarl*'s reaction thrust overcame the inertia of two hundred thousand tonnes. "Distance from Dock Twenty now eight hundred forty meters, climbing, acceleration factor zero by five, climbing," said Krynn. "The ship is sluggish. He dislikes the extra weight."

The main display had already told Kasak that much, and the repeater displays to either side of his chair augmented with further information. It had taken *Hakkarl* this long to cover just over three times his own length; though both ships of the combination had been uprated from standard, it appeared that someone, somewhere, had failed or forgotten to boost the cruiser's maneuvering drive to take into account the additional mass of a scoutship riding piggyback. Kasak touched keys on the command chair and noted that fact, then recorded the pertinent figures for his first-flight report. No matter just now about his future intentions for this ship, the conscientious execution of duty was a habit not easily broken—and besides, it would look strange even to those members of the crew not on the lookout for strangeness if he was not compiling such a report.

"Increase thrust."

The lattice of drydock webbing began to shrink a little faster, but still not fast enough. What if this vessel or one like him were in a situation where impulse and warp were both impossible but swift acceleration was vital to the survival of ship, crew, and mission? Kasak wondered. He leaned back in the chair and began composing a scathing comment intended to make it plain that while only the navy's officers and men went out in carelessly constructed ships, there was an increasing chance that the more careless constructors would start to go out—but without any ship at all.

And then the alarms went off.

"We are being scanned!" Askel looked up from his science station and punched data through to the captain's repeaters.

Kasak glanced at the information as it came up, then at the screen. The drydock continued to shrink in their wake, even more swiftly and yet still not swiftly enough. There were no other images moving there. Nothing had changed—yet. He was not about to wait. *"Degh . . ."*

Krynn did not raise her eyes from helm control, but her right hand anticipated the coming command and moved to rest lightly on the main thruster controls. *"SuH qaH!"*

Now Kasak knew he was being watched: the shift into Battle Language was not something any self-respecting spy could ignore. It was of no account. He looked once more at the unchanging screen, then made his decision. *"chuyDah HoS'a'!"*

"vanglI'!" Krynn pushed for thrust, boosting to

maximum in a single sweep of the levers. The ships vibrated slightly as their combined weight fought for a moment against the pressure of acceleration, then gave up the struggle. On screen, Taamar and its dock facilities became a bright, fuzzy blot as they seemed to jump into the distance—and then spawned a flurry of smaller specks that came glittering in *Hakkarl's* wake.

"Show mag six," he said, and watched as the screen image expanded, cluttered now with small ships against a distorted drydock background. "Identify."

"Gunboats," said Khalen. "Dock security contingent, twenty-plus."

"Sir," said Khitar, "I have a communication from head of security, Taamar facility. He orders this ship back to Dock Twenty at once."

Security Officer Marag laughed. "They haven't told him about the test," he said. "Too much for his brain to comprehend."

"More realistic this way," said Kasak to nobody in particular, even though his words carried all over the bridge. "Shall we see what *Hakkarl* can do?"

There was no reply, not even a cheer. If they were starting a test exercise early, and without the knowledge of the station security chief, then the testing was likely to be more stringent and the exercise more realistic than any of them had anticipated. Assuming that it *was* an exercise, and not any one of several other possibilities. But they were ready, whatever it was.

"Battle alert," said Kasak. "Secure for combat maneuvers. *Zan* Katta, weapons free." That did bring him a stare, which still did nothing to reveal potential spies and traitors, because no matter for how briefly, the stare came from everyone on the bridge.

Captain Kasak sat back in the command chair and stroked the palm of one hand over his forehead crest, silently inviting someone—anyone—to make a comment. No one did, certainly not while the fingertips of his other hand were doing a little dance along the grip of his holstered sidearm. Then he grinned wickedly and let the tension break. "Disrupters only. Set for heavy stun."

The release of breath was a soft sighing that was not really audible through the other sounds of the scout ship's bridge, but Kasak fancied that he heard it anyway. For just one minute there his loyal crew had truly begin to wonder what sort of mission this was, and then just as suddenly had been completely reassured. He silently thanked Marag for his comment, an observation which, coming from the ship's security officer, carried more weight than if it had been uttered by anyone else on board. Certainly a combat-hardened soldier's opinion was worth more than that of a desk-bound paper-pusher like the Taamar head of security, and he could plainly detect the amusement in Khitar's voice as the communications specialist relayed yet another message.

"More from Station Security, Captain. He demands that *Hakkarl* be returned immediately or he will personally take steps."

"Not without an environment suit, I trust?" said Kasak mildly. The laugh was better than the joke deserved, and it was not just crew members responding dutifully to their commander's wit. They meant it. "Ignore all further communications from that source. Weapons?"

"Preheat cycle completed, sir, running hot. Prelocks engaged on—" Katta hesitated, looking again at her board as if seeing it for the first time. "We have prelocks confirmed on all targets, Captain. All twenty-three of them."

"Screen: tactical."

He had never seen a tactical display so crowded with information. Velocity, trajectory, vector, status

—all of that and more for each of the station intercep-
tors, and each one of them overlaid by the green
triangle of a target lock. Once he gave the order to lock
on and those triangles changed to blue, they would
designate a certain hit. At least, so the designers
claimed.

"Helm, stand by on impulse power. Engage cloaking device on my command. Have the gunboats raised
their shields?"

Askel consulted a readout. "Not yet, sir."

"Good. Raise ours."

"Acting!"

"Helm . . ." Kasak watched the complex tactical
display, waiting for the first change in status aboard
the pursuing gunboats, the first indication from his
sensors that they might do more than follow. As they
detected the raised shields, weapons data went from
standby to active on five of them, and he had seen
enough. "Helm, impulse power, evasive corkscrew
down starboard, go! Engage cloaking device!"

With one hand Krynn hit maneuvering controls
that sent *Hakkarl-Tazhat* into an accelerating twist
out of the line of fire, and with the other she cut in the
cloak, so that neither Kasak nor anyone else on the
bridge were quite sure what produced the kick in their
livers that was like the effects of a very bad Saurian
brandy. All that concerned Kasak was the way in
which the gunboat formation broke apart as *Hakkarl-
Tazhat* vanished from screens and sensors and visual
all at once and all together.

Light flared from four of the gunboats as they fired
wild at *Hakkarl*'s last known position, and Askel
leaned over his console. "Incoming fire," he said, "at
five-two, five-nine, six-six, six-seven. All clean
misses."

"Zan Katta, you may return the favor."

Risking her captain's wrath, Katta stared at him,

knowing that what he had ordered was impossible. Her thoughts were shared by everyone. They were still cloaked, and no ship yet built could fire from cloak.

To even attempt it was to create a power drain massive enough to shut down the main drive, the gravity, the environmental . . .

And the life support.

Kasak slammed his clenched fist against the arm of the command chair and snarled at her. "I command! Obey! *baHwI', baH!*"

Katta blinked, swallowed—and hit all the firing controls at once. On the screen, coronae of blue incandescence bloomed among the gunboats as disrupter batteries stabbed lances of energy from target to target. By the time a certain startled Klingon gunnery officer could draw breath twice, the entire formation of twenty-three small ships was tumbling all over the screen and the sky it displayed, crews stunned and controls useless.

Hakkarl's power-consumption gauges had barely flickered.

Kasak watched for a moment in absolute satisfaction, then said, "Stand down from battle alert, secure from combat and evasive maneuvering—but remain cloaked. After this, every Imperial vessel in the quadrant will try to gain a sort of glory by making us look as foolish."

He stood up and stretched as if he had been slightly bored by the whole business. It was another mannerism, one for which he was well known, having once visibly yawned at the sight of a fleet of Romulan ships that outnumbered his command by seven to one, and the end of an engagement would not have seemed the same without it. "Cruise stations," he said to the bridge in general. "Forward angle on the screen. Once we are clear of the Taamar primary, come to warp

63

four. Maintain speed and course until I instruct otherwise."

Kasak turned to leave the bridge, then stopped and swung back toward his crew. Praise was not expected, nor was the giving of it a requirement of good command, but . . . Kasak eyed them all slowly, the gaze seeming to see more than perhaps it ever could, making the innocent writhe as much as the guilty. Finally he relented and permitted them the honor of a salute. "A good first combat," he said. "The others will be better." Praise, promise of glory, and veiled threat all in one. Klingon was an economical language.

The crew returned his salute as he walked to the waiting turbolift car that would take him to his quarters and to the other, less dramatic work that awaited all captains. A voice that might have been Krynn's or Katta's, but never Askel's, said quietly behind him, *"Oapla', joHwI."*

Kasak entered the lift and turned so that they could see his face, and its total lack of any expression. "Success, my lord," the voice had said. He would have both, the one giving promotion to the other. And perhaps a consort besides. The lift door closed just in time to hide his smile.

Chapter Four

THE U.S.S. *ENTERPRISE* slid down out of warp and into normal space in a coruscation of hard radiation that sleeted off her skinfield. Normally there was nobody to see the flaring Cherenkov corona that formed her bow wave, but this time she had an audience.

Vanguard and *Sir Richard* hung in the shadow of a planetoid, dark and silent to both the visual and the electronic senses of any who might be traversing a sector of Federation space where none but Federation vessels had a right to be. Still, their presence here was sufficiently unusual to raise eyebrows from the fringes of the Romulan Star Empire to the Imperial Palace on the Klingon homeworld and all points between, if they were spotted.

Which was why both ships were quiet, and their respective commanders probably flinched just a bit at the relative commotion made by the arrival of the starship. Frontiers and Neutral Zones and official protests had not stopped Klingon spy ships before and were unlikely to do so now. And the presence of the *Enterprise* herself would, if observed, likely cause comment. At the very least.

* * *

Jim Kirk sat back in the center seat and felt himself relax just a little bit. There was always just the smallest chance that something unexpected might be waiting for a starship dropping out of warp, and until the lack of surprises was confirmed he preferred to stay at yellow alert.

"Lower shields," he said finally.

"Hailing frequencies are open, sir," Uhura said, "and I'm receiving transmissions from both *Vanguard* and *Sir Richard.*"

"On screen, Commander."

"Jim, are you well? You sure look well! They can't be working you hard enough!" Captain Farey's face— or, more accurately, Nicholas Farey's bearded grin— came up in one section of the screen. Uhura had considerately windowed it so that both Captain Farey and Captain North were visible.

"Hi, Jim. Welcome to the back end of nowhere." Gytha North looked as lean and dangerous as she had the last time Jim encountered her. She had taken to wearing her silver-shot hair loose around her high-cheekboned face, but it would still be regulation and if necessary she would be able to quote him each and every pertinent paragraph. Captain North had always made a point of understanding Starfleet regulations. It made them easier to bend. "Admire the scenery. There. Didn't take long, did it?"

"Yes, Nic, I'm well, and, no, Gytha, it didn't," Jim said, and smiled thinly. "So much for the small talk. How much information did you two get?"

"That's Jim, straight to business." Farey shrugged. His expression turned suddenly grim. "Well, if you got Nhoma's signal, you know as much as we do."

"Understood," said Jim, getting to his feet. "Well. This may be a secure transmission—but we should have these talks in person. I'll meet you both in our transporter room."

"Er, Jim, there'll be three of us."

"Three . . . ?" Jim was momentarily at a loss before his memory dropped a name into place. "Oh, yes, Colonel Johnson." He paused to check how his next question would sound when it came out. "Why wasn't he on one bridge or the other?"

"Bridges for Starfleet captains and shuttle bays for constabulary colonels. That's what he told me." Nic Farey smiled a bit, not looking much upset. "In fact the man has had a lot more to do than stand in the corner like an aspidistra. Nobody bothered giving us an exact time of rendezvous, and 'best speed' as per signal can vary just a bit, so we—"

"Nic, Jim's waiting for us."

"Right. Sorry, Jim. We'll be with you in, uh, five."

Farey was as good as his word. Five minutes later, three whining spindles of light expanded out and became Starfleet officers standing on *Enterprise*'s transporter pads—actually, two Starfleet officers and one in khaki one-piece work fatigues. The name seemed all too appropriate, for Jim privately thought that the man wearing them looked tired. Too tired for what the mission had in store for him—even though there was nothing tired about the precision of his salute.

"Colonel Todd Johnson, Diplomatic Protection Group. Permission to come aboard?"

He was a big man, middling tall, solidly built, with dark, closely cropped hair. He seemed young to be a full colonel. To Kirk's eye Johnson looked like someone who had spent time as a duty sergeant before climbing the commissioned ladder. His rank tabs would probably have been new and shiny had they not been of the same material as his fatigues, a few shades darker for the sake of contrast but not enough to be an obvious target. DPG personnel were supposed to get in the way of unpleasantness before it reached anyone more important, but that didn't mean they had to dress to attract it.

"Permission granted, Colonel Johnson," said Jim. "Welcome aboard the *Enterprise.*"

"Thank you, sir. Excuse my appearance." He gestured at the coveralls, ignoring the fact that they were perfectly clean and had creases sharp enough to shave with. "I wasn't expecting a briefing as soon as you arrived. I didn't have time to change."

"The colonel was running an equipment maintenance exercise on board the *Richard,* and he won't order his people to do anything he hasn't already done himself," said Captain North. There was no inflection in her voice, but Jim thought he could hear disapproval in there somewhere. "He pushes hard. Sometimes too hard. You're not indispensable if you're there all the time."

"Sorry, Captain." Johnson was smiling; plainly he'd heard this more than once already. "But you can only trust equipment if you've checked through it yourself."

Nic Farey said, "And then you're quite sure whom to blame?"

"If you're still alive and unhurt, why blame anybody?"

They were walking along G deck from the transporter room to the main briefing room, and that was where McCoy and Spock caught up with them. The doctor was grousing as usual, but in a more understated way than usual and not, for once, trying to include Spock in his grumbling—for which the Vulcan looked as relieved as he was willing to let show. McCoy seemed to be suffering from some sort of depression, but Jim didn't ask about it; he already knew the reason, having given the order himself, and equally, knew that he would hear all the details just as soon as Bones had polished up his choice of phrases and was ready to hand them out.

For the first part of the briefing, the computer merely reiterated what all present knew already: the "request" by the Dekkan Planetary Council that all Federation personnel be off world within a certain time span, and the evident enthusiasm shown by the PDI terrorist organization to be responsible for those kinds of acts for which the council had stated bluntly they could *not* be held responsible.

Spock put the library computer back to standby and stared at its controls for a few seconds. "It would appear, from study of the available data, that even if the Planetary Council members reconsider their position—and that cannot be guaranteed—the PDI terrorists will put up an armed resistance to any such weakening of purpose, and given the historical context of similar situations, will give in only when it suits their purpose to be 'defeated by overwhelmingly superior numbers and firepower' or"—he looked around the table—"or when they are wiped out."

Spock's somber pronouncement fell with leaden finality into the middle of the discussion. Todd Johnson glanced briefly at the Vulcan and then nodded as if satisfied with what he had read there. "Mr. Spock is quite correct," he said. "He also knows, as do you all, that employing 'overwhelming firepower' is something that we must not do—and indeed, are not equipped to do."

"The terrorists know it, too," said Jim. "They know it because they're dealing with the Federation and not with the Klingon Empire."

"Impasse," muttered Nic Farey. "They can do what they like, because we can't do anything of the sort. Wonderful."

"So what *can* we do?" Gytha's voice, and her impatience or incipient frustration, brought the words out as an irritable snap, unusual enough during a high-level briefing to turn heads.

It was Spock who gave her an answer, and they could all see how inadequate he felt that answer to be. "Initially, Captain, we can do nothing at all. I have been reading through the finer print of General Order Twelve. Computer: correlate subsection 7.1, rules of engagement, with function of the present assignment."

"Working," said the computer's calm, synthesized voice. It took maybe three minutes to relay what Spock had requested, and when it was done they all sat in silence and digested what they had been told.

"This," said Johnson finally, "might as well have been written by the other side."

The Starfleet officers knew already about the dangerously tight restrictions on shipboard navigational and defensive systems, but what with one thing and another involved in bringing the ship back from near-leave to fully operational status, none of those aboard *Enterprise* had been able to find the time to wade through reams of impenetrable officialese and learn what else was involved in General Order 12. The fine print that Spock had mentioned made for unpleasant reading, written as it was by some bureaucrat light-years from any of the risks he was so casually dismissing.

Most of its instructions referred to ground units, in this case the five hundred men and women of Johnson's Diplomatic Protection Group. Among all the other "whereas" and "notwithstanding" jargon was the nasty requirement that, in order to indicate the peaceful nature of their mission, helmets and body armor were strictly forbidden "unless proven necessary by subsequent events."

"Which means," said the colonel, "that we aren't allowed any protective gear at all until someone gets shot at, maybe killed. Because until that happens, we don't have any need of protection."

"No weapons either. Not even hand phasers." Gytha North smiled crookedly. "You all heard that, I'm sure: 'Under no circumstances may any weapon be carried by Federation personnel unless and until conditions outlined in paras. seven through twelve are met or exceeded. In such situation issue of phasers may . . .' et cetera, et cetera, blah, blah, blah. But: 'this restriction is and remains absolute when taken in reference to hand phasers to avoid the potential of provocation that is concomitant with the carrying and/or wearing of any and all concealed weaponry.'"

She finished the quotation with a sort of bitter relish in her voice, then glanced along the table at the other Starfleet officers. "Dear God. Now, how many times have you gentlemen beamed down into known hazard without one of those little lifesavers at the back of your belt, eh?"

"There will be no beaming down here," said Spock. "Commanders Uhura and Sulu have advised me that the system's primary planet is at a peak of sunspot activity. Bearing in mind the prohibitions on sensor-related operations, navigational systems will be disrupted to a greater or lesser extent, but communication both to and from the planet and intership remains relatively immune. My analysis has also revealed a most unpleasant energy fluctuation. Its pattern is a natural equivalent of the electronic countermeasures employed against transporter beams. In effect, any attempt at particle transmission and coherent matter reassembly within the 4725 Cancri system would be . . . scrambled."

Jim's mouth tightened at an ugly and still-painful memory. He had seen what Spock so dryly described, most recently—*too* recently—on board the *Enterprise* just before the V'ger incident. He had lost two good friends on that occasion, and he preferred not to think about a similar accident involving the eight twenty-person transporters aboard each of the support ships.

Bones had evidently thought about it already, but had more on his mind than that. "It seems to be your day for making cheerful observations," he said. "Anything further to add?"

"Only to observe that unless this situation improves drastically during the next thirty hours, all landings and evacuations from Dekkanar must be undertaken by shuttlecraft," said Spock, "and to admit a certain surprise at your reaction, Doctor. With your well-known dislike of the matter-transporter system, I would have expected you to be pleased at the announcement rather than otherwise."

"Normally you'd be right, dammit. But not this time. Have you seen what's being done to my sickbay?"

"I have not seen," said Spock, pedantic to the last, "having been at the science station on the bridge during all of my most recent duty shifts." The Vulcan paused, and then continued more gently, "But I do know, and why it troubles you."

Jim glanced at McCoy. His guess about what had been bugging Bones was right. To put a starship's sickbay on full emergency readiness was a drastic step, but he had taken it earlier that day. The order had come through McCoy, of course, but even though they both knew what it entailed, the actuality was never pleasant to see.

The sickbay was designed to handle day-to-day health care for the four hundred–odd individuals of various species who made up *Enterprise*'s crew and who were working in an environment that was as safe as the ship's designers could make it. Minor illnesses and injuries and now and then the equivalent of an industrial accident were all that McCoy and his staff expected to encounter in the normal course of events. To all intents and purposes, it was a small-town hospital. That it should suddenly be stripped of all nonessentials and converted to the dressing station for a major disaster, cleared for a 500 percent increase in patients, and equipped for emergency trauma surgery on a massive scale was enough to unsettle even the phlegmatic chief medical officer.

That same step had been taken aboard *Vanguard* and *Sir Richard;* not only did the three ships have a combined crew complement of over a thousand souls, but there were Johnson's people to consider and most of all the civilians trapped on a planet whose government no longer wanted or protected them—and whose lunatic fringe seemed more and more likely to take some advantage of that lack of protection. That the standard evacuation of these civilians and the medevac of anyone injured during the operation was now restricted to shuttlecraft came as something of a shock to those who had been seeing matters in terms of mass beam-ups.

"And because of all this concern about provoking the Dekkani," said Captain Farey to the briefing in general, "we're here with a pair of support vessels and a starship designed primarily for deep-space exploration—but none of those vessels are capable of making planetfall! Jim, no insult to *Enterprise,* but Starfleet Command must have known what was needed for this operation—something that could go down there, fill up with people, and then leave.

Something big enough to do the job in only one trip—at the very least a couple of bulk transports to make this all a whole lot simpler," Nic finished irritably, breathing hard.

Jim looked at *Vanguard*'s captain and remembered when he, too, had been full of sound and spit. Maybe getting older and more sensible wasn't so bad after all. "It would be simpler still if we were serving in the Klingon Empire, Nic," he said. "You know how they respond to rebellions on their subject worlds. But I don't see anyone in this room wanting a transfer. . . ." McCoy stared at him, then looked once more at the tangle of red tape whose words covered the main screen and muttered something under his breath. "I missed that, Bones. Again, please?"

"What I said was, we're the good guys."

"That's the theory."

"And the good guys never shoot first, right?"

"Right."

McCoy sighed heavily. "That's what I was afraid of."

The *Enterprise* and her consorts came out of warp three days later, a respectable distance from the tangle of ionization and debris surrounding 4725 Cancri and its inner planets. Time-sensitive though the mission was, Jim and the other captains had agreed that there was no sense barging into such a mess any faster than safety permitted—and besides, a high-speed approach was prohibited as being too provocative.

Provocative or not, any approach was dangerous, and at any speed. They held station just clear of the system—and of the Dekkan long-range scanners—while *Enterprise* once again played host to the other captains and the DPG colonel during the last bit of peace and quiet any of them could expect to enjoy for the next several days. All three ships had been running on alert status for close on a week now, and Jim decided to take advantage of this short pause for breath before the heavy work began. He was senior officer here, and until Johnson was on the planet's surface and command of the mission passed to him, he was responsible for any decisions that might affect the other ships in his little fleet. After a quick consultation, Jim cheerfully gave clearance that all three vessels should maintain a listening watch but otherwise stand down from alert until they began their tippy-toe nonaggressive no-bumping-into-things approach. Feeling rather pleased with himself, he took the turbolift from the bridge and went down to join his guests in the officers' wardroom on C deck.

They were sitting quietly in the lounge area, watching Uhura's disturbing simulation of the approach to orbital insertion around 4725 Cancri IV on one of the big wall screens and, judging by the expressions on their faces, were not enjoying the view. Jim looked briefly at the screen and made a sound of faint but emphatic disapproval. "I've already seen this one," he said. "It doesn't get any better. Nothing on another station?"

There were a few halfhearted grins at that. "I just hope your entertainment channels are as good as they're supposed to be," said Nic, lifting the screen's voder remote and tabbing it to *active* with his thumb. "Show entertainment channel One, please."

"Hechu'! jISaHbe'!" barked the speakers an instant later. *"chuyDaH!"*

Nic eased the volume down to a tolerable level and tried to pretend he hadn't almost jumped out of his skin. "What interesting programs you people watch, to be sure," he said carefully, and stared as a Klingon warship powered its way across the screen on the thrusters its commander had just called for.

Captain North and Colonel Johnson looked at the screen, then at each other, then at Jim, and realized rather sheepishly that they had both reacted in exactly the same way. Very slowly they removed their right hands from the place on their belts where a phaser would have been. Gytha then sat up very straight, narrowed her eyes, and watched the Klingon cruiser for a few seconds more.

"Since when has *Battle Cruiser Vengeance* been available from the entertainment library?" Then she grinned. "And where can I get a first-generation copy?"

Jim laughed and saw Dr. McCoy laughing with him, though almost certainly for reasons of his own. Jim hadn't forgotten that crack about making a diagnostic psychologist out of him, and he smiled to himself at the thought that Bones wasn't so far from the truth after all. As usual.

"Have a word with our Mr. Freeman. He'll be happy to oblige." Jim sauntered up to the bar, got himself a drink, sipped it, and felt even more pleased at his inspiration to give everyone some time off— even though McCoy *had* been there before him and the only beverage readily available without resort to the processor was a jug of pungent mint julep.

He could see a bright, irregularly shaped speck through the viewports at the rear of the lounge. Seen naked-eye at five kilometers' distance, it was clearly one of the two support ships, but at such a distance impossible to identify as either *Vanguard* or *Sir Richard*.

Jim swirled his drink around its glass and watched for a moment. The three Starfleet vessels formed the points of an equilateral triangle, and the empty space between them was currently busy with a scurry of shuttlecraft that flitted from one ship to another and back again as pilot-qualified DPG personnel accustomed themselves to rapid transit without benefit of transporter beams. Every now and again Jim would catch a glint of light as one of the little wedge-shaped craft went into the tumbling maneuver that had become standard as the quickest method of presenting docking ring to docking port, but for the rest of the time they might as well not have been there at all.

Earlier in the ship's day, Colonel Johnson and two of his junior commanders had spent several hours out there in an engineering-section travel pod, watching the exercise for real rather than on screen and instrument monitor. Those same men were now standing by the viewports, close enough to feel the soft breath of chill that flowed eternally from the clearsteel no matter what level of field insulation might be installed to prevent from seeping in. And yet they weren't noticing. Indeed, they weren't noticing anything except what they watched through binoculars.

Professionalism could be taken to extremes, thought Jim, and took care to keep the thought away from his face. He had been accused on more than one occasion—(usually by McCoy)—of being too professional in his approach to command, but he had never been so single-minded as these young officers. They saw nothing of the strange, magnificent grandeur beyond those viewports, none of the worlds, the life, the civilizations, that had drawn him into Starfleet and out among the stars. They saw only what they had been trained to see—the movement of men and of ships. Maybe if the risk of imminent dissolution had been absent, they would have been acting differently, but somehow Jim doubted it.

Their colonel was rather more approachable, he thought, sampling the julep with appreciation. McCoy had outdone himself, as he always did when *Enterprise* was playing host to visitors.

Johnson had already been through the coldly professional stage of his career, and with that acting as a buffer against misplaced opinions, he had shown himself able to relax just a little more. But not enough, not yet. Jim always felt uneasy going into a hazardous situation in company he wasn't sure of. Maybe Johnson would eventually forget their difference in rank and unwind enough to talk to Jim as he talked to the other two ship captains instead of giving the impression of standing perpetually at attention even when he was sitting down. Then they might be able to get on a little better than they were doing now. Jim smiled; maybe he really *should* get some training in diagnostic psychology. Or maybe someone—such as Bones—could explain to the colonel that Admiral James T. Kirk resented his promotion just as much as the colonel probably treasured *his,* and then . . .

His gaze strayed to the ports and the view beyond, and all thoughts froze.

Two of the shuttlecraft were no longer just blinks of reflected light. Now they were identifiable vessels, framed between the warp nacelles and growing larger as they closed with *Enterprise* for yet another of the interminable touch-and-go docking runs. Except that this time they were both on approach for the same docking port, just one deck overhead. . . .

Afterward it seemed to Jim that his glass hit the floor and exploded into fragments a measurable time before he came down from his own vault—over the back of a row of chairs—with his hand already slapping the emergency override on the nearest communicator.

"Break right! *Break!*"

He was yelling and didn't care who heard him, didn't care about the dignity of rank, didn't care about anything except the twenty tons of metal on a collision course with his ship. All over the sky shuttlecraft flinched sideways at the sound of the one order no one ever paused even to think about. They simply slid to a dead stop until the emergency was resolved.

Except the two closest to *Enterprise*. They entered the break properly enough, but one was already far too close to the other for the arc of its turn to do anything but intersect with that of the other vessel. At first there was only a glittering puff of chipped-off thermoglaze as nose and tail came violently into contact; but an instant later one of the shuttlecraft began tumbling end over end as two of its maneuvering thrusters jammed at full power. And this time it was headed straight for the main viewports.

There was no running about, no screaming, no panic—not, as McCoy speculated later, because Starfleet personnel were any braver than ordinary mortals, but simply because there was no time to start before the incident was over.

It ended as suddenly as it had begun when the shuttlecraft jolted to a standstill as abruptly as if it had run into an invisible wall, only spinning on its own axis now until the pilot thought to cut all power. "What in blazes . . . ?" said Jim aloud in a voice that sounded ridiculously calm.

"Gotcha, ya haunless wee bugger," said Scotty's voice over an open channel. "Git away from ma engines." The Glaswegian accent that surfaced only under stress was thick enough now to defy understanding by most of the crew aboard the *Enterprise,* and even some of the other native Scots were probably having trouble. There was a moment's silence as the carrier hissed on empty air, and then the speakers crackled briefly with the unmistakable sound of someone clearing his throat. *"Ahum. Engineering to Captain Kirk."*

"Kirk here. Uh, thank you for that, Mr. Scott. Tractors, I presume?"

"Aye." Again Scotty paused, this time not so much to get his rogue accent under control as to consider how to say something that might be interpreted the wrong way. *"I, er, I wasna intendin' any insult to the colonel's pilots, Captain, but wi' all those little ships runnin' about this confined space I thought it best t' keep an eye on them. And t' keep all the tractor installations manned . . . jist in case somethin' should happen."*

Jim was finally able to let his grin of relief shine through. "It did happen, Scotty, even though the worst part of it didn't. Just stay on those tractors."

"I think, Admiral," said Johnson, very stiff and proper, at attention in his dress uniform, "I should check on the health of my men."

"And I think, Colonel, that you should first join me in a drink"—Jim looked the colonel up and down and thought he recognized the symptoms—"to celebrate that both pilots are still alive for you to tear their stripes off. Agreed?" He glanced out of the viewport at where the last act of the brief drama was taking place. The tractor virtuoso—probably Montgomery Scott himself, though the chief engineer had been too modest to say so—had one of the damaged shuttlecraft in tow and was drawing it down toward the hangar bay at the stern of *Enterprise*'s secondary hull. The other was being escorted toward the same destination by two engineering work bees.

"I . . ." Todd Johnson retained that ramrod-straight posture for a few seconds longer, then relaxed into a more comfortable stance. "Agreed."

"Good," said Jim. "I can particularly recommend the mint julep." He smiled at Bones, who after all his fussy performance over making up the drink was starting to look smug, and then eyed the floor where his own julep had landed. "At least this time it didn't melt the carpet."

"Captain on the bridge."

Chekov touched control keys on the center seat and waited the brief moment for confirmation before coming to his feet. "Keptin, you have the conn."

"Thank you, Mr. Chekov." Jim settled back and cast a quick glance down the latest pad screen before initialing it. "Status?"

"All stations and departments report green, Keptin, although we are already encountering a degree of interference from the primary. Systems requiring shutdown under General Order Twelve are holding on standby response."

"Communications remain unaffected, Captain," said Uhura. "You can advise the Dekkan Planetary Council of our approach at any time."

"Best do it now, before they pick us up and start getting agitated. Standard friendship messages, then tell them who we are and why we're here."

"Just that, Captain?"

"For the time being, yes. I think they'll understand that an exchange of pleasantries would be somewhat out of place at this stage of the proceedings. If they have anything to say, however . . ."

"Noted." Uhura smiled to herself as she turned back to the comm board. It was well known that when the captain was officially annoyed with someone or something, the first thing he did was to take refuge behind the punctilious good manners that were as close as any Starfleet officer could come to insult— and right now, he was *very* much annoyed with the Dekkani.

That annoyance had a lot to do with the approach

parameters worked out by Navigation. Sulu had worked well beyond the end of his shift to provide them, and by all reports had barely missed a beat even when it seemed likely he was going to be sharing the bridge with half a shuttlecraft. Initial speed was going to be no more than $.425c$, tapering right down as they entered the garbage-rich zone farther into the 4725 Cancri system. Given the present attitude of the Dekkani toward the Federation in general, and most likely Starfleet in particular, Jim liked the notion of a slow and cautious approach to Dekkanar almost as little as he liked what was at the end of it: an unshielded, defenses-down close orbit of a potentially hostile planet. Bad enough with only the *Enterprise* to worry about, it was far more than three times worse with a pair of equally defenseless ships tagging along.

Uhura took the transdator out of her ear and looked at the inoffensive piece of equipment as if it had bitten her. "Well!" she said, and then, louder, "message . . . acknowledged, Captain."

"One of *those* acknowledgments, Commander?"

"Yes, sir, one of those. Essentially 'Come, go, good riddance.'" She put the transdator back in place and touched a key to log the message and response, then shook her head in mock regret. "I hadn't realized until now just how well the comm translation circuits can handle idiom. What they used to call 'earthy and colorful.'"

Jim glanced at her sympathetically. "Contact *Vanguard* and *Sir Richard*. Let them know we've received approach clearances. And, Uhura, get a hard copy of all communications from this point on."

"It's already being done, sir. Even including the exact text of the Dekkani acknowledgment."

"Good. There's no sense in waiting any longer. Mr. Sulu, one-half impulse power."

"One-half it is, Captain."

"Take us in. . . ."

Sulu's approach was, as usual, a balance between precision and inspiration. Because they were already traveling well below light speed, all three vessels had to be flown. It was less exciting than Uhura's simulator approach, but more wearing on the nerves because of the extra time it took. And at a point just outside the orbit of 4725 Cancri IV.

"Keptin! We're being scanned!"

"Very good, Mr. Chekov, noted and logged. No active response at this time." Jim looked quickly at the data and didn't like what he saw. The sensors currently sweeping over his ship were the search and target–acquisition systems that usually preceded a phaser or a photon torpedo target lock. *Damn.*

"Go to yellow alert, shields to standby. Do *not* adopt any defensive posture, and do not power up weapons without my express order."

"Understood, Keptin."

"I know. Just making sure. Uhura, shipwide intercom, please." The communicator beeped obediently. "Attention all hands, this is the captain. *Enterprise* is being scanned by weapons-level sensors. Ignore the scan. This is not—I repeat, not—an act of hostility. Just bad manners. We're going to get a lot of behavior like this from the Dekkani before we're through, because right now they don't like us much. Don't give them reason to like us less because someone overreacted. We're not supposed to provoke them—don't let them provoke us. Kirk out."

They really don't want to make this easy for us, he thought gloomily, then shrugged the gloom aside. It could have been a lot worse: he could have ended up sitting behind a desk in Starfleet somewhere reading about all this.

"Mr. Sulu, at your discretion, take us into orbit."

Orbital insertion was trouble-free. *Vanguard* followed suit thirty minutes later and *Sir Richard* twenty minutes after that. And there they sat, the representatives of the United Federation of Planets, doing nothing but the starship equivalent of twiddling their thumbs until such time as the Dekkan government chose to acknowledge their existence and implement the transfer of Federation personnel. *For a government so keen to be rid of unwanted guests,* thought Jim after the first hour had gone by in silence, *they're in no great hurry to start shifting our diplomats out.*

In accordance with General Order 12, *Enterprise* and her consorts had shut down all of their active sensors, which might have shown up on other screens and been perceived as an unfriendly gesture. It didn't, as Captain North had pointed out, prevent the Starfleet vessels from maintaining a watch on Dekkanar—just to avoid any unpleasant surprises. All the surveillance equipment they were using worked on the same principle: passive systems quietly registered the presence of movement, heat, or radiation. The two support ships showed up as bright on-screen blips, reassuringly tagged with each vessel's name, registry, and ID code. A constantly changing pattern of communications and weather satellites tracked to and fro, emitting radio waves from their big transceiver dishes and infrared heat traces from their power packs—

—Then all of *Enterprise*'s alarms went off at once.

"Three vessels leaving the planet's atmosphere, Captain." Spock peered over the science console. "Make that eight—all heading directly toward us."

All around the bridge people scrambled to their stations—and stopped there, poised and ready for action.

Jim sat with forced calm in his center seat and waited for more information as he watched the eight computer-enhanced signals, bright with infrared from what could only have been old-style rocket exhausts.

"Analysis, Mr. Spock?"

"Sensors indicate rocket propulsion of a fairly primitive type."

"But propelling what? Guided missiles? Are we being fired on?"

"Difficult to say, Captain. The rockets are producing so much raw IR that a more detailed—"

"Best guess, and fast. What are they?"

"Keptin, range is now fourteen hundred kilometers and closing!"

Jim swiveled in his chair. "Spock?"

"Circumstances dictate caution, sir. If they *are* guided missiles—"

"Battle stations. Shields up, lock phasers on." Jim took one last look at the screen, blinked, then barked, "Belay that last order!" The rockets were shutting down. Within a matter of seconds all eight rocket flares had winked out, and without that inadvertent jamming the sensor-linked computer started to gain some hard data at long last. There was one more moment of on-screen confusion when the contacts multiplied, but then it became clear that this was not some form of deception but merely a dumping of strap-on fuel tanks before the original targets came coasting on toward orbit.

They were shuttles—clumsy wide-winged orbiters that reminded Jim sharply of the old *Enterprise* pictured on one wall of the rec deck. He let out a long-held breath between his teeth. "Will somebody please shut off that noise," he said, and somebody did, the red-alert siren expiring in mid-whoop as the bridge lights came back to normal.

"Sensors indicate life signs aboard all of the recently launched orbital vessels," Spock said.

The Dekkan shuttles continued on their way around the planet, each one shifting gradually under the impetus of its reaction jets so that by the time they went sliding around the curve of Dekkanar's horizon and out of sight they were moving in a loose arrowhead formation like a gaggle of geese.

"That's strange." Sulu touched controls on his helm console, and the cloud-whorled image on the screen became overlaid by a computer schematic. More controls created a projected flight pattern for the shuttles—a pattern which plainly indicated that if they had wanted to rendezvous with the Federation ships they could have done so as soon as they left orbit. "They'll be back in this location in . . . seventeen-point-two minutes," he said, almost to himself, "and then we'll see."

"What are we expecting to see, Mr. Sulu?" said Spock.

"Sir, I'm not sure." Another overlay joined those already on screen—more flight predictions based on trajectory, orbital velocity, and as many variables as Sulu could think to run into the computer. "But I don't like the look of it. Because I don't think they're carrying evacuees."

"And you think we'll find out in seventeen minutes?"

"Yes, Captain, I do."

"It is now sixteen-point-four-five minutes," said Spock. Jim swung the center seat around just enough to give his science officer a sidelong look. It was returned with the bland lack of expression that he knew so well. "Approximately," said Spock. "And counting."

"Of course. Thank you, Mr. Spock. Carry on." Jim took care to hide any suggestion of a smile. He couldn't think of any mission that had gone so far wrong as to stifle Spock's occasional exercise of the sense of humor he claimed not to possess.

Uhura's comm station beeped. She listened briefly, then turned toward Jim. "Captain, incoming communication from *Vanguard*. Captain Farey wants to know if you"—she touched the transdator again and smiled briefly—"if you saw the veterans' flypast or if you arranged it yourself."

"On screen, please, Uhura." Sulu's navigational plot broke up in shimmer and became Nic Farey's grin. It was more strained than Jim had last seen, and the reason was plain enough to see: *Vanguard's* bridge was just coming down from a red alert. "So they got you, too?"

"Oh, yes, they got us all right. Silly sods don't know just how lucky they were that I don't have a jumpy crew." Nic glanced pointedly over his shoulder. "At least I didn't until now."

"Why, what happened? I mean, they caught us on the bounce when they came up without warning, but—"

"So they didn't buzz you? Lucky man!"

"Buzz? Nic, what's been going on?"

"They—"

"Apologies, Captain Farey," said Uhura, interrupting. "Captain North for Captain Kirk. Priority One."

Nic Farey's image shrank into one-half of the screen, but where Gytha North's face should have come up on the remaining half, there was only static.

"Uhura? Jamming, or . . ." Kirk didn't want to say the immediate alternative, because saying such things in the past had so often seemed to make them true.

". . . hear us, *Enterprise?* This is NCC-2382 *Sir Richard* calling NCC-1701 *Enterprise.* Respond please. Do you copy?"

The voice came swimming up through interference like something that had lain drowned at the bottom of a pond. Then with a crackle harsh and sudden enough to make everyone on the bridge jump, sound and picture both came through loud and clear.

Captain North's eyes were dark and wide with something Jim failed to recognize for the first second. Not fright—that didn't go with the Gytha North he knew. And then he placed it: rage. It was leashed in as only command conditioning could do, so that there was no trace of it in her voice, but it had drawn the skin and muscles of her face down tight against the underlying bones until it became a still, expressionless mask. Only the eyes burned behind the mask like coals, and he thought how fortunate it was for good relations that the Dekkani could monitor only sound. Or maybe it wasn't so fortunate after all.

"We have had five red alerts in as many minutes, Jim," said Gytha. She was speaking slowly, probably as aware of the planetside listeners as anyone else, and picking her words with care. "We have come within the flexing of a finger of blowing each and every one of those flying freight trucks back to where they came from. And *they* have come within meters—not tens of meters, but meters—of ramming my damned ship! I tell you, if they're looking for trouble they're certainly going about finding it the right way."

"Captain North, that's enough." Jim sat back and looked thoughtful to conceal the fact that he was slowly counting to ten. Gytha wasn't about to do it, and somebody had to before somebody else got severely hurt or severely dead. He had reached eight when *Enterprise*'s red-alert alarms all went off in wailing chorus once again.

"Chekov!" Jim barked, counting forgotten, and was just quick enough to freeze his weapons officer's hand in midair as it came slapping down on the shield-activation toggle. "Not without my express order, Mister, and the word hasn't been given yet."

"But look at this!" Chekov's other hand moved, fingers splaying over touch pads, and the faces of the other captains were banished to window inserts in the viewscreen as a tactical display filled it almost from frame to frame. "A classic attack profile, Keptin. In a classic attack formation. A *Klingon* attack formation."

Jim glared at the computer-animated blips. Pavel was right. The Dekkani shuttlecraft were swinging back around the curve of the planet, but they were no longer an untidy gaggle of metal geese but as neat a formation as any he had ever seen. "Spock, scan for weapons. Because I don't think they have any."

"Scanning, although Captain, the passive systems—"

"Spock?"

"I can detect no weapons, Jim. This guarantees nothing."

"It guarantees we won't shoot first. Stand down from red alert." Jim got to his feet and walked around the bridge so that he could look over Chekov's shoulder at the weapons console. "And turn the alarms off, please."

Almost before their last echoes had died away, the sirens were back in full cry again as one of the passing shuttles illuminated the *Enterprise* with some archaic form of targeting sensor. The sensor didn't achieve a lock, wasn't even trying for a lock, and had been activated only for the instant needed to set off every automatic warning on the ship.

The fifth shuttle did exactly the same thing, but spiced its electronic harassment with a flyby so close that it passed up between the warp nacelles and all but scraped the top of the primary hull. "Sirens, someone," said Jim for the fourth time as he returned to the center seat. There was a weary resignation in his voice and his face and his very posture, that of a man faced with the prospect that his next duty shift—and the rest of the mission—looked set to be one very long day. . . .

Chapter Five

HAKKARL hung dead in space.

All his systems were shut down, even to the running lights, and the only suggestion of movement around that whole huge dark bulk was the firefly glimmer of a work pod's lights as Askel and Chief Engineer Aktaz, aboard the pod, made a final exterior inspection before proceeding to the next stage of this first-flight checkup. For three hours now the engineer had been virtually a part of his diagnostics board, looking up from it only for long enough to make sure that Askel was directing the remote sensor probe correctly. The science specialist found the look more than slightly insulting, but not so much that he troubled to take issue with it. At least, not yet.

"Structural analysis, main drive nacelles, external casings," mumbled Aktaz, more to himself than to the diagnostics recorder.

Askel listened for a few seconds as the engineer went off into a long monotonous checklist that was no more interesting now than it had been when they were inspecting the other end of the hull. It was at times like this, and there had been a few before now, that Commander Askel really understood the sheer size and complexity of a battle cruiser. And how incredibly boring it all was. Askel's interest lay more in the complexities of the mind, in the multifarious ways of plotting, and in the equally varied ways of suppressing those plots—or turning them to a different use.

There had to be a plot involved here. The smell of intrigue was one his nostrils had grown accustomed to recognizing, and they had recognized it aboard *Hakkarl* almost at once. That Captain Kasak was working so determinedly to suggest that there was no such thing made Askel all the more suspicious.

Every Klingon officer was involved in something or other, be it only jockeying for power and promotion within his own line families. For Kasak to expect his first officer to believe that of all captains in the Imperial Navy he, the famous sutai-Khornezh, was without some complex subterfuge to better both career and position was tantamount to calling him a fool to his face and before witnesses. But until he learned the details of Kasak's scheming, he could not be certain just how deeply he had been insulted. For the present it was enough to know that once that information had been obtained, Imperial Intelligence had agonizer booths enough and to spare for the captain and all who had assisted him.

Unless, of course, there was more profit in supporting Kasak than in handing him over to the appropriate authorities.

That was the one great problem about working for I.I. The bureau valued any ability to see both sides of a problem; it meant that agents could better understand its complexities and more easily work against it from the inside. But it also meant that the advantages of a given stratagem were as plain to an I.I. operative as basic, blatant treachery usually was to a member of Imperial Security. And the intelligence for which the organization was named was also a faculty that enabled its members occasionally to see that their loyalties need not always lie with the more obvious side.

Nal komerex, khesterex, the saying went. "That which will not grow will die." Askel always thought of it inverted, being thus more appropriate to his present station: *nal khesterex, komerex.* As did his captain of the moment and, curiously, a Thought Master among the *Doy'tS* line of humans long ago whose use of the saying, once it had been translated into Federation Standard, which Askel understood, made the most sense of all. *That which does not kill us, makes us stronger.*

". . . dreaming, Commander?" Aktaz's irascible voice cut through his thoughts. "I said, the analysis has been completed. We can proceed."

Why were engineers and surgeon specialists always so easily irritated? thought Askel as he absently shifted the travel pod's flight controls. Was it because the machines they worked on constantly broke down and needed their services? Shrugging the thought aside, he opened a channel to the cruiser.

"Askel to bridge."

"Bridge." It was Krynn who responded. Krynn, one of the two females in the crew. One of the captain's two favorites. One of the two who most bore watching —for reasons other than the obvious.

"Engineering reports completion of external checks. Restore power to all systems. We will observe. Out."

"Affirm. Acting. Bridge out."

Yes indeed, most efficient. Perhaps Krynn was too efficient, if there could ever be such an officer on a Klingon ship. It was a matter of small account to Askel, unless Captain Kasak's plan involved some privateering on his own account before returning *Hakkarl* to the Taamar drydock, and unless Kasak's security and intelligence officers agreed with his misuse of imperial resources. Of course, if the profits were high and the ship was indeed to be brought back intact, they might be persuaded to agree. If that was the case, then so far as Askel was concerned *nobody* was too good at his job. Or hers.

He watched with interest as the battle cruiser came back to life, like some vast monster from the old legends aroused from sleep. First came the glimmer of the skinfield, not so much an illumination as a haze like that of heat, spreading out over the main hull and then up the boom to the command pod, running along the generator grids that covered *Hakkarl* like a protective net. Running lights were next, jeweling his ghost-gray armor—proper adornment for so mighty a vessel. Last of all, and brightest, were the anticollision warnings, the safety beacons, and the insignia spots that made *Hakkarl's* imperial trefoils glow against the darkness of space under the gaze of myriad naked stars.

Askel watched and felt his liver shift in his chest at the promised glory of it all.

"Captain," said Krynn, "mains are back on line. Blue lights on all systems. Power to max at your discretion."

Kasak checked the readouts before he nodded. "Good. Then have the pod brought back on board and we— No. Signal to *zan* Askel. Hold station. *Tazhat* will exercise separation sequence from *Hakkarl.* Observe and report."

He waited until the signal had been acknowledged, then studied the data once again. "Maneuvering thrusters forward, one-half power."

"Affirm." Krynn pushed for thrust, and *Tazhat* vibrated slightly, a rumbling that was felt in the bones as power graphs flickered and screens began to register more than drift. The entire console swiveled on its plinth until Krynn was aligned with another and quite separate bank of controls, these shrouded with security covers that retracted into slots as she keyed in an unlock code. At their own stations on the bridge, other officers did likewise.

"Zan Khitar, interlink status?"

"Interlinks live, full communications confirmed."

"Good," Kasak said again. "Helm, on my command, execute a full combat breakaway to cloak. Make one-quarter impulse on both. Affirm action." He glanced once around the bridge and smiled. The members of his crew were nervous, as might be expected, but they were as eager as their captain to see how this ship fulfilled its expectations. They would see soon enough. Kasak sat straight-backed in the command chair and stared straight ahead out of the viewscreen and toward the naked stars. *"Degh,"* he said, and his helm officer tensed. *"yIchu'Ha'."*

"Acting," said Krynn, and tabbed all the release toggles together.

Neither Askel nor Aktaz was exactly sure what to expect or what to look for. Certainly the first suggestion of movement as the thrusters powered up was imperceptible except on instruments. Despite their respective specializations, and despite the numerous computer simulations they had watched in the past, they had yet to watch the actuality of a separation. They saw it now.

When the monoweb filaments connecting *Hakkarl* and *Tazhat* were degenerated, the smaller vessel was supposed to push clear of the battle cruiser with pressors. Nothing dramatic—no flash of explosive bolts such as occurred when a ship's boom broke away from its main hull. So at least went the description and the simulations. Reality, especially under the command of the sutai-Khornezh, was somewhat different.

Instead of the leisurely parting that they had seen

on computer screens, *Tazhat* seemed almost to leap away from the father ship. The impulse drive conduits on both ships glowed red, and a brutal kick of acceleration sent them surging out on divergent courses. They moved so fast that before Askel's brain could comprehend the full implications of what he saw, they had diminished to the apparent size of a child's toys. Toys whose outlines were already hazy, evaporating as the cloak took effect. *Tazhat* and then *Hakkarl* shimmered and were gone.

"*Kai* Imperial Engineering!" Aktaz laughed aloud and pounded his fist against the diagnostics board, not noticing or not caring that Science Specialist Askel was failing to share in his delight.

What Askel had seen was not a matter deserving applause, but one deserving curses—at Kasak for such a consummate move and at himself for having failed to foresee the possibility of such a development from the first instant he had been assigned to fly the inspection pod. The captain's latest tactic was masterful indeed. Even if Askel survived long enough to be picked up by whatever Klingon vessel next passed through this quadrant, he would not last very long afterward. A cool specialized area of his mind was already calculating how long the power and air in the inspection pod would last, assuming Aktaz . . . died and only he remained to use it.

Imperial Intelligence took a dim view of operations masters who allowed their surveillance subjects to give them the slip in so inglorious a fashion. Askel looked at the chief engineer's back and wondered when he should kill him—before or after a distress call had been sent. Certainly sooner instead of later; no reason to wait until the air turned bad. In fact, no reason to wait at all. His eyes fixed on a certain spot at the nape of the engineer's neck, and he flattened one of his hands into a chopping blade. . . .

And the sky outside the viewport was abruptly full of ships.

The angular masses of metal swallowed up the stars as they condensed out of cloak less than two hundred meters distant. *Tazhat* was once more in his accustomed place above the battle cruiser's main hull, hanging there for several seconds while the mono-web connections regenerated before settling onto *Hakkarl's* back.

"Opinion?" The voice from the communicator was Kasak's own, and sounded as pleased with events as the sutai-Khornezh ever permitted.

"Impressive." Askel might have wanted to say a great deal more than that, and not about the ships, wanted indeed to roar like a stormwalker and let someone feel the teeth of his anger, but to do so would be to confess what he was and why he had feared such an act of desertion by this ship and this captain. "All operations were flawless."

"And recorded?"

"Affirm. Is the one gratified by the performance of this new ship?"

"I am content. Return. There is much to do."

Askel looked at the ships, and at Aktaz the engineer who would never know how close he had come to service in the Black Fleet. There was indeed much to do, and a deal of that involved revision of his own ideas. Either the captain was genuinely innocent of the plot that I.I. suspected he had hidden somewhere, or he was infinitely more subtle than any of them suspected. For either reason, Askel's place was by his captain's side. He stared at the pod's command console as if he had never seen it before; then he engaged the thrusters that would take him home.

The eight Dekkani shuttles passed all three Federation vessels ten times before changing their orbit. In those ten flypasts, they had set off the alarms on twenty-two occasions, not all of those occasions sequential. They were in a low polar orbit now, as far from the Starfleet geosynchronous positions as it was possible to get. It was not much of a respite.

Jim had heard more bad language on the bridge in the past hour than ever before. His crew seldom swore, they were usually too busy with *doing* to trouble much with *saying,* but orders and circumstance meant that right now they could do nothing at all, except exercise a vocabulary of invective that should have gone on tape for xenosocioanalysis. Mr. Freeman would have welcomed a chance to take the more complex usages to pieces; there was probably a doctorate waiting in there for somebody.

It was impossible to say if there was any sign of fraying nerves among all the fraying tempers, but Jim had already put a call through to Bones, summoning him to the bridge to lend a professional ear. McCoy would be the first one to notice whether everything was running smoothly or not.

"What the billy-be-damned blue blazes is going on out there?" said the voice from the turbolift behind him even before its doors were fully opened. Jim didn't even blink. Apparently Bones had decided for himself already that things weren't running smoothly at all.

"They're trying to annoy us," he said.

"They're doing a damned good job of it." The chief medical officer stalked out of the lift angrily, and its doors shut behind him with what might well have been a mechanical sigh of relief. "Can't you *do* something?"

"Bones, you were at the briefings; you know damned well I can't." The cursing was infectious, dammit, thought Jim, mentally damning his own damning before realizing ruefully that he was chasing his own tail. "None of what they're doing is offensive—"

"Oh *isn't* it!"

"You know exactly what I mean. Under the rules of engagement. They're just acting like a bunch of kids, ringing doorbells and then running away."

"Don't you know what to do with kids like that, Jim? You catch them at it one more time, and you tan their little hides."

"A photon torpedo isn't a slipper, Bones, and we can't detune the phasers enough to just deliver spankings."

Chekov exchanged a significant glance with Sulu and Uhura. Muffled laughter escaped from all three of them.

"Mr. Chekov?" said Jim. "If you can make the phasers do it . . ." he persisted. Sulu and Uhura suddenly became terribly interested in their control consoles, while Chekov made a small snorting noise and went red in the face.

And then *everyone* went red in the face as the bridge lights shifted and the alarms went off again.

The noise and the scarlet lighting lasted only a matter of seconds before Spock shut them both off. "Another nonspecific targeting scan, Captain. Directed by one of the orbiters as it passed apogee."

"Not so far out of range as we thought, Mr. Spock."

"It would appear not."

"Good psychology, properly applied," muttered Bones. He caught the quirky glance directed at him and shrugged slightly. "I'm not giving their actions any sort of approval, Jim, so you needn't get that look in your eye. But they know what they're doing."

"By not poking at us all the time? Obviously. You jump harder from rest than from halfway through the last jump. And that's not psychology, Doctor, it's good tactical sense."

"Different words, same meaning."

"That is not in fact the case, Doctor," said Spock. McCoy rolled his eyes in mock anguish and didn't care who saw him. "There is indeed a sound tactical reasoning behind the Dekkan action," Spock continued. "Although our passive sensory systems are a pale shadow of the active-scan units, if they received a signal of sufficient duration I could analyze the unique features of the Dekkani targeting controls and by a subprogramming input override response to all but a full prelock contact."

"Tune them out, you mean? Then why didn't you say so?"

"But I did, Doctor, adding sufficient detail only to make the procedure coherent."

"'Coherent' is *not* the word that I'd have used, Spock. Not by a long shot."

Spock said nothing. He merely raised one eyebrow the merest fraction and held it there until he had turned back to his viewer. For all that McCoy had the last word, Jim couldn't help thinking that Spock had won the point. At least his ship's surgeon had stopped grousing about the alarms going off.

Until the next time.

Hakkarl was running at an easy warp 6.2, well within capabilities for those uprated engines that had no other demands on their energies right now than to drive the ship and power his enhanced sensor suite. Captain Kasak had insisted on the sensors being fully activated, holding that the prestige gained during their departure from Taamar would all be lost if they were caught unaware by another ship of the many that were doubtless searching for them at this moment.

Any who want to find this *ship will have to look long and hard,* thought Askel as he took his place in the small inspirational theater aboard the scout ship

Tazhat. Not only the sensors but also the cloaking devices were up and running, with no diminution that the science station could reveal in the power curves of the battle cruiser's warp engines. It was becoming increasingly clear that for once Design Engineering had told the unglazed truth about its latest product. *That* was sufficiently unusual for the captain to have made special note of it in his report.

"All's well?" said Marag from the door.

"Blue lights," Askel said. "What's this about?"

"Inspirational theater." Marag took a seat. "We're to be inspired."

"To do something Security can monitor before you die of boredom?" Marag showed just the points of his side teeth in an expression that only loosely could have been called a smile, but said nothing. It was true enough that on this ship, with so small a crew and a minimum rank among its members of lieutenant commander, a security officer had little to do.

Other members of that crew, those not on duty monitoring sensor input, trickled into the theater, nodded or waved casual salutes according to their mood, and settled down to be advised, instructed, inspired, or whatever else it was that the captain had in mind. They could all just as easily have gathered on the bridge, but with the computer relays and general lack of space in which to move, the meeting would have been, at the very least, intimate.

The screen hummed, glowed, and flicked into life with a picture of the bridge. Captain Kasak was in his command chair. Behind him Surgeon Specialist Arthag sat in Askel's place at the science station. Arthag appeared to be on the crew roster only because a ship was required to have a surgeon. So far he had treated two small electrical burns and a finger nipped by the unsecured lid of a diagnostics board, and he seemed relieved to be doing something that would take him out of the empty quiet of sickbay. With so many other things on his mind, Askel was more than willing to let him do it.

"The flight goes well," said Kasak. *"This ship can do all that has been claimed for him. A lesser captain and a lesser crew flying a lesser ship would be content with this alone. I am not. I have said I was content. It is not so."*

Askel sat up very straight and began to listen hard.

"This," the captain said, *"is my intention. To give Hakkarl a first flight worthy of his capabilities—and worthy of the crew I chose to fly him. The Roms have done what I now plan, testing their cloak and their plasma torpedo, but since the interference of the g'daya busybody Organians, no ship of the Empire has done so. Until now. In ten standard minutes we leave neutral space and enter that claimed by the Federation."*

And suddenly Askel *knew.* All the pieces fell into place: the planet in Federation space, torn by dissension that had led its people to order their Federation guests off-world and so leave themselves in need of a protector; their own lack of authorization and their departure from Taamar's Drydock 20. That had been no exercise but a theft, so that no Organian could blame the Empire's policymakers for the doings of an independent privateer, no matter how much the Empire stood to gain through those same doings.

All of this and so much more made sense at last, as the captain continued to address a theater—and a ship—gone totally silent with shock or disbelief or admiration. Askel had one source at least for all of those emotions: himself. The disbelief did not last long, for I.I. had required him to believe things far more unlikely than this, and to gather evidence about them. This dramatic play was not merely possible, it was capable of such vast success that all concerned could wallow in glory and everything that glory brought.

Marag stirred. The security officer had been sitting still as a statue while Kasak was speaking, but now he came to his feet. Askel tensed, watching and waiting for his reaction so that he could match it. There was a small pellet pistol in its customary place within his tunic, and if Security's response was such as to spoil his chance—*all* their chances—for advancement beyond that of a lifetime's service to I.I., then Askel was ready to use the pistol and justify its use afterward to whoever needed explanations.

It was not required. *"Kai* the captain!" roared Marag. *"Kai kassai, Klingon!"* All the others in the theater followed his example, stamping and saluting. Askel relaxed; it was going to be all right. It would be even more right once he had learned which of these enthusiasts were the *khest'n* covert Imperial Security operatives and what their true feelings might be. And had acted accordingly. But not right now.

Askel stood up slowly and walked across the theater through a steadily increasing atmosphere of suspicion about why he among all of them should not be cheering his friend the captain. Askel ignored the stares and the leaden silence until he reached the communicator panel near the wall and switched it on, then turned to face the captain's accusing eyes and fixed them with his own—yellow, hot, unblinking.

"Bridge," said Kasak's voice from the comm grid and from the screen.

"They are cheering the one down here," said Askel, his voice quite neutral.

"And you?"

"This one wished to speak instead of cheer."

"Then speak."

Askel smiled, at the screen and at the other members of the crew who had watched him with such doubt, a smile with all his teeth on show. He raised his right hand, empty of weapons, and when he closed it in salute the renewed shouts of approval all but drowned his words.

"Success, my lord."

"Captain, I have a transmission from Colonel Johnson. The shuttles are ready to go."

James Kirk scribbled his initials on yet another duty pad and glanced up at the main viewer. It showed the same scene as before, a planetscape overlaid with tactical traces as Chekov kept an eye on the doings of the Dekkani orbiters. Other than that, nothing. Certainly none of the communications that he wanted to see. "Uhura, are the Federation diplomats ready to leave the planet?"

"Still no contact, sir, due to a combination of deliberate signal interference and all this sunspot activity."

"All right, Uhura, understood. But keep trying."

"If I could just run enough power into the system, those upgrades to the duotronic circuitry should be able to burn a decohesive tight-beam squirt clean through without annoying anybody."

"Except the Dekkani, because right now they're in the business of being annoyed at anything we do— and Starfleet Command, once they found out, which they would, from the Dekkani. I've been thinking about it, too. I've even considered dropping messages in bottles."

"They would think we were bombarding them from orbit, Keptin," said Chekov unhelpfully. "Or trying to bribe them with the promise of full bottles next time around."

Jim pulled a face at that and returned his attention to the screen. At least the Federation people on

Dekkanar would know where to assemble for the evacuation. It was standard procedure in these operations that planetside personnel would be landed— either by transporter or by shuttlecraft—only at designated sites within areas of diplomatic immunity, and evacuees would have made their way to those same sites for pickup.

At least the PDI terrorists hadn't tried to interfere. So far. If they were there at all. Jim blinked, shook his head slightly, and put *that* hopeful, potentially dangerous notion right out of his mind. *Don't assume,* he told himself severely. Assumptions led inevitably to carelessness and to surprises of the most unpleasant sort. Worst of all, they could result in casualties.

"All right, Uhura," he said wearily, knowing perfectly well that things were moving out of his direct control. "Open a general channel."

"On line, sir, and standing by."

There was a trace of perspiration on his hands and an uncomfortable tickle of impending moisture on his upper lip. "This is Captain Kirk of the *Enterprise.* Commence rescue operation." Jim pressed his palms lightly together as the green confirmation lights came up on his armrest console. "Go quickly, go carefully, and may your gods go with you. Kirk out."

"It's not like you to be so worried," said Bones very quietly from behind him.

Jim twitched, caught off-guard. He didn't, couldn't, deny the little start. He hadn't even heard the turbolift doors open and shut. "It's not like me to be this angry, either."

"No." McCoy took a quick look around the bridge. Everybody was on station; everything was in place and running smoothly. "A word with you in private, Captain."

"I can't leave the—" Jim started to say, then shrugged. He could indeed leave the bridge, at least for a short time, and Bones wasn't about to take no for an answer anyway. "Mr. Spock, you have the conn."

The lift door closed and Bones said, "Sickbay." Nothing else.

Jim turned, stared at him, and raised his eyebrows to invite another comment.

"It's not just the anger, Jim; you're pushing again."

"Until Johnson establishes a ground control, I'm in charge of this."

"When did your duty shift end, Jim?"

"Never mind that. Bones, I have to get back to the bridge. If we ever establish communications with whoever's in charge down there—"

"—Uhura will find you. I think this is nothing more than a reaction to that last mission, trailing up and down the Neutral Zone, waiting for something to happen that never did. Now you've got some action and you're going to make the most of it." Dr. McCoy shook his head. "But that's not everything, is it?"

"No, dammit! It's the fact that if Dekkanar and the Federation's diplomatic corps had been willing to listen instead of just talk, we wouldn't be sitting here in the first place!"

"The fault's on both sides, then. Is that what you really think, or are you working with advanced hindsight?"

"Stop trying to psychoanalyze me, Bones." Jim spoke without heat, but there was something final about his tone of voice that made McCoy hold back on whatever else he might have said. "Of course the fault's with both. You must realize that an organization as large as the United Federation of Planets can afford to be magnanimous in a confrontation with one small world that isn't even a member. Bend a little. I don't think anyone even thought to make the effort to be generous; otherwise Colonel Johnson and his men wouldn't be walking into a mine field right now. What was it you called the Federation? The good guys? Well, maybe. We try; we all try. But we're not there yet."

They stood in silence as the lift car came to a standstill and its doors opened. Bones stepped out into the corridor, hesitated, then swung around and jabbed a finger at Jim's chest. "Well? Sickbay's this way."

"I was going back to the bridge."

"Yes, you were. Until I changed my mind. I was going to tell you to go back up to the bridge, supervise the shuttle departures, finish whatever extra duty you've awarded yourself, and then come down to sickbay for a routine checkup. And then I thought to myself, Leonard McCoy, you've waited fifteen days over schedule for this officer's last medical. Don't let him get away again. So come along."

"Bones . . ."

"Jim, do you want me to invoke all those fitness-of-command regulations? Because I will if I have to."

"Doctor, I'm up to here with regulations, and now you're the one who's pushing." Jim raised his hands in mock surrender—and then slapped one of them against his forehead. "And you're right, I must be getting tired. Or old, or slow." Intrigued, Bones watched as Jim made for the nearest communicator wall mount with what had to be the beginning of a silly grin spreading over his face.

"I should have thought of this hours ago," he said over his shoulder. "Engineering, this is Kirk."

"Engineering aye," said the voice of Montgomery Scott.

"Scotty, are things running smoothly down there?"

"Aye, sir, all's well. If ye could just keep the alarms from goin' off so much, we'd be delighted."

"If you can, er, pull the same people you had on duty during the shuttlecraft drill, I think something could be arranged." There was perhaps a second's silence at the other end of the connection, and then the speaker crackled as Scotty's laughter overloaded it.

"Now, there is a happy man," said Jim to Bones as the sound of orders being issued came drifting out of the comm grille.

"The tractor-pressor teams are already on their way to station, Captain," said Scotty, still chuckling. *"An' then we'll see how those damn hotshots want t' play— rough or smooth. Engineering out."*

"Tractor-pressor units aren't classed as weapons under the current rules of engagement," Jim said, "and they don't even register on most low-grade sensors. All we need now is for Spock to be able to detune the automatic alert systems, and those Dekkani shuttles can go fly a kite."

"Unless they want to get serious," said Bones.

"Enterprise can handle getting serious." The door into sickbay hissed open and Jim stepped inside— then stopped and looked slowly from side to side at what had been the chief surgeon's lab and office. He remembered Bones's complaints at the initial briefing about what emergency standby had done to his sickbay—remembered them with more clarity than he might have expected—but he hadn't had a chance to see it for himself. Until now.

The place was stark, and there were no longer any concessions to comfort at all. Even the holoprints had been removed from the walls. Silvery emergency blankets and folding standby beds were now stacked where the few chairs had been, sealed ready-dispensers of medical supplies—mostly sedative painkillers and trauma dressings—were set in any remaining floor space, and the elaborate micro-diagnostic equipment had been replaced by heavy-duty anabolic protoplasers and medical tricorders locked off at their coarsest setting. Jim stared at it all, and only slowly became aware that one corner of his mouth had quirked back in an instinctive expression of disgust, not at how the place now looked but at what that look implied.

"I don't care who can handle getting serious," said McCoy bitterly. "Just that it's always my staff people who have to clean up afterward."

"It won't come to this, Bones." Admiral James T. Kirk was standing almost at attention now, his face somber, his voice quiet and serious. "If it's in my power to avoid it, you won't need to use the place like this."

"Jim," said Bones, "I hope to God you're right."

Every alarm the designers had ever fitted went off at once, a solid wall of noise slapping through *Tazhat's* overcrowded bridge and reverberating back from every console until it was enough to rattle the teeth.

Kasak sutai-Khornezh sat bolt upright in his command chair and glowered at every single member of his crew, not assigning specific blame but more than willing to hand it out on a more general basis if he had to. "Shut off that *khest'n* noise," he snarled in a voice so soft that the klaxons should have drowned it out, "before I shut off the one responsible."

The silence on *Tazhat's* bridge was so sudden and complete that it echoed. "Better," said Kasak. "But not much. Explain."

Askel stood up, saluted, and presuming on his friendship immediately assumed an easy posture, then caught the expression in Kasak's yellow eyes and snapped right back to attention. "One of the purposes of the first flight is to establish the development of faults in a new design," he said.

"This is already known." The captain leaned forward, looking as predatory as any Klingon of the Imperial race might do whose liver had just been jolted in his chest. "Enhance."

"Sir, one of these faults has just become apparent." He touched a control on the science console and the bridge viewscreen went blank. "If the one will permit?"

"All right, *zan* Askel." Kasak leaned back and dropped that dangerous rank-linked formality. He could see relief spreading across the bridge like ripples in a pond, although no member of the crew was so presumptuous as to relax until instructed. "Carry on."

"Acting," said Askel. "Engineer Aktaz, put the interlink schematics on the screen. Also the monoweb connectors."

He spoke for the next several minutes, indicating the operation of stress points between the two ships, both while joined and when separate. The combat breakaway had altered pickup alignments between the beam-linked repeater arrays, and the pickups had been shifted still further out of sync by vibration since the ships reconnected. "This is why no alarms were sounded when *Tazhat* and *Hakkarl* first rejoined," Askel explained. "Signal cross-transmissions were sufficiently strong at that time so that this did not register as a fault. Whereas now . . ."

"And how is it to be repaired, Science Master Askel?"

"The receptor and transmitter installations on this ship must be released from their locked calibrations and coded for signal homing on source to and from *Hakkarl*."

Kasak looked thoughtfully at his science officer. Askel was Imperial Klingon, but the captain wondered idly if there might not have been a Vulcan fusion somewhere in the ancestry of his line. "What must be done to achieve this?"

"A full systems shutdown to prevent overload. Otherwise once one pickup is unlocked and recoded it will become the sole transceptor channel for all data passing between both vessels—and if that happens, we'll be resetting circuit breakers for a week."

"Indeed." Kasak allowed a smile to cross his face. "Then this is an eventuality to avoid. *Zan* Khalen, present heading and location?"

The navigator flipped a schematic onto the screen. "Heading is standard, location is as indicated. We are on course. Without power, we cannot maintain warp speeds, and to avoid relativistic and temporal distortions we should not drift at a high sublight velocity. Therefore time to target will be seven-point-six hours at point-forty-five c."

"Work time is estimated at six-point-two hours, Captain," said Engineer Aktaz.

"Then our speed will not decay significantly," said Khalen. "We will enter the outer planetary system during the period of shutdown, above the ecliptic plane to avoid most potential obstructions, but power will have been restored long before there is need for orbital maneuvering."

"Good." A shutdown approach was a tactical bonus Kasak had not anticipated. "All is well." The captain studied his crew, all of them standing by for his word of command. He nodded, once. "Action."

Jim leaned back and watched another quartet of Starfleet shuttles start their run from *Sir Richard*'s hangar bay down to the planet's surface. His mind ran over the problem in simple arithmetic for what he hoped was the final time. There were four shuttles on each ship, with room on board each shuttle for seven of Johnson's people and one Starfleet crewman to bring it back. And there were five hundred Diplomatic Protection Group personnel to shift. That meant something like eleven flights for each shuttle—five round trips and one final descent before starting it all over again with the Federation refugees. He grimaced and rubbed his eyes; even on this small scale, the niggling time-and-motion puzzle of logistics had the ability to take over all his thought processes and leave no room for anything else. Better leave it to Spock and the computers.

Every flight was a potential target, but so far the Dekkani and the PDI had kept quiet. Even the orbiters had ceased their intermittent harassment of the Starfleet vessels, recognizing perhaps that there was too much potential here for matters to get out of control. They had played their part, indicating to the all-powerful Federation that their ships, tied as they were by red tape, were not quite so powerful after all. If Scotty's guess about the purpose of all the posturing was correct, this forthcoming round of negotiations would probably begin on a basis of restrained aggression and progress through disposal of the more outrageous demands and arguments to something that at least resembled a sensible dialogue.

Just so long as nobody with a gun tried to interfere.

It was right then that the alarms went off again. Jim muttered something under his breath and glared at Chekov. "What is it this time—more Klingon attack formations?"

"No, Keptin." Chekov sounded so uneasy that all at once the hackles on the back of Jim's neck began to rise. The viewscreen flickered and the image changed from *Sir Richard*'s shuttles to a crank-winged shape that was equally familiar but far more ominous. "This time it's *Klingons!*"

Jim stared at the screen. The other Federation ships

were not yet aware of the new threat, shielded from it as they were by their geosynchronous positions on the farther side of the planet. As usual, it was all up to the *Enterprise*—and it was *that* which put a sort of smile back on Kirk's face, because General Order 12 had just taken on a whole new meaning.

"Uhura?"

"I've been trying, Captain. The usual greetings on a standard hailing frequency. They haven't responded."

"Nothing at all?"

"Not even a standard ID, Captain. Just static."

"Good. In that case I shall quote one of the other provisions of General Order Twelve." Quick grins were suppressed all over the bridge as the crew's recent familiarity with that damned order allowed them to pick up immediately on what Kirk was about to say.

" 'On the approach of any vessel when communications have not been established, Starfleet safety-of-personnel requirements indicate that said vessel should be treated as potentially hostile until proven otherwise, and in consequence a standard defensive posture should be adopted.' "

"Changes of situation and shipboard status duly noted and logged, Captain," said Spock. There was a cool satisfaction in the way he said it, though the Vulcan would never have admitted any such thing.

"Thank you, Mr. Spock. You may restore all sensors to active status. Raise shields and bring weapons to operational readiness." There was no leaping for positions on the bridge this time. Everyone was there already.

"Uhura, transmit on all frequencies: 'Captain Kirk, commanding U.S.S. *Enterprise,* to all Federation vessels and personnel. We have detected a ship entering this system. Ship has refused to answer hails or transmit IFF/ID. Visual indicates ship to be a

113

Klingon K't'inga class battle cruiser. *Enterprise* will intercept. Continue evacuation procedure. All ships are cleared for battle stations. I repeat: battle stations. Kirk out.' And, Uhura, keep an ear open for what the Dekkani have to say."

He glanced at the battle cruiser's sinister outline on the long-range display. For all the menace that it represented, the Klingon warship was more easily dealt with than all this sitting around.

"Mr. Chekov, lay in an intercept course. Mr. Sulu, full impulse power. Take us out."

Chapter Six

ENTERPRISE WAS NO MORE than a few seconds clear of orbit when the yelling began from planetside. The approaching Klingon ship was still millions of kilometers beyond the range of Dekkan Central Control. What they saw, and what they now reacted to, was the trio of so-recently defenseless Starfleet vessels going into a maneuver that could either be defensive—or a preparation for attack.

"The entire Dekkan Planetary Council's screaming down there, Captain," said Uhura. She pulled the transdator from her ear and reset its systems for reduced transmission volume before reluctantly putting it back. "And some of their language is getting beyond 'earthy and colorful.'"

"Anything of importance, or just opinions of Starfleet in general?"

"Opinions of the fleet commander in particular," she returned dryly, "and imaginatively worded ones at that. They are *not* pleased."

"Mmf." Jim looked again at the K't'inga class battle cruiser on the screen. "Give them something else to think about. Patch that Klingon ship through to the planet on visual for a few minutes—enhanced imagery, so they're in no doubt about whom it belongs to—and then give me an open line to anyone who wants to listen."

Uhura nodded and began working with the visual-image coders, building her picture around that on the main screen but thoughtfully adding declassified schematics and silhouette data until the shape, provenance, and destructive capabilities of the Klingon ship were made plain even to the most uneducated layman. "Transmitting now, Captain," she said, "and opening your general transmission in seven minutes. Until that time, you're not available to Dekkan callers?"

"Seven minutes, unless it's more important than what they've had to say so far." Jim had had enough of the council, the Dekkani, the planet they lived on, and the whole damned mission. "Advise Captains North and Farey to make no independent reply to planetside queries. All information must be channeled through *Enterprise.*" He swiveled the center seat a little. "Time to interception, Mr. Sulu?"

"Six-point-three hours at point-forty-five c, sir. Much faster and we'd start running into time-relativistic distortion."

"And miss the whole party? Not a chance. Hold her steady at point-four-five."

"We may need the extra time to sort out whatever has happened here," said Spock, sitting back from his viewer and looking puzzled. "I think, Captain, that you should see this." Even without that unprecedented request for a second opinion, his expression and tone of voice were already sufficiently unusual to have Jim out of his seat and up to the science station.

Spock touched controls, and schematics scrolled across the monitors, but none of the output made sense. Jim looked at one particular power consumption readout and then back at the main view-screen, frowning.

"I have restored full power to all of the science sensors," Spock said, "and correlated with the information available in the main ship's computer concerning this class of Klingon vessel, but there are more anomalies than matching data. This is most unusual. And more unusual still, despite the Klingon vessel's nominal crew complement of five hundred thirty, I can pick up life signs for only eight."

McCoy had emerged from the turbolift as Spock was speaking, and now he peered over the Vulcan's shoulder at the display whose readings mirrored those of a medical tricorder. He tapped its screen, an irritable tapping he regarded as the last remedy for recalcitrant electronics when all else has failed. "Have you tried reading for non-Klingon life-forms?" he said.

"Yes, Doctor, I have. To no effect. The possibility of rebellion or theft by a servitor race has already occurred to me."

"And what about disease?"

"This unit has detected the life signs of eight Klingons, all in perfect health. Unless they are the fully recovered survivors of some strange plague, I see no reason to assume illness aboard this ship"—Spock evidently saw McCoy's next question coming—"or any accident involving biological or chemical weapons."

Bones humphed and shrugged his shoulders. "It's damned strange, whatever's behind it."

"Stranger even than that," said Uhura.

"Strange in what way, Uhura?" Jim asked.

"Captain, as you requested, I ran image enhancement on the Klingon ship before putting it through to the Dekkani Council. Most of that was just additional detail work, but I've been processing the residual signal and . . . well, it's done something very peculiar to the Klingon's outline. On the main screen now."

Even with full magnification and the resolution-boosting circuitry already built into the *Enterprise*'s main viewer, a battle cruiser at a distance of some twelve light-hours was still an infinitesimal speck from which the viewer could only infer details. It had done the best it could, assembling the usual twenty points of similarity against whichever silhouette in its memory banks was a closest match and then generating a computer-corrected image based on that assumption. It was only when Uhura had cross-checked that she discovered there was more to this particular Klingon battle cruiser than the viewscreen's cursory first glance suggested. Much more . . .

"What the . . . ?" Jim stared at the scout ship riding piggyback on the battle cruiser and tried with no success at all to work out what function it might serve by being there. He turned back to his science officer, who was studying the screen with an expression of mild interest that usually concealed intense curiosity. "Any opinions, Spock?"

"At present, Captain, my opinions are uninformed and consequently of little use. However, interrogation of the library computer should presently alleviate the situation, if only by providing data for enhanced guesswork."

"At least it starts to explain the limited life signs," Bones said.

"Except that there are no known Klingon scout-class vessels with a crew of less than twelve," Jim put in. "This one's still running light on personnel, and it doesn't explain the cruiser underneath."

"Captain, the computer now indicates several explanatory possibilities," said Spock. He brought the data up on his department monitor and raised one eyebrow at what he saw there. "Fascinating."

"How so?"

"I ran only a very fast and shallow inquiry scan in search of similarly attached vessels, Captain, and yet five of the examples the computer provides are of Earth origin; they cover a period from the third to the seventh decades of the twentieth century, and . . . one of them involves a ship known as *Enterprise.*"

"Captain, I'm getting a transmission in clear from the Planetary Council. Will you reply?" Uhura's voice cut through the amused confusion in Jim's head; part of his mind was insisting that Spock had just made a joke, while the rest was refusing to believe any such thing. At least this news was sensible.

"What message?" He looked toward Uhura. "And what sort of language?"

The comm chief laughed softly. "Very polite language, for a change. They want to speak to *Admiral* Kirk."

"Do they indeed?" Jim wasn't sure how to take this: being referred to by his full rank had invariably meant trouble in the past, and if some Federation bureaucrat had gotten involved with the Dekkan councillors and was starting to throw his weight around, he would find that weight swung both ways. "Put them on the screen."

The Klingon battle cruiser disappeared in shimmer and became . . .

. . . A Klingon face.

Jim had already returned to the center seat and composed himself to receive whatever message secessionists transmitted to admirals. McCoy had not. Instead he stared at the image on the screen and sat down hard on the nearest thing convenient.

"Doctor," Spock said very calmly, "that is probably

not the best method of input through a keyboard. Move, please."

It had been one of those oversights in a busy operations schedule: what with getting down to orbit, organizing the landings, arranging when and how to evacuate DPG and Federation personnel without either offending the Dekkani or risking injury to anyone involved, Jim realized nobody had gotten around to advising the chief medical officer of just exactly what the inhabitants of Dekkanar *were*.

Kirk took a longer breath than was absolutely necessary to begin a conversation, and let it out again slowly before he felt entirely capable of speaking to the face on the screen. It belonged to a ferociously white-whiskered old Dekkan male whose forehead, while lacking the lobster-back ridge of a pure Imperial race Klingon, was still sufficiently knobbed and furrowed for the family likeness to be unsettlingly plain.

"You are the Kirk Admiral, the fleet commander," said the old Dekkan.

"I am Admiral James T. Kirk, yes. But when I command a ship my title is Captain."

"So." Hot yellow-irised eyes stared from the screen for a moment, then turned away as their owner relayed the information to someone else beyond range of the video pickup.

Jim could distinguish at least three additional voices and wondered when he would see the three faces, assuming one of the voices wasn't originating on the incoming Klingon warship. . . . He muted the mike on his own pickup and glanced quickly over one shoulder at Uhura. "What about the battle cruiser? Transmissions, energy surges, anything?"

Uhura checked the comms console and shook her head. "Communication silence, sir." She looked at the viewer, where the white-haired Dekkan was still in discussion with his off-screen companions, and tapped controls on her board at top speed. "Voice analysis and the ambient sound of this transmission indicate that all four voices originate from the same point source."

"Well done, Uhura!" Jim's mouth stretched into a brief, tight grin.

"I am Varn Chief Councillor," said the old Dekkan, coming back on line and making Jim freeze the last remnant of grin from his face, *"and I am Varn Political Leader. You will address the council and the party through me."*

Jim stared at him for several seconds, expressionless and saying nothing, while he sifted his own immediate and irritable response out of the more diplomatic statement that the situation required. "Councillor Varn, I need say no more than was said when our ships first entered orbit. Our purpose is to escort the Federation personnel expelled from Dekkanar to safe haven aboard our ships and then to leave."

"Your ships are military. You came with soldiers."

"Our ships are armed, yes, but they are not military. They are exploration vessels that are often required to explore dangerous and unknown territory. Their weapons are defensive."

"And the soldiers?" Varn's old voice grew sharp. *"Will you say that soldiers are not military?"*

"I do say it. They are not soldiers. Their job is to defend our people against those of your people who would use violence. Or do you deny the existence of the group calling themselves the Phalange for Dekkan Independence?"

"PDI is a gang of bandits. Their title is grandiose, their intention no more than theft. They do not represent the council or the party."

"But the council and the party have said they cannot protect Federation personnel against these . . .

bandits. Therefore the Federation must act to protect its own."

"With soldiers?"

"With whatever is necessary. At present, with nothing more than men and women in uniform. Our present regulations forbid these uniformed crew members to carry weapons until weapons are needed."

"Soldiers without weapons? This is foolish."

"Less foolish than causing hurt or death by accident, Chief Councillor Varn." Jim shifted in his seat, the movement of a man bored with pointless talk and intending to bring it to an end. "If there is no more to be said than this, which has all been said before, then I and my ship have work to do."

"Wait!"

Aha. Jim lifted his hand clear of the cutoff switch and looked back at the screen with an expression of studied disinterest.

"Kirk Admiral, what of this new ship reported to be entering our system?"

"That is a part of our work, Councillor. It is a warship of the Klingon Empire, and it has no business in this galactic sector, much less this system."

"Klingons . . . ?" The councillor's voice was a case study in innocence. *"Why would Klingons come here at this time?"*

"Perhaps they heard of Dekkanar's falling-out with the Federation and wish to offer protection to a nonaligned world against potential invaders," said Jim with a saccharine smile. "Perhaps the form of that protection will be an offer to join the Klingon Empire. Perhaps they were invited."

Councillor Varn stared at him, and the heat went from the Dekkani's eyes until they looked like chips of muddy topaz. They looked, thought Jim, like the eyes of someone realizing he just might have made a mistake. Like someone who might want to speak quite soon to one of the diplomats at present leaving his planet. Well, let *him* ask for the meeting—but not right now. "We will doubtless speak of this again, Councillor. For the present, good day." He turned away from the screen and only then said clearly, "Kirk out.

"Uhura, standing order for Communications: all transmissions originating from the surface of Dekkanar will be monitored as usual, but no transmission from the Planetary Council will be acknowledged or replied to until further notice."

"Noted and logged, sir. And if they or the Klingons attempt to open communication with each other . . . ?"

"Jam the frequency and let me know at once."

"Sir." She worked a moment at the main console, then tabbed an activation toggle. "Jamming circuitry is enabled." Uhura smiled wearily. "Of course, that does mean there'll be another alarm going off."

"One more won't make much difference on this ship," said Jim. "And I think we could go back to standard illumination." The bridge lights flicked back to normal. "Better. The ship will remain at condition one, but there'll be time enough for a full red alert when we reach intercept range. Until then I prefer to see what I'm doing. And now, Mr. Spock"—he returned to the science station—"let's see what *you've* got."

Spock touched controls on the library computer, bringing its memory buffer back on line. "The parameters I set, Captain, were most basic: known historical examples of a similar arrangement between two ships. Once fed into the computer, these parameters were of necessity expanded to include atmosphere craft. It was at this point that the search began to prove successful."

"You said there were five examples from Old Earth, Spock. I'm curious."

"Most are military," said Spock, "which is hardly surprising. During the twentieth century the military had first demand on governmental funds."

"As usual," said Bones, standing off to one side and speaking almost to himself. Jim glanced quickly sideways, but his science officer let the comment pass as one not needing a reply.

"The first example and the last, however, are civilian, and are, I believe, of as much significance as all the others combined. Especially the final example."

Spock pressed a control and fell silent, allowing the dry, synthesized voice of the library computer to speak for him. "Nineteen thirty-eight," it said. "Operator, Imperial Airways, London, England. Short S-twenty-three Empire class flying boat *Mercury* carrying floatplane *Maia*. Purpose: extended-range mail delivery. First nonstop transatlantic mail flight.

"Nineteen forty-four. Operator, Deutsches Luftwaffe, Germany. Unmanned Junkers Ju-Eighty-eight bomber carrying Messerschmitt Bf-One-oh-nine or Focke-Wulf Fw-One-ninety fighter. Name: *Mistel Two* combination. Purpose: crude guided missile, forward fuselage converted to carry three-point-eight-tonne shaped-charge demolition warhead."

"Stop," said Jim. He turned to Spock. "How old is the K't'inga class of battle cruiser? Old enough to warrant using one like that? To carry a warhead?"

"Doubtful, Captain. Latest intelligence reports indicate that, like Starfleet, the Klingons have a policy of constant upgrade and refit—except of course when ships are sold to the Romulan Empire, and stripping out appears more the order of the day. It is not beyond speculation that there is a Klingon engineer with talent equal to that of Mr. Scott, since the effective result to many of their vessels is similar to what has been done to the old Constitution class *Enterprise*—a new ship built on the structure of the old. I find it unlikely that any situation could arise where this ship would be used as a disposable weapon. Almost certainly the same applies to Klingon vessels."

"Point taken," said Jim.

"Nineteen-fifties," the library computer continued. "Operator, USAF Strategic Air Command, America. Convair B-Thirty-six carrying Grumman FF-One Goblin hook-recoverable parasite fighter within aft bomb bay. Purpose: point defense during mission. Also: Convair B-Thirty-six carrying Republic F-Eighty-four-F trapeze-launched fighter semi-scabbed onto bomb bay. Purpose: extended-range recon missions.

"Nineteen seventy-seven. Operator, National Aeronautics and Space Administration. Boeing Seven-forty-seven Shuttle Carrier Aircraft carrying Orbiter *Enterprise-One-oh-one*. Purpose: ferry flights, airworthiness tests, and manned free-flight tests during initial phase of space shuttle program."

But the Klingons saw no need for orbiters or for research programs and no need for any of the rules and regulations that bound the Federation. "What about our intruder? What category does he fall into?"

"That thing's military, Jim," said Bones. "Otherwise it wouldn't be here. It wouldn't *dare* be here!"

"The K't'inga class has never been anything *but* military, Doctor," Spock said. "However, some of its later variants have converted their troop-carrying capability into research space. Although I can do nothing more than surmise from the information presently available," he said, evidently picking his words with care, "I suspect it is possible that the Klingon fleet has been experimenting with fully computerized onboard systems and that we are on course to meet one of their prototypes."

"You mean an M-Five clone?" Jim and Bones said much the same thing at once, both men simultaneously imagining the devastating consequences should another central command computer—this one programmed by Klingons—decide to run amok.

Spock looked at the schematics readout and shook his head. "More probably a ZD-Eight modification. The most reliable information available at present indicates the Klingons' continuing refusal to adopt centralized artificially intelligent units."

"They don't trust smart machines," translated McCoy. "I always thought there was *some*thing good about the Klingons, if you only looked hard enough."

"I suspect that the smaller craft contains the control systems," Spock continued, "and the battle cruiser's remote-command structure is designed around them. Although the Klingons are scarcely safety-conscious and are therefore notoriously profligate with lives during the testing of new equipment, it seems most likely that the scout detaches itself before passing maneuvering instructions to the cruiser."

Bones gestured toward the viewscreen. "If that thing's new, Spock, then it's been kept secret. You know the Klingons well enough: they might not have much concern for safety, but when it comes to security they're red hot. So what in hell is that ship doing here?"

Jim was staring at the screen as if hoping to read some hidden answer from it; he didn't need to hear Spock's reply. He had pulled enough science station duty in his younger days to know his way around the monitors, and those energy readings had niggled at him. In a ship of the battle cruiser's size the curve had indicated no more than shutdown decay, and even when the crewed scout had been added to the equation its energy readings were borderline residual. Even the vessel's motion was no more than an unpowered freefall into the gravity well of 4725 Cancri, and it was a bad system to enter at the best of times, never mind blind and unable to maneuver.

Something most unpleasant had happened to that ship—*those ships,* he corrected absently—and as had so often been the case, *Enterprise* just happened to be right on the spot. Except that right now the spot was six-plus hours away.

Jim stifled a yawn, and realized with pleasant surprise that he actually had some time to call his own before they reached the interception point. Six-plus hours of leisure. Enough time to catch up on at least some of the sleep he'd missed.

"Uhura, if you could log me off shift, please?" he said, and headed determinedly for the turbolift. "And fend off Councillor Varn if he gets importunate. I'll speak to him later . . . this morning, isn't it?"

"Later tonight, Jim," growled Bones. "You're two shifts out. Leave it. Go, go." He restrained himself from actually making shooing motions, but not by much.

"Throwing the captain off his bridge is mutiny, Doctor," said Jim, but the effect was spoiled by another huge yawn. "Spock, you have the conn again. Good morn—ah, g'night, everyone."

"Good night, sir," said Spock and the rest, but until Jim was in the lift and for once on the way to bed without any interruptions, he didn't really believe them.

The bridge was dark, and almost silent. Kasak could hear only the sound of his own breathing and, as if in the far distance, unless he adjusted the gain on his helm headset's receptors, the voices of Askel and Aktaz as they worked on the remote transmitters. He and the rest of the crew had donned environmental suits at Askel's suggestion and without argument. Kasak loathed the all-over constriction and the strange smells that always lurked in the suits no matter how new or how clean they were, but the alternative meant being unprotected if the central life-support system decided to shut down. He and his crew had all served long enough to have seen the aftermath of an environmental accident, and it had never seemed a sufficiently pleasant way to die for any of them to find running such a risk appealing.

For all that, Kasak tried not to breathe through his nose more often than necessary.

It was only after he had suited up that he began to realize just how long six hours of shutdown was likely to seem. Complaining would be of no use; the work had to be done or *Hakkarl* would rapidly become just one more piece of junk that had left the imperial yards with such high hopes and never come back. He did not much relish the prospect of returning to Taamar without the major portion of his command. Still less did he like the idea of continuing with his scheme for the planet Dekkanar in only a scout ship, lacking the battle cruiser's destructive potential. He did not intend to use his weapons, of course; the whole point of the plan was to entice Federation ships into firing first, thus outraging the Organians. But no captain in the Klingon Imperial Navy felt anything except unease without considerable—and preferably overwhelming —firepower at his disposal.

Kasak glared at the blank monitors, the useless sensors, the dead screen, and curled his lips back from the points of his teeth. This enforced blindness, not knowing who or what was out there, was unsettling in view of what navigational intelligence had said about traverse of the Dekkan system. Before systems shutdown, Navigator Khalen had triple-checked their projected route for debris and had pronounced it clear. Khalen had been most cautious before making his announcement, and with good reason: Kasak had informed him, in front of the rest of the crew, that even a minor collision would prove fatal—for him, even if for nobody else.

That had been two hours ago. The navigator was still alive, and the ships were undamaged except for whatever Askel and the engineer had been doing down among *Tazhat's* electronic entrails. Kasak snorted softly, regretting it a moment later as one of those in-suit aromas reminded him of its presence. He began punching up the codes to access the first-flight Captain's Log on his pad screen, then augmented his previous observations about whoever in Design Engineering had been responsible for the intership data link. He had no idea when he would deliver his final report, but when he did—he, Kasak, the captain whose stratagem had acquired an entire planet for the Empire—that data-link designer would be finished. And not merely so far as his career was concerned. He would be terminated. Kasak had done it before. On one occasion he had been so enraged that he had simply drawn his duty sidearm and disintegrated the offending designer where he stood gaping across the bridge. After that incident had been passed around, design engineers had grown very skilled at devising reasons not to accompany Kasak sutai-Khornezh on the proving flights of their own ships.

He closed the file, closed his eyes for just a moment, and then locked off the pad screen. "*Zan* Askel, progress report," he said to the microphone array within his helm.

"*Blue lights, Captain,*" came Askel's voice. "*Progress continues. We are testing each transceptor for individual homing as we unlock and recalibrate. From Aktaz: completion estimate is now reduced by point-*

three hours. We will advise when the systems can be set for warm-up cycle. Askel out."

Kasak made a mental note to add positive notations to each officer's file. Possibly even a commendation. But that, and indeed anything else stored in his own memory, would stay there until all of this was over. Mental notes were easier to change than hard copy, and awards one day could so easily become demerits, or worse, the next. It made the life of a captain so much simpler if the justification of changed reports didn't need to be done in public. . . .

Wearing heavy-duty work coveralls and a clear-view visor, Science Specialist Askel took care to keep his facial muscles well under control even when Aktaz wasn't actually looking in his direction. Inside, however, he was laughing. Because both of them were full commanders and neither was in the mood to argue seniority based on date of graduation, they had divided the labor equally. It meant in essence that Aktaz performed the engineering tasks of freeing the transceptor heads and installing the new signal-seeker hardware. After that, the more ticklish operation of recalibrating and cross-checking fell to Askel. It was hardly such heavy work as lugging the electronic power units in and out of their location slots—an awkward and often dangerous business in zero-G, when their mass was far less controllable than just their simple weight—but it was boring, repetitive, and, given the captain's reaction to less than perfect work, just as dangerous. That, at least, was what Askel had said.

For an Imperial Intelligence operations master it was also the perfect opportunity to set things up in preparation for whatever the future might hold.

Askel had already decided that his most immediate advantage lay in Kasak's scheme for personal and political advancement. Perhaps the captain meant to capture Dekkanar by double-bluffing both the Federation and the Organians—a plan so elegant that Askel was almost eager to see it succeed. Or perhaps Kasak simply intended to turn privateer and gain wealth and glory by becoming a thorn in Starfleet's flank.

Still, the Thought Admirals of the Advanced Strategies Board might object to any or all of Kasak's plan. That was why the sternmost data transceptor had been programmed not just with the ability to home on its mate in *Hakkarl*'s hull but also with an override that enabled it to transmit messages from Askel's science board on *Tazhat* without any tiresome need to go out through Communications. The installation would operate quite normally until he cut in his override, and that would act only for the nanosecond required by a tightbeam tachyon squirt. Since the aberration would show as nothing more than a brief signal fluctuation, nobody else would know. Aktaz certainly wouldn't mention it, least of all to this captain whose view of shoddy workmanship was already notorious, and Askel himself didn't intend to breathe a word. Not that the thing was any more than theoretical until the mains were back on line and he had a chance to test it.

But at least it was *there*.

The chimes at midnight pulled Jim out of a sound sleep and back to the realization that he had dozed off facedown with his uniform and boots still on. And his mouth open. *Yech*. It felt as if someone had been storing used dilithium crystals in it. He sat up and swatted groggily at the wake-up's off switch. There was no doubt at all in Jim's mind that another six hours' sleep would have been just what the doctor ordered—indeed, just what Bones had *been* ordering.

At least he was awake enough to suppress two-way

vision on the communicator before opening a channel to the bridge. Spock was on the other end, looking as usual annoyingly crisp and well rested. "Good morning, Mr. Spock," said Jim, hoping his voice sounded more the way his first officer appeared than the way its owner felt. "Current situation report, please."

"Good morning, Captain," said Spock formally. *"I have continued sensor scans of variable intensity, but the intruder ship still reads as virtually dead on all scopes.* Enterprise *is continuing to close, with a present estimated intercept time of forty-seven minutes."*

He paused an instant to recheck something, then stood up and moved to the science station. *"Reduction in range has enabled me to confirm that this is indeed an augmented modification of the K't'inga class cruiser. Within forty-five minutes, therefore,* Enterprise *will be entering the two hundred twenty thousand kilometer extreme firing perimeter of their main disrupter batteries. Do you wish to hold off out of range? Given the intruder's present course and heading, it would be simple to run parallel with him for"*—Spock glanced sideways at another monitor—*"at least three hours before further action became necessary."*

And for you to get some more of the sleep you need. The Vulcan had said nothing of the sort and would never have dreamed of doing so, but his suggestion was clear enough. Jim thought about it for a moment, then dismissed Spock's offer. Even though he still felt in need of a shower, a shave, and a fresh uniform, his brain had kicked itself back up to full running speed and there seemed small purpose in letting it relax back into the warm dark for any shorter time than the six-hour absolute minimum he needed to fully recover.

"Thanks, Spock, but no. There's no point in letting the Klingons get farther into the system than necessary," he said, more briskly. That briskness helped put another thought into his head, one that had been wandering around as he fell asleep and had evidently been biding its time ever since. "Is there any reason to believe that this ship is a derelict?"

"Thirty-two-point-four-four percent probability," said Spock, *"based on scanning observations that suggest the existing crew are presently incapable of operating the vessel by themselves. The ship is following an uncontrolled course into a populated system and toward an inhabited planet whose present traffic patterns are in excess of those laid down as safety-minimal. Under the current laws of space salvage, all of these facts constitute sufficient reason to consider and treat the offending vessel not merely as salvable but as an actual and continuing hazard. Of course, acquisition by salvage of a military vessel that is the property of a known sovereign power is somewhat frowned upon. Even if we can somehow persuade the entire crew to request political asylum in the Federation, we will be obliged by law to hand the ships back to the Klingon Empire."* Spock paused. *"Eventually."*

"Spock, did you ever consider a legal career?"

"No, Jim, I did not." There was a smile in the voice if not on the face. *"Vulcan law, while precise and elegant, has always been less aesthetically challenging than my present career, and as far as Earth's legal practices are concerned"*—Spock shrugged, a very small, massively dismissive rise and fall of one shoulder—*"A system where parties hire professional exponents of argument, and where those who can afford to hire the best, most skillful or indeed most persuasive arguers are most likely to win any given case regardless of its actual merit, strikes me as singularly lacking in logic."*

And I always thought he just didn't like court-

martials, thought Jim. *Well, there go several thousand miles of books.* "Thank you, Spock. No further questions. I'll be there in fifteen minutes."

"Captain on the bridge," announced the duty comm officer as James T. Kirk—looking and feeling much more like a starship captain—stepped out of the turbolift.

"Magnification up three points, pan right to left along the command pod and boom," Spock was saying.

"Thank you, Mr. Mahase," Jim said to the communications officer. "Log me in, please." He looked at the Klingon warship on the viewscreen, its hull crosshatched with the amber rectangles of camera angles, and then at his science officer. "Are you directing or producing this one, Mr. Spock?"

The Vulcan vacated the center seat. "Neither, Captain. Otherwise I would have called on Mr. Freeman's talents. These are visual records for Starfleet."

Jim glanced at the ominous shape filling the screen as he sat down, scribbling on the duty pad Spock handed him. "Ah. Of course." Another glance at the battle cruiser. "Yes, that thing most certainly has the potential for hostility. Any further contact with its crew?"

"Mr. Mahase?" said Spock.

"Nothing whatsoever, Mr. Spock, Captain," said the Eseriat. "When Commander Uhura went off shift she left a comprehensive list of suggested approaches and analyses that she had already tried and which needed to be repeated. I regret to admit that I experienced as little success as she. I think they're either deaf or dead," he finished irritably, "or doing a good impression of it."

"Not dead at least." Spock flashed up the life-sign sensor on the main screen. "Still eight, still healthy, although deafness is not beyond the bounds of possibility, as a side effect of explosive decompression."

Jim studied the Klingon ship, or more accurately, ships, since a slight alteration in approach vectors was giving a clearer view of the scout riding on the cruiser's primary hull. "Magnification up seven," he said. "Let's see what we can see."

Whatever else the high-mag scan revealed, it showed no trace of the structural damage normally associated with a hull blowout: no ruptured plates, no fans of frozen air around the point of venting. And yet . . . And yet there was that lack of energy readings, and the life signs that suggested too small a crew even for the scout ship alone. Theories jostled for prominence in Jim's mind, as they had doubtless jostled in Spock's—with as little apparent success. More and more he kept coming back to the library computer's examples, trying to force their historical realities into some shape that would fit modern uncertainty.

Might this vessel have been designed as a long-range ferry similar to the sleds employed by Vulcans, something more capable of self-defense than a warp shuttle and perhaps intended for high-ranking imperial officials? Hardly. If a Starfleet admiral needed to travel any great distance within the Federation, he used an existing vessel, and if his mission was delicate or the territory dangerous, he used something like the *Enterprise,* rather than a specialized ship that shouted its function and its occupant to even the most casual observers. There was no reason to believe that a Klingon Thought Admiral would act any differently —although the speculation had a convoluted entertainment value of its own.

If the scout ship wasn't a double-range courier, which in any case was unnecessary with warp technology; and if it wasn't riding a flying bomb, which was improbable; and if it wasn't some means of giving the cruiser additional protection, which the K't'inga needed like a cat needs pajamas—then what in blazes *was* it?

It's something controlled by computer, and the smaller ship has come along as an observer.

That thought came back up out of the tangle of discarded notions and seemed to bounce off the front of his brain with a flat solidity that Jim felt sure was almost audible. It wasn't the only possibility, but it was certainly less unreasonable than most of the others, in practical terms at least.

It *was* unreasonable in a great many other ways, however, especially when the one considering it had suffered more than his fair share of problems with megalomaniacal computers. Daystrom's M-5 had been only one of them, and far from the worst. There had been too many others. V'ger, that unpleasant echo of NOMAD, was the most recent. To be coming into firing range of something with the same potential, but programmed with a Klingon military mind-set, was more than disturbing; it was downright scary.

James Kirk had never been ashamed to admit to fear—for his friends, for his crew, for his ship, and sometimes for himself, at least privately. He was afraid now, for all of those things and more. If this robot battle cruiser somehow reactivated and was subjected to the same provocations around Dekkanar as had been flung at the rescue ships of Operation Backtrack, Jim could imagine how it would respond. And the requirements of General Order 12 wouldn't mean a damned thing.

Granted, Spock had talked about the Klingon distrust of artificial intelligence and machines with the capacity to make their own decisions, but facts obtained by espionage could be incorrect, out of date, or the result of disinformation. The Vulcan had also suggested that the scout ship might be some kind of master controller. If it was then it would be better for all concerned—perhaps even the Klingons, considering that their new baby had apparently thrown some sort of tantrum already—if *Enterprise* took the whole thing into tow.

The only problem seemed to be in letting those eight Klingons know just what was going on. The situation around 4725 Cancri was quite troublesome enough without starting some sort of panicky small war out here on the rim. Jim then considered towing first, boarding second, and communicating last of all—once it had been established that communication was possible. Jim began wondering what sort of strain the *Enterprise*'s tractor beams could take, then decided his chief engineer should be up here; no need to set up the briefing room for what looked like one of the quicker tactical discussions. "Engineering, this is the captain." It wasn't Scotty who answered, but Roz Liddle, one of the new draft of lieutenants. "My compliments to Commander Scott, Lieutenant," said Jim, "and I'd be grateful if he could drop whatever miracle he's working on and get up to the bridge. Kirk out."

The turbolift doors hissed open behind him and McCoy strode out. "Since you won't come to the doctor, I guess the doctor will just have to come to you," he said with mock severity. "Yeah. You look better. But I've got you rescheduled for that checkup later today."

"Later today is fine, Bones, just so long as it's not right now. Chief of security to the bridge, please."

"Dammit, Jim, what did I do wrong this time?"

"Security's not coming for you. I'm assembling a boarding party," Jim said over his shoulder, then swiveled the center seat around to face McCoy.

"Bones, get someone from Medical with knowledge of Klingon physiology. Have him rig a suitable medical pouch and then get him to the transporter room."

"Let me get this straight: you're sending a boarding party over *there?*"

"Only eight crew aboard, and they evidently can't control it. Damn thing's a hazard to system traffic."

Bones took a deep breath and grimaced ruefully. "I took the time to read up on what those battle cruisers can do, Captain, and believe me, that ship is a hazard to a damn-sight more than traffic!"

"Recalibration complete, Captain," said Askel, stalking onto *Tazhat*'s bridge as though it were his ship and not Kasak's. "Blue lights all across the board."

The captain let that small impudence pass, at least for the present—although his mind noted it down against the commendation he had been considering for his science specialist. Time would tell which one would be erased and which set down for Command to see. Certainly Askel seemed confident enough in the quality of his work, for he had taken his visor off and tucked it beneath one arm. Kasak noted that as well; it was a flamboyant gesture worth remembering, even though by rights Askel should have spoken privately with the captain so that such a gesture might first have been his own.

Perhaps he is *ambitious after all,* thought Kasak, *and endeavoring to enhance his reputation among the crew. No matter. At least, not yet. And not on this ship.*

"Power has not yet been restored," Kasak said aloud, mildly critical after a meaningful glance at the still-dark chair repeater screens. "If the one's statement is correct, then why not? Explain this to me, *zan* Askel."

Kasak sutai-Khornezh was never so dangerous as

138

when he sounded patient and understanding. Too many subordinates had fallen into the error of assuming that because, against all reason and expectation, their captain appeared calm, a mistake or breach of regulations had been overlooked. No Klingon captain ever overlooked anything of the sort.

"It is for the one to order restoration of power," said Askel, "and for others to obey that order."

"So." Kasak nodded in sage agreement, but inside he was showing his teeth in a smile that was more than half a snarl. Askel had not shown such careful respect for the privileges of rank after the external check. Then he had addressed Krynn even though he had known the captain was also present on the bridge, and without needing or requesting further clearance she had begun the battle cruiser's power-up sequence. Askel could as easily have spoken to her now, or to Kasak, by way of the comm array all wore within their suit helms or their visors; and he could just as easily have advised the captain that his ship was not in fact evacuated to hard vacuum, instead of which he had chosen to make a dramatic personal entrance. It had been a good attempt on the first officer's part, to impress and, an instant later, to cover his mistake. Neither had worked, both knew it, and honor was satisfied.

For the moment.

Kasak unsealed his own helm, removed its headset, and then opened a shipwide channel on his chair communicator. "All stations, commence all-system warm-up. On my command, action, affirm action."

"Acting," said a chorus of voices, and data displays all over the ship came glowing back to active status.

"And beam a security team in *here.*" Jim indicated the command pod of the Bird of Prey on a three-view projection.

Security Chief Tomson studied the diagram, then operated controls to run through its deck plan. "I'd suggest another here, in the engineering section," she said. "Just in case somebody has second thoughts about being taken in tow." She smiled the icy smile that had become her trademark, a smile that had all the humor leached out of it. "Warp drives can be useful to a saboteur."

"Two teams of twelve, then, and a medic with each one. Do you approve, Bones?"

"As much as I've ever approved dealing with the Klingons, yes." Bones didn't look at all happy with the arrangement, but he was putting his best face on it.

"Captain, we're now on a parallel course and starting convergence to transporter range." Sulu followed the information with a tactical schematic. Behind the overlay, the Klingon battle cruiser and its scout grew steadily larger on the screen.

"Yon's a big bugger, Captain," observed Scotty. He had all the politely leashed enthusiasm of a hungry man staring at a roast of beef and knowing he was going to have first hack at it.

"Can the engines and the tractors handle it?"

"Handle that wee thing?" *Funny how sizes change depending on what's being called into question,* thought Jim, and hid a smile. "Och aye, no problem. It's well under the critical handlin' mass."

"All right, then, people, let's move it. Ingrit, you and your people use the emergency transporters on Q deck; that way we'll put all of you over at once. If memory serves, Mr. Scott's people used to be quite good at slipping things unnoticed onto Klingon ships." He returned the smiles, noticing that even Tomson's had a touch of amusement in it this time, and then went back to being serious. "Set phasers on

140

heavy stun—and remember, this is a rescue, not a raid."

"Aye, sir, noted and logged. I should—"

A siren began to yelp, and Jim turned quickly, looking toward Uhura in case it was the jammer she had installed. Her shake of the head was only half completed before the bridge lights snapped back to red and all the other alarms came whooping in. Jim looked at the screen, at the suddenly climbing energy output that could only mean a main drive powering up, and immediately he *knew.*

The Klingon ships were coming back to life.

There were no dramatic open-handed slaps at the controls in the arm of the center seat; the time for that was past. Instead, Kirk's index finger came down very lightly, opening the one internal channel that meant something right now. "This is the captain," he said, his voice unnaturally calm and sounding huge over the intercom. "Red alert, red alert, all hands to battle stations. Secure for combat maneuvers. This is not a drill."

Kasak had always thought that to emerge from any form of blindness was a pleasant thing. He had learned that he was wrong. When the first thing one saw was a Federation starship at almost point-blank range, the ignorance of unsight was to be preferred.

"wIy cha'!" he barked over the screeching klaxons, and glared at the tactical display as at the naked throat of his worst enemy. The Federation vessel was already too close, running almost in formation with *Hakkarl* and sidling nearer with every second. The display was running wild as all the sensors on both his ships came close to overloading it with data—and all that data had to do with the Starfleet vessel's readiness for combat.

Kasak showed all his teeth. He saw that his own crew was just as ready, weapons showing lock and preheat, shields at attack standard. *"baHwI'—cha yIghuS!"* He saw Katta's hand poise over the torpedo controls, fingers spread wide for volley fire, and the Federation starship pinned by the triangle of a target lock. They would all go to the Black Fleet together. And then, as he looked at death and glory in the maw of the enemy's phasers, his head cleared and his blood began to cool.

"We want them to shoot at us," he said so that all his crew could hear. "But in a time and place of our own choosing, where it will do us the least and them most harm. That time and place is other than here. Communications specialist?"

Khitar stiffened at the honor of hearing his title used in full, but remained immobile at his station. "Standing by," he said.

"Open a standard hailing link to the Starfleet captain."

Khitar was not the only one to turn and stare, but he was the first to compose himself and get back to work. "Affirm," he said, his voice far from steady.

"Yes," said Kasak sutai-Khornezh, and stretched luxuriously in the command chair. "Before the Organians decide to interfere, let's have a cozy little chat."

Chapter Seven

"THEY'VE DONE *WHAT?*" snapped Captain Kirk. Of all the surprises that had come sneaking up behind him with a sockful of sand since the mission began, this was one of the most improbable.

"Opened a hailing frequency, Captain," said Mahase. Just to be sure, he rechecked the comm board for a third time. He had made the first two checks because he hadn't believed his ears, or the transdator stuck in one of them. "It's a Federation frequency, too, prefaced with the level three friendship message and greeting."

"Is that so?" Jim stared at the screen, and the battle cruiser that filled it. For just the merest instant he hadn't a notion what to do about the situation; then command conditioning, years of experience, and his own wit came back on line. "Reply to them, Mister; reply, and use level four." He rubbed his chin thoughtfully. "I'll be damned if I'll let any Klingon commander out-polite me."

"Yes, *sir!*"

"If that's the situation, do we stand down from battle stations, Captain?"

"We will do nothing of the sort!" Jim swiveled his

143

seat around so that he could stare at whoever had spoken. "Ah yes, Lieutenant Stewart. Bear in mind, Lieutenant, that the *Enterprise* was designed principally for research and exploration. She can defend herself against attack—but that ship out there was designed first and foremost to *make* such attacks. So why would we want to give up our small advantage of readiness by standing down?"

"Demonstration of good faith, sir. Indicating peaceful intent." Larry Stewart looked faintly uncomfortable to have brought himself to such exalted notice with what had evidently been the wrong thing to say. He tried to set matters right. "As per General Order Twelve, now that communications have been established—"

"Lieutenant," Spock said severely, sounding like what he was, a teacher whose prize pupil was getting uppity, "it is the captain's place to interpret regulations, not yours."

"Spock, please." Jim held up one hand in a gesture for silence that looked more like some sort of benediction. "We're talking here about doing things by the book. The lieutenant hasn't seen enough service to know that books provide guidelines, not rigid fences."

"If the flexibility of rules is to be a part of his education, Captain," said Spock, "might I suggest a tour with Captain North?"

"Noted, Spock." To unfamiliar ears the Vulcan sounded angry; only Kirk and the small core of *Enterprise* veterans knew that Mr. Spock had deigned to make a joke in public.

"Reply acknowledged, Captain," said Mr. Mahase. "The enem— Sorry, sir, the *Klingon* commander wishes to speak with you."

"Does he indeed? Then put him on the screen."

It was the first time that most of the younger crew members had seen a Klingon of the Imperial race except for those depicted in Mr. Freeman's sterries of *Battle Cruiser Vengeance,* and an entertainment tape, even one that had originated in the Klingon Empire, had none of the impact of the real thing. For those accustomed only to holos of the ordinary-looking fusions, the face that now glowered from the viewer was a disturbing one.

To Jim's more experienced eye, it had all the characteristics of a line long kept pure. There was the naked dome of skull with its high, bony crest, rising above a swan-back sweep of thick black hair that from in front had the appearance of horns; the heavy brows above yellow-irised eyes that burned within their deep sockets like something lethal hiding under a shelf of rock; and the coarse beard and whiskers surrounding a mouth that looked as though it could wear a smile only if one was surgically inserted. And then the mouth *did* smile, in a slow and careful sequence of muscular contractions, its owner evidently quite aware that what passed for smiling among humans was very different from that acceptable to his own people.

"Kai kassai," the Klingon said in that guttural voice Jim knew rather too well for comfort. *"HoD QaSaq jIH. Ha'Qarl QaSaq. gavanneS lo'laH gholwIj. HIja'neS nuqneH?"*

Jim muted his voice-pickup before glancing toward Spock. "What's wrong with the translator circuit?" he muttered, trying not to move his mouth; lip-reading was not unknown in the Federation and among its opponents.

"Hold transmission and repeat on request," said Spock to the still-open channel. Then he shut off his own mike. "I took the liberty of putting comms on a ten-second-plus variable delay. The Klingon instruments will read it as a slight signal breakup, requiring no more than a repetition. If they register it at all. I

145

wanted to hear the Klingon commander's introduction for myself before switching to simultaneous translation."

As Jim listened to Spock with one ear, he could hear with the other that the Klingon had also swung sideways in his command chair and was snapping orders at someone offscreen. With the translators out, his words made no sense, but almost certainly he was tearing several stripes off his own communications officer.

"And?" Jim asked when a pause in the lecture seemed to require it.

"His manners are exquisite," Spock said. "Too much so. He has already employed two honorifics where—excuse me, Captain—none were appropriate or required. This approaches the level of insult, though of the most delicate kind; one that is doubtless appreciated by his crew, but otherwise unnoticed because of translator limitations. Therein of course lies the humor. I caution you not to match him like for like."

"Match what, Spock? What did he say?"

"He is Captain Kasak," said the Vulcan. "Kasak of the *Hakkarl.*"

"That's not an unusual opening; I've picked up similar ones on Freeman's tapes. Where was the insult?"

"He then said: 'I am honored to salute my worthy adversary. Do me the honor of telling me what you want.'"

"Oh. I *see.*" Jim stared at Spock very hard. "And he really thinks that he can get away with that?" He could sense and almost hear the bridge crew around him; the older hands fizzing with indignation and the inexperienced wondering what all the fuss was about. They would learn, in time, that Klingons were seldom this polite even to one another, except when addressing a very highly ranked superior. Using any form of address so exalted that it became absurd was always an insult: a captain would customarily promote a slacking ensign to admiral or, far worse, general, somewhere in the course of a dressing-down. To do the same to a Federation officer in the near-certain knowledge that he could not react—because he was unlikely to speak even basic Tlhinganaase, and his translator would filter out the subtle nuances that gave the words their weight—would be a rich jest indeed.

"DaH choQoylaH'a?" said the Klingon captain, not waiting for anybody's clearance to resume transmission. *"jISov! qaboQtaH DIvI' Hol vIjatlhtaH."*

This time, every translator on the bridge was active, even though the main comm system was still switched off. They heard nothing overtly impolite. *"Can you hear me now?"* Captain Kasak said, and then, *"I know! To assist you I will speak the Federation language."* Only those who knew Klingons of old were able to pick up the patronizing undertone to his choice of words.

James Kirk kept the way he felt under a perfect, near-Vulcan control, as Spock stepped forward like a good first officer and handed him a pad screen. Jim glanced down at it, and more than ever had to fight to keep all expression from his face. There were words on it, but not just the usual data-for-signature.

These words were Klingonese.

"Thank you for that consideration, Captain Kasak," said Jim in English. He hesitated for a moment, just long enough to see the sidelong smirk of satisfaction start to cross the Klingon's face, then sprang Spock's trap. *"batlh jiH, 'ach 'utlI'be',"* he continued, and though his larynx immediately sent a note of protest to the pain centers of his brain, he gave every syllable its full value. *"pup tlhinganlIjqu' Hol naDev wIyajlaH."*

Jim cleared his throat daintily and gave Kasak an amiable smile. There was no indication on the Klingon's harsh features that what had been said had registered at all, but his impending smirk had collapsed into a thin straight line that left his mouth like the slot of a data-solid reader. That was proof enough.

"I am honored, but it is not necessary," Jim had told him. "We understand *your* Klingon language perfectly here." It might have been the carefully placed emphasis or the discovery that his secret joke was not so secret after all—or it might just have been that Kasak had pledged himself to speak in the enemy's tongue and had learned too late that such a step was now unnecessary and consequently a humiliation.

"Enough of these courtesies," Jim said before the Klingon could brood long enough to do something they might all regret. "We're both captains of our respective ships: shouldn't we begin to speak as such?"

Kasak stared at him as though considering something much more violent than words; then settled back into his high-backed chair and nodded. *"Very well. We shall indeed speak as captains. But first, one further . . . courtesy. The only one remaining. Your name and your ship?"*

"Of course." He would have thought that *Enterprise* was already close enough to the Klingon battle cruiser so that its occupants could read name and registry from her primary hull. Evidently not. "My oversight. This is the Federation Starship U.S.S. *Enterprise,* and I am Captain James T. Kirk."

The Klingon jerked upright from his posture of studied indolence as though someone had run an electrical current through his chair, and stared from the screen with unsettling intensity. There was a heat in his eyes that would have been more appropriate had he been squinting down a gunsight rather than along a communication link that spanned fifteen kilometers of empty space.

Jim had never become truly accustomed to the reactions his name or his ship were prone to create in the most unlikely circumstances. In their long career together, he and the *Enterprise* had left a lot of friends behind them in a great many different places. They had left enemies as well, dangerous enemies with long memories, in places and on planets that he had no intention of ever visiting again.

And then the moment was past, and Kasak was relaxing back into his command chair again. To be arrested and taken in charge for illegal entry by one of the most notorious ships in Starfleet was probably enough to give most Klingons a turn for the worse, reflected Jim. And even without involving the Organians, it couldn't look good on their reports.

"Captain Kasak, you are doubtless aware that the star system we call 4725 Cancri is in a Federation-listed sector," Jim began. "So why do I find a warship," he paused, then very deliberately corrected himself, "or rather, *two* warships of the Klingon Empire in an area of space prohibited to them by treaty, by accord, and by accepted practice?"

Kasak stared at him and then past him, with eyes like yellow flints. *"Ask your Vulcan about the condition of both my ships until bare minutes ago."*

"Kasak," said Spock, and saluted with spread fingers, refusing to be nettled by the Klingon's insult. "I am no one's Vulcan. I hold captain's rank in UFP Starfleet, and I am science officer of the *Enterprise.*"

"Two captains . . ." Kasak muttered something off-screen that the pickup relayed as *"They must be running out of ships."*

"I agree with your contention that your ships were

without power when they entered the system perimeter," Spock said. "But I state that without power a ship will continue in the same direction as its last course set under power. Therefore I reflect my captain's curiosity as to why a course had been set toward this system at all."

"Would you accept that this vessel combination suffered a systems failure during first-flight shakedown?" From the way he said it, Kasak didn't seem to care about acceptance or denial, but then both Kirk and Spock knew how much face-saving was involved in holding command of a Klingon ship, and accepted the aggressiveness for no more than what it probably was: posturing to impress subordinates.

"In the case of a new or refitted ship, Captain," said Jim, "I would accept that almost anything is possible. But regardless of your shakedown problems, Captain Kasak," he said, stubbornly probing for something he felt sure the Klingon was avoiding, "it still begs the question of why you were heading toward this system in the first place. For the record, I should like to hear your explanation of *that*."

"Certainly, Captain Kirk." Kasak looked sideways through the warm and comfortably humid mists of the bridge, and received immediate nods of readiness from Askel and from Khitar on Communications. "Prepare your comm board for a transfer of the distress signal we received." He watched the moments of fussing on the Federation ship and heard the muttered speculations. *They have no patience,* Kasak thought. *A few seconds more and they will know, but still they have to debate and wonder what it is I send them.*

"Ready to transmit," said Khitar.

"We are ready to receive your transfer," said the gray humanoid who sat behind Kirk and off to the left in

the big, bright circular bridge. Kasak looked quickly toward him and suppressed yet another smile. *Ready to receive it, yes: but to accept it? That must yet be seen.*

"Transmit," he said.

It took less time to do than to say. Almost immediately after the word of command, Khitar sat back from his console and announced, "Transmission completed." Askel leaned over the comm board, did something to the controls that made lights chase each other across the readouts, then straightened up and walked over to his accustomed place just behind the command chair.

"*Now* it's completed," Askel said, drawing an inquisitive look from the captain and another from the communications specialist. "I fed a scramble signal into it from one of the intership transceptors and sent a random squirt in the other direction at the same time. Let the Feds try to analyze it, if they have five years to spare." With malevolence in both his face and his voice he added, "Unless *zan* Khitar would prefer that I make cracking our codes a little easier for them?"

Khitar said nothing. Nothing at all.

"Captain Kirk, have you received my transmission?" said Kasak, taking care not to smile at the wrong time no matter how he felt inside. There was a long silence from the bridge of the Federation ship, but nobody had thought to cut the visual connection when they shut off the sound, so Kasak was able to enjoy the spectacle of his message cassette being passed from hand to hand as gingerly as if it were coated in one of the more interesting contact poisons.

Finally Kirk reopened the voice channel. For many seconds he sat in his chair and stared alternately at the cassette, at its printed copy, and at Kasak's face on his own viewscreen. Meanwhile, the sound link spat and whistled through the interference of two sets of shields, transmitting nothing of more interest than the fact that the Federation captain was breathing hard.

"This," Kirk said at last, *"is a forgery."*

"Then I am scandalized, Captain Kirk, that I should have come so close to precipitating an incident because of an untruth."

The Starship captain looked straight at the viewscreen, and straight out of it, as if he stood nose to nose with Kasak rather than on his own bridge. Kasak presumed that this was what was called a "dirty look." He was not impressed; any Klingon cadet proctor could do better, and make it feel worse with the live end of his shock wand.

"Do you really expect me to believe this?" said Kirk again, after another swift and silent discussion with his two officers. Kasak still dismissed the Vulcan as unimportant—why else would he serve on a ship commanded and crewed by non-Vulcans? The other, Makhoy—if he was a surgeon specialist, why had he the name of a soldier?—was more interesting. He had the fire, the passion, the *klin;* and sometimes, for no reason at all, his body moved like that of a Rom. That fascinated Kasak, because he had seen Romulans move, both in the cube and in the Year Games, and while he might have expected it of the Vulcan, to find a human with the same kinesics as a Romulan was to find a human who deserved much closer examination. There was a story behind Makhoy, more probably several, and given adequate facilities and sufficient time, Force Leader Marag could extract them all.

"No, I don't expect you to believe it," said Kasak. *"Then why send it?"*

"Because you should have evidence of the false signal that led us astray." The Federation captain stared toward his viewer and toward Kasak. He was a worthy adversary indeed. Kasak had called him so in jest, but it was true. He was quick, wise, and difficult to deceive. That would make his final defeat so much the sweeter.

For he *would* be defeated. Kasak had sworn it before the naked stars in the instant when the name of the man and the name of the ship had shown him just what a gift had fallen into his hands. Kirk would eat deck scrapings and dust from the soles of Kasak's boots for every one of the vermin tribbles he had transported onto Captain Koloth's cruiser—and even that would not begin to make him suffer as Kasak sutai-Khornezh had suffered. At the last he would be denied even the Black Fleet, and his spirit would wander through cold darkness between the living and the dead, bewailing its fate for all the years to come. . . .

Captain Kasak dragged himself out of the dream and waved one hand idly in the air, as humans did when they dismissed a matter of small account. "We picked up a distress call," he said calmly, daring Kirk to call him a liar to his face. "This was during the initial exercises for *Hakkarl*. We had a ship beneath us that was new and fine, one that would strike fear into all wrongdoers."

Surgeon Specialist Makhoy made a snorting sound and hid part of his face behind one hand.

"And even in the Klingon Empire, the one does not receive warnings of the imminent invasion of an unprotected planet every day."

"Not unless you listen to your local station," he heard Makhoy mumble amid chuckles from behind his hand.

Kasak chose to let that pass; but the remark and the ill-timed laughter joined all the other notes in the locked file at the back of his mind. It would be a useful lever later, when it came time to learn what stories Makhoy had to tell. "This planet was in the Federation sector; but *Hakkarl*'s long-range scans could detect no Federation vessel coming to assist. Therefore we came instead."

"Captain," said Kirk, *"you will excuse me, please. Has it not been true in the past that the Klingon Empire enters Federation space only when it sees a chance for profit or expansion, and preferably both?"*

"Thanks to the *g'day't* glowbugs— Excuse me. Thanks to the wise and farseeing policies of the Organian people, the Empire is not at war with the Federation." Kasak spelled it out as though to a small and backward child. "Is it not, therefore, the duty of all to further friendly relations between our two races by offering whatever assistance is at our disposal— whenever and wherever it may be required?"

Kirk cleared his throat again, not as he had done after speaking Klingonese, but in that significant way Kasak had heard humans use before. He supposed it might be the eroded remnant of a shout for attention by the leader of any given group, but now it merely sounded as if one was announcing to the other that he felt unwell. *"So far as offering assistance is concerned, Captain Kasak, a K't'inga class battle cruiser seems like an overenthusiastic response to me."* He looked again at the cassette whose message Askel and Khitar had labored over for almost a day, until it sounded just right. *"And I still don't believe this. Neither what it says nor where you say it came from."*

"Believe it or not, Captain Kirk, we came here in good faith, and when this new ship developed faults in the propulsion and life-support systems, we almost lost our lives. Allow me and my crew to believe we came so close to the Black Fleet in the service of something useful."

"Captain Kasak," suddenly Kirk sounded very tired, *"you could almost be in politics. If your ship is back to full and proper operation—and my ship's sensors tell me it is—then I should be grateful if you*

and it would make best speed back within the boundaries of the Klingon Empire."

"Not quite, Captain Kirk." Kasak noted with great satisfaction that Kirk rolled his eyes and concealed a groan, almost as if he knew what was about to happen. "Since it was a respect for the terms of the Organian Peace Treaty that brought us here and placed our lives and our vessel in jeopardy—"

"So you say," muttered Makhoy from behind his captain.

"—then under the terms of that same treaty, I, my crew, and my ship may rest and resupply at the M-class planet known as Dekkanar."

"Captain," said Kirk, *"for some strange reason I have been expecting that statement from the moment you opened hailing frequencies."*

"Then, Captain"—Kasak allowed himself a broad smile that showed the points of his teeth to best advantage—"since you have had so much time for preparation, I see no reason why either of us should linger here a moment longer."

Askel could not believe his own boldness. He had not only made his first use of the transceptor override, but he had done so through Communications in full view of its department head and of the captain.

He had even risked testing Khitar's resolve with that stupid excuse about the double-random signal, and he had been proved right. For all his ability—and the very fact of Kasak's selecting him as crew said everything that needed saying about *that*—the communications officer was lacking in any form of courage. Even though he had certainly noticed something irregular about the readback following Askel's signal, he hadn't dared say anything about it. Either the captain would respond as he always did when equipment misbehaved, or Askel would deal with him personally. Having weighed the relative prospects, Khitar had chosen silence as the safest course.

That was just as well. Those for whom Askel's signal was intended were not the ones with whom Captain Kasak would have wanted to make contact. Not yet, at least. But it was essential that Imperial Intelligence be made fully aware of what was happening here. The message Askel had just transmitted outlined Captain Kasak's first intentions, as the captain had relayed them in the theater: to become the protecting power for this planet once they had thrown the Federation off it, and to so obtain the planet for the Empire by provoking an Organian intervention if such became required—but until then displaying no loyalty to any other than himself.

Now things had changed, and Askel suspected that the change was not one for the better. Meeting Starfleet ships had always been a part of Kasak's plan, that much was beyond question, but meeting this particular ship and this particular captain had put a different complexion on the matter. The science specialist had seen Kasak's reaction to the names of Kirk and the *Enterprise,* and though the captain had covered it instantly and well—well enough at least to fool those who didn't know him—that reaction had been enough to make Askel's liver shift in his chest.

Kasak had wanted to kill.

This new attitude had nothing to do with the plan, and Askel had decided there and then that another message would have to follow the first if everything was not to fall apart. Perhaps Kasak would restrain himself, and be satisfied with the ignominy that would fall on Kirk for the loss of an entire planet; that revenge would be sweeter than a simple killing, reflecting as it did what had happened to Kasak all those years ago. But Askel could not bring himself to believe in it. It was approaching the time when his own plan would need to be set in motion if he was to salvage anything from all of this. Even his life.

"Of course it's a forgery, Captain; but it's a particularly good one." Commander Uhura had come back to the bridge, and for the past half-hour she and Mr. Mahase had been shredding down the supposed distress signal and subjecting even the least crackle of subspace static to a battery of cryptology tests. "It's so good that I'd raise the question of whether it originated aboard the Klingon ship at all."

"So maybe someone on Dekkanar *did* invite them after all."

"It's entirely possible." Uhura waved several sheets of hard copy and then slapped them down on her working console. "Even though nothing was ever detected, we've taken the thing apart, and the carrier wave, the signal corruption, all of it points to a planetside source of transmission. Although whether the planet was Dekkanar or the Klingon homeworld remains to be determined."

"Wonderful." Jim scrubbed the heels of both hands into his eye sockets in a weary gesture that had as much to do with how fed up he had become with the Dekkani as with how little sleep he'd been getting lately. "The Klingons have always been capable of this sort of deception, so I guess I really shouldn't have put it past them." Jim glanced up at the viewscreen.

The Klingons, for their part, seemed unconcerned that they were the focus of attention for four hundred-plus pairs of eyes or species-variable alternatives, or that every available sensor, camera, and recording device was being run over their vessel. Instead, they seemed more concerned with their own punctilious observation of Starfleet's mandatory traffic limits.

Tazhat's crew held their linked ships exactly at the boundary of minimum separation, five kilometers bang on the nose.

Just how exactly came out an hour later during an engineering grid-laser scan to cross-check the Klingon battle cruiser's dimensions against official intelligence figures. One of the many additional figures that came out of it was that the Klingon ship was holding formation at a distance correct to the millimeter and eight decimal places.

"Very impressive, I'm sure," said Jim, not sounding impressed at all. "But how does the ship perform under combat stresses?"

"If you're asking for opinions," said Bones from his usual place behind the center seat, "then mine is that I'd rather not find out."

"I doubt the Klingons know themselves." Scotty was on the bridge as well, having brought the station-keeping data up in person. Jim knew that his chief engineer would sooner turn teetotaler than admit to anything like interest in the Klingon ship, but now that he had lost the opportunity to take it apart, he was gazing at the battle cruiser with a wistful expression on his face.

"Well, Mr. Scott, what do you think of him?" Jim took care to use the correct pronoun for the Klingon ship, and was amused when Scotty snorted something that might not have been Gaelic but was certainly rude.

"A bucket o' bolts, sir. Oh, aye, it'll be the usual." Jim raised his eyebrows. "Cheap an' nasty rubbish, all but the guns. And automated forby. I wouldna like to run a ship on automatics an' then take it into any sort of combat. Not even this one." He patted one of the bridge railings affectionately. "No, I dinna think the *Enterprise* would have much trouble wi' that thing."

"Um." Jim leaned forward a bit and looked more

closely at the steadily increasing raft of data that various departments were accumulating about the Klingon cruiser. A lot of it was as opinionated as Scotty, and a lot more was inspired guesswork, but the general view seemed to bear out what had just been said.

He sat back again and stared at the battle cruiser's hulking outline on the screen. "Still, I echo Bones on this one. I hope we never have cause to learn what it can do." Jim put his thoughts of the Klingons aside for a moment. "Estimated time to orbital reinsertion, Mr. Sulu?"

"Three-point-seven hours at present speed and heading, Captain."

"Good. In that case, Uhura, patch me through to Captains North and Farey. It's been too long since I had an update."

"He is an *admiral?*"

Askel heard the edge in Kasak's voice and scowled inwardly. He would have preferred that his captain not find out any more about Kirk's career than he already knew, and had said as much, but Kasak was now standing behind him and speed-scanning the data as it appeared on the library computer monitor in the captain's private office, so there was no way to prevent him from extracting the information. Intelligence had been working hard where James T. Kirk was concerned. The human's name had a considerable entry against it, and Kasak had demanded to see the lot.

Seeing it had not improved his temper. As he grew calm again, he was grateful that some errant need for secrecy had brought him behind a closed door, because it was never good for a crew to see their commander lose his temper and his control so completely. He had only bared his teeth at first, but later he had raged, and twice now he had flung the collated hard copy across the room. This latest piece of outrageous information was as much as he could bear.

Kasak took a deep breath of the warm, moist air, and then another, but it was only with a third that the burning began to fade from his chest and from behind his eyes. "That Kirk should be an admiral by now is a thing that I can understand," he said slowly. "But that by all accounts he should resent the promotion is an insult!" Askel stood by the computer console and said nothing, his face devoid of any expression that might be misconstrued. "An insult to the rank, to the institution of rewarding merit, to the others like him who have lived long enough to earn such rewards, and to ambition itself."

"If it pleases the one to say so, then it is so."

"And what do you say, Thought Master Askel? What is behind the careful phrases that will not give me offense? Speak."

"He is an admiral who would prefer to be a captain. You are a captain who would prefer to be"—Askel hesitated for an instant, debating the wisdom of his words, before he went on—"to be the captain of your own ship, one that is not taken from you after every flight. To be your own master instead of their servant."

"Be careful," said Kasak in a voice that had gone flat and dead. "Be very careful indeed."

"Killing the speaker will not kill the truth," said Askel. The boldness of his words took Kasak by surprise, disarming whatever threat or action his statements might have provoked.

"So."

"And killing Admiral Kirk will be a poor satisfaction."

Kasak stared for several seconds at his science officer, then turned a chair out from the desk and sat down. "How are these issues connected?" he demanded, curious.

"In this fashion: your rage would have you kill him by some means not offensive to the Organian *wewwI'vethpu',* and once he is gone, what then?"

"He will be my servitor in the Black Fleet," growled Kasak, "and I will slay him again a thousand times, laughing."

"This will be in any case. But would it not be a more elegant revenge to make him you, and you him?"

"Explain," Kasak said, using Battle Language to indicate his impatience.

"Kirk resents his promotion to admiral," said Askel, "because it takes him from the bridge and the direct command of his ship, and from any further chance of gaining glory."

"And?"

"Death in action is an eventuality he must have faced before, many times. He will be prepared to face it again, and to accept it if need be. Therefore the killing of Kirk will be a lesser punishment than to let him live."

"Why?" Kasak continued to use Battle Language, for though his irritation with Askel was fading, his idea was of sufficient interest to require minimal prompts. It had occurred to him that Askel would have continued even if his captain said nothing at all, but Kasak had decided that his science, first, and executive officer needed to be reminded who was in command on this ship. It would teach him humility and a sense of place; and if it pushed him into losing his temper, then Kasak already had several punishment details in mind that would do the job just as effectively.

Askel probably suspected something of the sort, because Kasak could actually see the other officer pulling himself back under full control. That was sufficient: superiority had been reestablished, so the captain could become magnanimous once more. "Relax, 'Kel," he said, gesturing to the computer console's chair. "Relax, sit down, and continue at your own pace."

Askel remained where he was for a moment, standing quite still, and inwardly Kasak went tense. If he *had* pushed too hard, as he had done to other junior officers in the past, then this was the moment to be most wary. There was something about being criticized and then patronized immediately afterward that touched a raw nerve in the Klingon psyche. Then the science specialist nodded—a short, sharp jerk of his head—and sat down, and the moment was past, until the next time.

"Captain Kasak," he said, "all know that the Federation is weak and lacking in the true *komerex klin,* that strength of purpose which gives Klingons their superiority. It is unable to punish even its own criminals as they deserve. Sentence of execution has been erased from its books of law except as penalty for a few most particular crimes. Incompetence is not one of them. Therefore"—he leaned forward and began counting points off on his fingertips—"one can safely assume that even after you disgrace Kirk by causing the Organians to hand over this planet's development to us, he will not be terminated by his own superiors—"

"And this," interrupted Kasak, amused and confused in equal measure, "is intended to be more stimulating than cutting out his liver?"

"Yes, sir, it is. Because after that, do you believe Starfleet will ever give him command of his own ship again? They will enforce his rank and the duties of that rank, and leave him to rot behind a landbound desk. Oh, they'll call on his experience, and allow him out once in a while to inspect vessels in close orbit, but if ever he travels out among the naked stars again, it will be as a passenger on some other captain's ship, where he will be of no more account than a piece of baggage." Askel grinned savagely and closed his fist. "And always he will know and helplessly remember how he was brought so low, and he will speak your name with curses. As you have spoken his for far too long!"

Kasak gazed at him through eyes half-hooded by their heavy lids, and said nothing at all.

". . . initial upheaval downstairs after the ships went to battle stations, but things have calmed down more or less."

"Noted, Gytha," said Jim, more relieved than he was willing to admit. He and the *Enterprise* had been away from the action for almost twelve hours, and he kept thinking of a line from one of Freeman's more peculiar tapes: "Anything can happen in the next half-hour." He remembered vaguely that the line had been delivered as someone called battle stations. Well, at least most of the possible shocks hadn't happened. But the PDI had made its presence known. "Anything further on the fight planetside?"

"Negative on that, Jim. Somebody started shooting at Johnson's people as soon as they landed. Three hit, including the colonel. Nothing serious, but after that the DPG had clearance for self-defense." Captain North smiled dryly. *"It all got very peaceful very fast. Evacuation is proceeding, and Nic has some good news for you."*

It was indeed good news, unmitigated by *buts* or *maybes*. *Vanguard's* geosynchronous position was such that she was now on the dayside of Dekkanar and able to run a direct astroscan on the system primary. Her science officer, Lieutenant Commander T'rell, had observed, logged and later confirmed that the sunspot activity had passed its peak and was tapering off rapidly. *"If it continues into recess at its present rate, Captain,"* she told Kirk, *"the last phases of the personnel evacuation may be safely undertaken by transporter beam. I shall of course continue to monitor."*

"Thank you, Commander," said Jim. "Kirk out." He closed the channel and smiled. Things were finally starting to look up. Now if he could only work out what to do about the Klingons.

Uhura's comm board beeped, and Jim thought, *No. . . .*

She touched the transdator in her ear, frowned slightly, and said, "It's *Hakkarl,* sir. Captain Kasak sutai-Khornezh wishes to discuss a matter of importance."

Jim turned enough to lift an eyebrow at her; that use of full title and line, rare between Klingon and human, suggested that this might be more than just a social call.

"Recorders and voiceprint analysis up and running, Captain," said Spock softly.

"Let's hear what he has to say."

The Klingon was no more beautiful now than he had been at first sight. Age and experience had left their mark on his face, and it was probably one even a Klingon mother would find hard to love, but Jim was getting used to it. "Captain Kasak," said Jim, and nothing more.

"Captain Kirk." Kasak was still speaking Federation Anglish, and this time he was showing no sign that doing so annoyed him. As far as anyone on *Enterprise* could tell, the Klingon had more on his mind than that. *"Within this system and holding separation distance from a Federation starship, may it be said that I am within Federation space?"*

He already knew as much; he had known it before

he came here, and Jim had taken him to task about it since. So what was going on? "Captain, this sector is officially nonaligned, but the planet 4725 Cancri IV is under Federation territorial protection. So, put simply, yes, this is Federation space."

"And you in your rank as admiral are the most senior Federation officer?"

Jim hesitated, wondering how in hell he knew that, then remembering that his Klingon intelligence file was probably hefty. Even so, he didn't have to act as if he liked it. "Yes."

The Klingon's yellow eyes had gone cold and wary, though Jim had the feeling they weren't watching him, but someone—several someones—on Kasak's own bridge. *"Then, Admiral Kirk"*—did he really come down harder on that "Admiral" than he needed to?—*"I and my crew require and request that at this time you grant us your protection and political asylum within the borders of the Federation—"*

And all hell seemed to break loose.

Chapter Eight

"STATIONS!" BARKED KASAK as he cut the transmission link. The whip-crack imperative of Battle Language had a more immediate effect even than the heavy disrupter pistol he had drawn the instant he spoke his final words to Kirk. Six of his crew dropped back into their proper places. Surgeon Specialist Arthag and Security Officer Marag stood right where they were, watching the pistol and remaining very still. Neither had a duty station on the bridge and they were there only because the captain had ordered them present to witness his discussion with the Federation commander. They were not alone in their surprise at what they had just heard.

Or in their desire to extract the traitor's lungs and make him eat them.

Kasak knew it. That was why he had brought the pistol. It wasn't meant for use—unless that was absolutely necessary—but to buy him the moments he would need for talking. After *that,* either he would no longer need the pistol or he would need it as he needed breath: to live.

"Better," he said, and having framed out what he would say an hour and more ago, went on, "and it pleases me that all of you are loyal." One or two were surprised by that; the others heard only sarcasm and responded according to their custom, with glares of silent hatred or snarled curses. Kasak nodded slowly, having expected nothing else. "Otherwise I would not have dared to act in this fashion. Or in this." And he returned the weapon to its holster.

It was not an act of such daring and trust as he intended it to appear, for he did not reseal the strap that looped across the pistol's grip to hold it secure, and he was comfortably at ease with the speed of his own gun hand. If anybody made a hostile move, Kasak knew well enough that he could have the weapon clear of its holster again fast enough. But it was the gesture that mattered, the gesture that was meant to impress, and it succeeded. There was some muttering, but all made acceptably relaxing movements as they settled back to listen.

For his part, Kasak did not relax until Arthag was seated at Damage Control and Marag had perched himself at the position normally occupied by Environmental Engineering. Both systems were now on automatic, their overrides run respectively through Engineering Central and Medical Sciences, but the chairs were still in place. Most important, Force Leader Marag was now almost a full radius of the bridge away from his supposedly treacherous captain, and given Marag's well-established reputation, that was still barely far enough.

"Now that you are willing to listen," said Kasak, "hear what I have to say and study it well." He leaned back in his command chair, and swept a long, slow stare across the faces of his chosen crew.

This was the moment for which they had been selected, handpicked both for their abilities and—far more importantly—for the frequency with which they had served under Kasak in the past. Loyalty aboard a Klingon ship was a difficult thing to ensure at the best of times; there was too much jockeying for future position, for arranging the downfall of a superior if that downfall would bring with it more benefits than would continued support.

He had always taken care to judiciously spread his own personal glory among his subordinates, even when their accomplishments were of a lesser magnitude than his. In that fashion they were continually reminded of the source of their most immediate advantage, and furthermore they were continually presented with indications of their captain's esteem. At no time would such a policy, even in its most blatant form, be considered an attempt to buy the loyalty of a crew member or an entire crew. The usual interpretation was that a given captain was recognizing the part played by his crew, individually or collectively, in his latest success. Just as, if they were responsible for his failure, he would kill them.

Their faces showed Kasak that they knew this. There was not a single Klingon on *Hakkarl*'s bridge who had failed to benefit in some way from service with this captain. For all that he could be cruel, his cruelty had never been pointless: it was widely known that the sutai-Khornezh regarded energy wasted to no purpose as wasted energy and nothing else. But if there was some advantage to be gained . . . There were stories about that, too. Stories to scare cadets with.

It was this same attitude that controlled his granting of benefits; he did not hand them out purely as a bribe in the hope of future support, as some captains were known to do, but as payment for hard striving in the duties Kasak set. And when they were so earned, he gave them immediately, publicly and with much praise.

"An attempted mutiny is not in itself a mutiny," said Kasak. "But an attempt to act without thinking first is always thoughtless. And unwise. There are other captains who would have left you dead. All of you. Or you might have left me dead, and then none of you would know the reason why I spoke as I did to the Federation Captain Kirk."

"And maintain shields at full power," Jim said. "That ought to buy us time to think of something else." Mr. Scott said something skeptical that Jim almost lost in the whooping of the red-alert siren, but he could guess the content. "We won't be firing first, no," he went on. "And not because of the rules of engagement. At least not ours." He looked up at the blinking alert lights, decided that by now everyone had gotten the message, and ordered the alarm shut off for the nth time today. "I'm more concerned now about the Organians sticking their noses into this mess."

"Phasers locked on target, Keptin," said Chekov from the defense station. "But it looks as if those Cossacks are just *sitting* there."

"Easy does it, Mr. Chekov. Hold fire. They'll sit there until they've sorted matters out between the captain's faction and the rest. And then the winners will make their move. Whatever that's likely to be."

In the instant after Captain Kasak's astonishing request for asylum, as the comlink image broke up on a scene of imminent chaos and death on *Hakkarl*'s bridge, Jim had sounded yet another red alert and called for immediate defensive and evasive action. The shields had never been fully down since interception, but they had been reduced to standby intensity as one of those token gestures of good faith Lieutenant Stewart had been talking about—and they had come right back up to maximum in the first of the seven seconds at full impulse power that had flung *Enterprise* far away from the Klingon cruiser.

The Klingons had an unfortunate propensity—demonstrated for the first time at Donatu V and all too frequently thereafter—of resorting to an unrestricted level of violence when settling in-ship disputes. Since the ultimate demonstration of this tended to be the detonation of their own warp drive system (and consequently all other parties in the area), high-speed retirement to a safe distance had become the standard response for anyone caught in the vicinity of a Klingon crew reconciling their differences about internal politics.

Jim eyed the main screen's readouts and felt somewhat more at ease to see that Sulu had already enabled an override circuit linking *Enterprise*'s own warp engines to a tight-focused sensor scan locked on the battle cruiser some hundred thousand kilometers distant. In this particular situation, at the first hint of matter-antimatter overload, the override would cut in and wrench them from their present station-keeping position to warp factor four in less than a second. Even that savage and stress-laden acceleration was cutting matters far too fine, since by their very nature certain parts of the energy pulse were themselves warp-capable. This time there were more sweaty hands on the U.S.S. *Enterprise* than just those of her captain, as they and he watched and waited.

And then waited some more. . . .

Although he was hearing it with his own ears, Askel still found it hard to believe that any Klingon officer of Kasak's fame should lay himself so open to ridicule. Had he or any of the others spoken of the captain's history in his hearing, as Kasak was speaking of it now, he could and would have burned them on the spot and been applauded for it. What the rest of the crew thought of his tale of tribbles being deliberately introduced to infest a ship he couldn't tell, apart from the usual and instinctive reaction of disgust. Askel loathed the useless fluffy little horrors as much as any of them, even though he had gained a few seconds of amusement when he discovered that his people's word for them, *yIH,* exactly matched a human noise of distaste. However, it was plain that while they found the rest of Kasak's tale of ability passed over something to be regretted, they were unable to understand why the captain was subjecting them and himself to this embarrassing and humiliating ordeal.

Until he named the Federation starship and the Federation captain who had been responsible.

And then Askel understood. Mentally he lashed himself for his obtuseness, for missing the links that an Imperial Intelligence operations master should have spotted even before Kasak began to speak. And then he calmed somewhat, knowing that he was blameless, since he had lacked essential data. He had not known, for instance, that Kasak put revenge on Kirk and the *Enterprise* above his own reputation.

That *he* was convinced, however, did not mean that any covert Imperial Security operative had also taken the unusual step of believing what he or she was told. Captain Kasak was still in considerable danger from . . . whom? Without seeming too obvious about it, Askel began to watch the other faces.

"I hear you wondering among yourselves," Kasak said, "if the one has taken leave of his senses." Now, that was exaggeration, for whether through shock or because they didn't want to miss a word of what he said, nobody had spoken since he began. "You wonder then if what you heard him say to the Feds was something spoken only in your imagination. I tell you it was not. I said it. But I spoke those words not to betray the trust placed in me by the Empire, or the honor given me by those I command on this first flight. I used them as I would use any other weapon: against my enemy."

Laughter bubbled up under Askel's immobile face, threatening to disrupt his composure with an unseemly outburst. Of course! Once the clues were assembled, the science specialist found himself having to fight down an impulse to leap cheering to his feet. It was so simple and yet so brilliant that it deserved to—no, it *had* to succeed.

"Kirk is torn now between his suspicion of my true motives and his hope that what I said to him is true," Kasak continued. "The longer we can maintain the illusion that we would meekly deliver *Hakkarl* and *Tazhat* and all their secrets to him in exchange for what passes for life somewhere in the Federation, the more blinded with anger he will be when he learns that the only truth is his own fear of our superior race! When we power up and begin to move away, oh, so slowly, he will see his great prize and all its glory snatched from his grasp. And how will he try to close his grip, *zan* Katta?"

Katta twitched from immobility as if waking from a doze during some dull lecture at the Academy, and her answer was the hasty rattle of words Askel had heard from his own students in just that situation. Except that Katta's answer was correct. "The one will act like any wise commander: free fire at impulse engines to disable the prize; precision fire to sever warp nacelles, thus preventing destruct option; finally tractor towing."

"Exactly, except for the Organians. Kirk may call down fire on us, but I doubt if it will leave his phaser tubes. While we, who have been visiting a planet permitted to us under the light bulbs' own peace treaty, will be the innocent victims of Starfleet aggression. Now what would an Organian make of that? Krynn?"

Askel covered his smile with one hand, admiring Kasak's technique. He had begun this so much on the defensive that he had needed a disrupter as backup, and now if it went on much longer he would be setting off-duty work assignments and written examinations.

Krynn answered in much the same manner Katta had, as student to teacher. "Terms of Organian Treaty regarding development of planets located in Treaty Zone. Respective signatory parties to send envoys. Purpose: demonstration of respective abilities to develop planet in peaceful useful manner. Rights granted to party showing best ability or most acceptable to native population. Failure to abide by terms of agreement: physical interdiction of offending party from planet, which is then ceded to nonoffending party."

"And what do we learn from this, bearing in mind that our distant line-cousins the Dekkani have already ordered the Federation from their planet? Marag, what does it tell you?"

"That Kasak sutai-Khornezh still has a mind sharp enough to cut throats," rumbled the force leader from somewhere deep in his chest. "Since we will be there when the Feds leave, these Dekkan cousins might be persuaded to accept us as their new protectors. And if a Fed starship goes so far as to fire on us, or even to attempt it, the planet and its surrounding spatial zone will become part of the Imperial zone of influence— and the one will have exacted his revenge, gained much glory, and won the Empire a foothold in Federation space."

Marag rose from his seat and came to a full salute. "The one is no traitor," he said. "All of Security is with him."

Whether that was Marag making a somewhat cumbersome joke about the fact that he alone was overt security on this mission, or a barely veiled warning to the coverts who acted as one or other department head on this ship where all of the crew were heads of department, Askel didn't really know.

"Captain, *Hakkarl* has just reopened the comm channel," said Uhura. "Message is: 'Still on course to Federation planet 4725 Can IV, still awaiting your reply.' That's all." Uhura took the transdator from her ear. "And that is, in fact, all. It's the only signal that has left the Klingon double-ship combination since we broke contact, and they haven't received anything."

"That includes the subspace transmission detected by Lieutenant Mahase during the Klingon transfer of their spurious distress call, Captain," said Spock. "It is a closed-satchel code of the type favored by my father the ambassador, but in this instance neither Communications nor Cryptography—"

"Nor even Mr. Spock himself," Uhura chimed in generously.

"—has been able to make sense out of the signal content," Spock continued without missing a beat. "My own opinion is that it constitutes a decoy intended to make us believe there is more of significance going on aboard the *Hakkarl* than there actually is."

"You're saying the transmission is just gibberish."

"Yes, sir. Although there is a chance that the signal does in fact contain information, and is directed toward whichever imperial orbital facility built this particular cruiser. If that is so, then I speculate the signal content to be congruent with those of the automatically deployed drones carried by experimental Starfleet designs for such a purpose. Essentially the Klingon ship has reported its own imminent destruction."

"To cover their defection," Kirk said.

"Presumably. I should not be surprised if we receive a request for clearance to point-detonate several photon torpedoes so as to leave an appropriate heat and radiation footprint. The number of torpedoes requested should provide a reasonable indication of what sort of accident was reported."

In fact, the request to time-set twenty photon torpedoes came in from *Hakkarl* less than two minutes later.

Jim turned to look very hard at Spock, raising both his eyebrows. Spock responded as he usually did, with the raising of only one.

Twenty photon torpedoes going off at once would make an estimable flare. It would not look much like an accident where the warp drives of both cruiser and scout had run totally beyond control. That would require more torpedoes than the Klingons and all the Federation vessels put together had on board. Instead, it would resemble a situation in which shutdown had begun but failed to take effect. Even that was an impressive bang, and Jim was relieved that he wouldn't have to stay and watch it.

"Uhura." Jim swung his chair around and grinned a bit at his comm chief. "I'm sure you've already made the appropriate signal to *Sir Richard* and *Vanguard* concerning what's about to happen."

"Yes, Captain. And to the Dekkan Planetary Council. I did that in the sequencing squirt to Colonel Johnson."

"Right." He shook his head slowly and ruefully; there wasn't really much else he could do in the circumstances. "Very good, Uhura. Thank you. Advise the Klingon captain that he may begin deployment of his own torpedoes. Advise him further that we have locked *our* torpedoes on his command pod. And if that isn't an accurate statement, Mr. Chekov, please make it so."

"Change of lock confirmed, Keptin."

"Messages acknowledged, sir. Captain Kasak advises you that he intends a low-velocity launch and will complete the deployment process using tractors."

"Sensible of him." Jim touched the call key on his chair communicator, Scotty having hurried back to Engineering when it first looked as though sudden demands might be put on his beloved engines. "Mr. Scott, have you been monitoring this?"

"Aye, that I have. This lad's got it all worked out."

"Then it's practical enough from an engineering point of view?"

"Och aye, he's done his homework right enough, though he's overdoin' the torpedoes jist a wee bit . . . or not, maybe." Jim knew quite well the sound of Scotty having second thoughts. He waited. There was a sudden scraping noise over the pickup as Scott consulted one of the heavy-duty engineering-section pad screens. *"We've been runnin' a few computer simulations, Captain, based on what we scanned in the last close pass. If the engines on that Klingon tub are boosted, an' the waste-heat readin's are suggestin' as much as thirty-five percent, then he's calculatin' the big bang jist right."*

Boosted engines had not come up for discussion before, and Jim didn't like having the news sprung on him in such a backhanded fashion. The way things had been jumping today, it wasn't anybody's fault, but Spock's various opinions about the cruiser *Hakkarl* had already been enough to make Jim wary of what other little surprises the ship might have in store.

"Mr. Spock," he said, "when you have a moment, I'd like a program initiated to collate what we've learned so far about the Klingon vessel. At present the information is all over the place, so that I've only now been told that Mr. Scott thinks it has a boosted warp drive. If somebody somewhere on this ship has any more theories that might give the Klingons an advantage, I want to know about them."

Jim knew he was drifting along the outermost edges of irritability. At present that didn't matter, but once the diplomatic part of this mission got back under way, he would have to be careful. The six hours of missed sleep were taking their revenge.

"Torpedo deployment completed, Keptin." Chekov tapped controls on the weapons console. "Tactical on the viewer."

The swarm of red-glowing fireflies that were the Klingon torpedoes looked as ominous to James Kirk as they always did, regardless of the fact that this time they were tracking away from *Enterprise* rather than toward her. His next order wasn't so much the issuing of a command as the utterance of a private desire.

"Right. Mr. Sulu, let's get out of here." There was no need for course or speed instructions: they were continuing on their original course back to Dekkanar, and since Sulu had no more love for Klingon ordnance than his captain, they would be moving just as fast as they were able. Since *Hakkarl* had already been advised of Jim's intention, it was the Klingon helm officer's responsibility to keep up. *Enterprise* was not staying in the vicinity of four teratons' worth of explosive power, not for the sake of a dozen newly surrendered battle cruisers.

Sulu pushed her sublight velocity to the limit and held it there for almost five minutes, watching as the countdown numerator spindled down to zero. The

Klingons were thirty thousand kilometers off to starboard and the same distance astern, a whisker over half a second behind them. Their helmsman's reflexes were evidently of the sort that made steel traps hide their teeth in shame, and Jim made various mental warning notes to himself on just that subject.

"Aft angle on the viewer," he said. "Shields four, five, and six to maximum power and deflection angle, all hands brace for possible flux turbulence."

And as if on cue, the torpedoes went off. There was a sudden blink on the screen, a pinpoint of intolerable brilliance that expanded violently into a flare of unleashed energy. *Enterprise* seemed to quiver in the same instant that the glare of the detonation reached her viewscreen, and a low rumble like that of her warp drive shivered through the starship's hull and decks as a warp-speed disturbance passed through her systems. Artificial gravity flickered maybe half a G to either side of normal. Uhura's transdator, lying on the communications board, emitted a multiple-harmonic squeal that could be heard across the bridge and would certainly have deafened her. One of sickbay's diagnostic beds claimed that the three tricorders resting on its mattress pad were suffering from high blood pressure.

And then it was over.

Jim took a quick look around the bridge and noted that everything seemed to be where he had last seen it, then glanced at Ensign Penney. "Damage report, Yvonne," he said. "Then defense station weapons status readout. Uhura, signal for a similar condition report from the Klingons, please. And thank you, Mr. Sulu; that was nicely judged."

The reports came in on all three ships, and every one of them showed the reassuring "no damage" flash Jim had expected to see. But there was one additional item in the report from the Klingon ship that he definitely had not been expecting, and it took him just a little bit off-guard.

Kasak wanted to come calling.

And Askel wanted to know why.

"It will deepen Kirk's trust in my good faith, that I will cross to the vessel of an enemy and meet with him face to face," Kasak said. "And he will be all the angrier, and easier to provoke into rashness and stupidity, when his trust is so humiliatingly betrayed." The speech sounded easy, not naturally so but with the ease that came with careful rehearsal. Askel guessed that the captain had known his latest decision would not go by without someone asking about it, and he had prepared his answer accordingly.

It might have worked with the rest of the crew—except of course for the security operatives, whom Askel, to his chagrin, had not yet uncovered—but surely Kasak did not expect his science specialist to swallow the same bait. Except that as they continued to discuss the matter in the mess room, it became increasingly plain that, yes, the captain was expecting just that.

Unless of course, Askel reflected to himself while Kasak punched up food and drink for them both, *the captain is expecting nothing of the sort and is provoking me for another test reaction.* He determined, in that moment while Kasak's back was turned, that he would provide no such thing. He would be more serene than a sleeping Vulcan, more difficult to read than an unwritten book, and he would use that position of strength to do some subtle testing of his own.

He had already sent another intelligence communication, during the flurry of activity that accompanied the shepherding of twenty live time-set photon torpedoes. His message had been primed in the same instant that Krynn sent *Hakkarl* in pursuit of the Federation starship, and he had transmitted it under cover of the magnificent explosion. Even if it had chanced to be overheard by some snooper either on the *Enterprise* or on his own ship, it would have sounded just like any other flux-distorted random squawk.

And now, thanks to Kasak's sudden desire to pay deceitful social visits, it had all to be done again.

He looked at the tray of fruit nectars and plain pastries, selected one of each, ate, drank, and tasted neither. "When and how many?" he asked finally, all business.

Kasak sipped at his glass of sweet fruit nectar before he replied. "At once and alone."

Askel was immediately wary of the real motive behind Kasak's sudden decision, and his mind began to race. "This may not be," he said, taking great care over the inflection of his speech. It would hardly help if he put the wrong weight on the wrong word and Kasak turned stubborn, because the last thing Askel wanted was for his captain to go alone to meet James T. Kirk. For various reasons. "It would be wrong if the one went unaccompanied. It would lack propriety. A captain of such repute should have an honor guard. . . ." His voice trailed off when he noticed the way Kasak was looking at him, a strangely speculative look that turned Askel's liver to lead within his chest. *He knows about I.I.,* he thought. *He knows about I.I. and he knows about me!*

None of that could be seen on Askel's face, of course. Nobody attained the rank of operations master by letting people read what they were thinking, and several operations masters in the past had gone so far as to wear dermally implanted prostheses of cosmetic plastic to permanently mask their features. Askel was not one of these, although with further advancement he might become one. At present he hid his thoughts by not allowing them to show, ever—except deliberately, for effect. In this instance it was just as well, for his fears were banished by Kasak's next words.

"Then the one will accompany his captain onto the *Enterprise,* together with others yet to be named," said Kasak. "And we shall wait until we achieve orbit, so that the stripping of the ship of all but a watchkeeping crew will not seem strange."

"Honored, Captain," he said. "And the others?"

"Yet to be named, I said. But Marag certainly. It is always good to have security in a hostile environment."

"Agreed." Though he ran that one several times through his mind and sifted all the layers of meaning out of it, Askel still wasn't sure whether it was a simple statement or some kind of very subtle joke at someone else's expense. And not necessarily that of the security chief. Marag had, however, already stated that he approved of Kasak's plan. Though he might question this latest development, his inclusion in the boarding party would put most of those doubts to rest. "Do we beam across?

"No. We will use a shuttle. Though its intensity is slackening, the present level of sunspot activity prevents our use of the particle transporter." Askel shook his head and drew breath to say something, but was silenced with an upraised hand and a grin so that he knew at once and mirrored it with one of his own. "At least, so they will believe aboard *Enterprise.* You know and I know that with *Hakkarl*'s extra power at his disposal, *Tazhat*'s transporters can easily burn through naturally occurring interference. But the Feds don't know it yet, and they will only find out as a very unpleasant surprise. So." He finished his own pastry, drained the last mouthful of nectar from his glass, and stood up. "Hangar bay, ten minutes after orbital insertion. Duty uniform and sidearm, but dress sash with all decorations and commendation clasps. Let's go talk to the Federation."

"Oh, God," said James Kirk very softly, and meant it. *"Six of them?* How could terrorists get their hands on six armed orbiters?"

"Because my people couldn't get to the landing field, except on foot," said Todd Johnson from the main viewer. He was cradling the bandaged mess that something low-velocity and heavy-caliber had made of his left elbow. He and his men had been observing Starfleet's self-assigned rules of engagement right down the line from the first moment of setdown, so they hadn't been wearing any defensive armor when they put their own bodies between the Federation civilians and whatever the PDI chose to throw at them. The middle of a terrorist attack had never really been the place for medics, and for all the availability of modern medical care aboard the orbiting starships, Johnson had been patched up with field dressings and torn strips of fabric as if he were a soldier in one of the ugly wars back on Earth a few centuries ago.

"Noted and logged, Colonel. We'll take all appropriate precautions.

"If we'd been able to beam-jump across from the embassy grounds . . ." Johnson didn't bother to finish the sentence.

Jim sympathized: he knew exactly how the DPG commander must be feeling, including the slug through his arm, and even that wasn't as painful as knowing for certain that he could have done something to change the situation had circumstances been different. Having a force of nature working against you—in this case the lethal sunspot interference in the transporter beam—was infinitely worse than twenty-twenty hindsight.

The background noise of the channel was suddenly brutally dominated by the rapid-fire hammer of some sort of automatic weapon, and immediately afterward by the screech of multiple phasers. They had the unmistakable top-frequency whine of a stun setting, and Jim's mouth quirked in a harsh smile. Despite all the malicious provocations, supported or at least connived at by Varn and the rest of the Dekkan Planetary Council, despite the brutal stupidity of the PDI, even despite being perforated by a chunk of metal that had made a jigsaw puzzle of his elbow joint, Johnson was holding a full two steps down from the intensity of response that the rules of engagement now permitted. Jim began to understand how the colonel had acquired his tabs so young.

"According to my science officer, we'll be transporter capable in just over four hours."

Good. Once all this is over, your Dr. McCoy and my elbow will have to get together. In the machine shop. There's not much for him to heal any more.

So that's what a stiff upper lip sounds like, thought Jim, wincing inwardly at the thought of what Johnson had dismissed so dryly. *I've often wondered.*

"Affirmative on that, Colonel," he said aloud. "Keep your head down till then. Kirk out." The screen blanked out, then once more filled itself with the image of the Klingon battle cruiser.

"Looks like fun down there," said Bones. "A whole barrel of laughs." His voice had the hard edge that always crept into it when he was confronted by the more avoidable human stupidities.

"Our people are doing their damnedest not to get pulled into the spiral, Bones."

"I know, I know. Jim, we may well be the good guys, and we may be shooting only to stun, but that still doesn't make it any more acceptable. It doesn't make us *right*. If the Federation hadn't sited their Firechain installation on Dekkanar, we'd have one reason less to drop those young people into that shooting gallery down there."

"You are an idealist, Dr. McCoy." Spock meant it gently, perhaps even as a compliment, but Bones was in no mood to hear any such thing. He didn't interrupt as the Vulcan continued to speak, but he simmered in a restless silence and wasted a whole clip of furious glares on the armor of Spock's passive exterior. "In your own words," Spock went on, "the evacuation site has become a shooting gallery. To extend the analogy, therefore: are the targets in such a gallery guilty of aggressive behavior? If a third party defends the targets from harm by standing in front of them and advises the marksmen that this passive defense will become active if the shooting continues, who then carries the burden of responsibility? I put it to you that a moment spent looking at the viewscreen will indicate that the situation has changed very little. The Firechain system has prevented such scenes on an infinitely greater scale."

"Are you *sure* you never cherished any secret desire to practice law, Spock?" said Jim quickly, before Bones could dominate what was left of the discussion. The doctor, he had noticed, was displaying all the indications of someone prepared to defend a wrong opinion to the death.

Something came through on Uhura's console and she acknowledged. Her slow sideways look toward the screen revealed the transmission's source before she said anything.

"It's time, Captain. Klingon shuttle is departing scout ship *Tazhat* as of now. ETA seven minutes."

"Thank you, Uhura," said Jim, and turned back to the screen. For a moment there was no change, and then a tiny bright speck drifted free and curved away from the cruiser. "Mr. Tomson, Mr. Matlock, designated honor guard, please make your way to the landing bay reception area." He turned to Spock and McCoy. "And now, gentlemen, if you'll agree not to continue your difference of opinion in the turbolift, don't you think we'd better get down there and say hello?"

By the time they reached the shuttle observation gallery, Montgomery Scott was there already. Supervising, he said, except that he was dressed in a standard uniform instead of the radsuit that was his normal duty wear. It was far more likely that he was making sure the Klingons didn't dent anything important with their ship during the landing cycle. There was no insult intended, at least no more than usual, and certainly not a Klingon-specific one; when it came to unfamiliar shuttlecraft pilots, Scotty was like this with all of them.

"Doctor, Mr. Spock," Scotty greeted them absently in the manner of a man with things on his mind, and then turned to Jim. "Captain, how long are these Klingons goin' to be aboard?"

"Captain Kasak has requested political asylum," said Jim. "That could well mean they'll be with us until we transfer them to a courier ship off Star Base Twelve."

"Ach, isn't that jist great."

"Objections, Scotty?"

"No more than usual, sir. I jist don't like the idea of those creatures messin' about wi' the *Enterprise*, that's all."

"Not to worry," he said, trying to sound reassuring. "I don't intend to let them have the run of the place, just in case one of them changes his mind about the benefits of life as a Federation citizen."

"So long as they dinna come near Engineering." His

voice had that tone of finality Scots engineers had been refining over four centuries when warning lesser mortals out of the private property of the engine room. The refining process had probably begun when the first of them helped build some maritime steam engine somewhere along the Clyde near Glasgow, then got shipped out with it so that the ship's captain would have someone aboard who knew what to do when the ruddy pressure cooker acted up. That had been back in the nineteenth century of Old Earth. By the twenty-third the breed of men who went by the title of chief engineer had evolved. It no longer mattered whether they were men or women or Scots or even human; they were all of a piece, a race of callused-handed, tech-minded, hard-drinking miracle workers who could persuade a dying warp drive not only to work again but to do so at peak efficiency. One did not cross a chief engineer lightly, and the wise did not cross them at all.

"Scotty, if they get past the dorsal K deck, you can do as you think fit, because none of the rest of us will be in a fit state to care."

"Aye. You're right. I—"

"Attention, attention," the annunciator interrupted. *"Incoming shuttle is now entering final approach phase. All nonessential personnel please evacuate the area. Landing bay systems please stand by."*

"Here they come," said Bones. He twiddled with the memory selector and the scan parameters of his tricorder, then locked off and snapped the memory head shut. "As of now, don't get sick, any of you. Not unless you're Klingons."

"Thank you for the warning, Doctor," Spock said. "Falling ill had not been among my present intentions. As any humanoid life-form whatsoever."

Scotty was paying no heed to the cross-chat behind him. He had swung a control console out from its recess in the insulated rollover of the observation gallery clearport, and it was already alive with a crawling glow of vector and velocity indicators. "Landin' bay control room, this is Chief Engineer Scott. I'd like to bring this one in myself."

"Control room here, Mr. Scott. Your request is noted, logged, and approved. I'm transferring control to your station."

"Thank you, lassie. Advise shuttle: disengage all manuals at this time, bring drive and maneuverin' thrusters to station-keepin'."

"Manual controls off line. Three, two, one, mark. Incoming shuttle now secure and holding station. You have control."

Scotty rubbed his hands together, interlinked his fingers and flexed them until the knuckles cracked, then twiddled them in the air like a concert pianist about to play. "Right," he said, "let's show them what a proper landin' looks like."

"Scotty, behave. No power fluctuations, if you please. I don't want our guests rattled around the inside of their shuttle like ice in your whisky glass."

"Och, Captain, I'd never dream"—a deliberate pause and a slow, wicked smile—"of puttin' ice into a dram o' good Scotch whisky. Or of that other wee matter either." He turned back to the console and began touching controls on the main panel. "The atmosphere containment field is up an' runnin'; bay doors are comin' open as of now."

Below them, the great clamshell doors began to retract, opening to reveal at first no more than a slice of darkness, but expanding steadily until at last that slice became a blunted, starshot wedge of the ancient night lying beyond the man-made fragility of *Enterprise*'s glowing interior. Those stars seemed to dance and shimmer as their glitter passed through the containment field that kept the airless cold at bay, but one of them blinked with a steadier rhythm and the harsh blue-white light of a visual location beacon. The shuttle hung immobile in the grip of the landing-bay tractor for the few seconds that it took Scotty to run his final sequence of checks, and then began to move smoothly closer.

For all his chief engineer's tacit mock threats, Jim had never seen a better landing. The shuttle, a squat chisel-nosed vessel, settled onto the floor of the bay with a lightness that would have put most feathers to shame. Its grim gray thermoglaze and imperial trefoils looked distinctly out of place aboard a Federation Starship. The beacon that had been no more than a particularly bright blink at two kilometers was now a strobing lightning flash within the confines of the hangar deck, leaving purple afterimages on the retinas of those who chanced to look straight at it. Jim was not the only one who felt heartily relieved when some Klingon hand reached out to switch the damned thing off.

Either the Klingons inside the shuttle didn't know about the atmosphere containment field or they knew but didn't trust it. Whatever the reason, the hatch didn't open until the fantail doors had been shut and proof of breathable atmosphere provided by the appearance of Commanders Tomson and Matlock and their honor guard of security personnel.

At Colin Matlock's suggestion, none of the security people wore their standard helmets or armor, but Ingrit had insisted on the Type IV phasers that all of them wore in plain view at their uniform belts. No matter how friendly these Klingons had become, they were still Klingons, and it would be all too easy for a well-intentioned gesture of going unarmed to be misinterpreted as that most dangerous thing to suggest where Klingons were concerned, a sign of weakness.

The shuttle's hatch swung out and up, its boarding ramp out and down, and one by one, six more of that small and select band of Klingons who had managed to set foot aboard the U.S.S. *Enterprise* stepped out onto her deck. "Honors, hut!" said Ingrit, and stepped smartly to one side as the file of security guards formed a double rank. One of them raised the boatswain's pipe that hung from its lanyard around her neck, and piped the visitors aboard.

Jim and the others could hear the pipe's shrill squeal even up in the observation gallery, and they could see momentary confusion on all the Klingon faces in the instant before the foremost of them realized that he was being paid a courtesy. That officer relayed this information to the others, provoking very human-seeming sidelong glances before all six responded with a salute.

"Well, that's over," said Jim, becoming uncomfortably aware that his nails had been digging into the palms of his hands from the instant that Scotty touched the shuttle down. He reached forward to the console communicator panel. "Kirk to honor guard."

"Security chief here."

"I think Rec One will be an appropriately neutral ground for whatever Captain Kasak wants to discuss with me."

"Affirmative, Captain. Rec Deck One. ETA four minutes. Tomson out."

"Four minutes. That gives us about two, gentlemen. Shall we?"

"Why not the officers lounge, Jim?" said McCoy as they headed for the turbolift. "One of the privacy areas."

James T. Kirk shook his head decisively and gave Bones a crooked smile. "Because that's exactly what they'll be expecting, somewhere small and private. The rec room's as far from that as we've got on this ship. It'll keep them confused and off balance, give us something of an edge, and it'll give Kasak a surprise to make up for the ones he's been springing on me."

"Ye dinna think he's serious about this political asylum business, Captain?" said Scotty.

"No. I won't believe that until there's a crew of my choosing aboard his ship and it's safely on the way to spacedock."

"I will feel more at ease," said Spock as he stepped into the turbolift car, "when the data we requested from Starfleet Intelligence on Captain Kasak gets here. The name Kasak has an uncomfortable ring of familiarity about it, and yet not so familiar that I am able to place the context."

"And you're almost ready to concede defeat and admit it annoys you, Spock?"

"No, Doctor, in fact I am not. It is an inconvenience, but by no means an insoluble problem. Current transmission time to Starfleet Headquarters is some three-point-seven-three hours, so the information may well arrive while we are entertaining its subject."

"Now *that* I want to see."

"Just be prepared to duck, Bones," said Jim. "If Kasak has run across the *Enterprise* before, I doubt he'll remember the occasion kindly. Few Klingons would."

"Och, now, that Captain Kang was all right, once we got things sorted out."

"Funny thing, Scotty, but I seem to remember you trying to cut his head off with a claymore."

"That wasna a claymore, Captain; it was a Scottish regimental basket-hilted broadsword an' well you know it."

"But I notice you're not correcting me on the way you wanted to use it."

"Aye, well . . ."

"Just watch him, that's all. I don't know what's at the bottom of all this. If it's nothing more than a bunch of dissatisfied Klingon officers defecting to put their opponents in a bad light, I'll be pleasantly surprised." The lift slowed to a standstill. "And very, very grateful . . ." They stepped out of the lift car and into Rec One.

And into yet another demonstration of the near-proverbial speed with which starship gossip traveled.

It had been something like ninety seconds since Jim had given his instructions to Security Chief Tomson, and already the rec deck had more crew members in it than was usual at any one time. It seemed to Jim that all the off-shift personnel who weren't there already were strolling with elaborate high-speed nonchalance in from the corridor or out of the number two turbolift. He found himself wondering what Kasak's people would make of *Enterprise*'s multispecies crew, because he had noticed that all of the Klingons were of the Imperial race. That suggested at the very least a certain elitism, and at worst racial intolerance and xenophobia. It also suggested that the more eyes there were watching them, the safer it would be for all concerned.

"Attention, everyone," he said, projecting hard to cut through the murmur of many speculating voices. The background noise faded away as quickly and as smoothly as though someone had rotated a gain control. "You all know more or less what's going on here. I haven't got time for a pep talk, much less a briefing. Just be careful. These Klingons are all Imperials and are probably unfamiliar with the way a mixed crew works. Show them. And remember, your Starfleet commissions state that you're all officers and gentlebeings. So act that way. Even the ensigns . . ."

The laughter had barely died before both turbolifts hissed open and there were Klingons on the rec deck.

"Captain Kirk," said Ingrit Tomson, doing the honors in a neutral voice that came from an expressionless face, "may I introduce Captain Kasak sutai-Khornezh, commander of the Imperial Klingon Vessel *Hakkarl,* and officers of his crew."

"Captain, greetings," Jim said carefully.

"Kirk," said Kasak, giving the consonants their full *Tlhinganaase* value, though whether as compliment or veiled insult was unclear. "Greetings. As it is our intention to speak with one another as equals, it would please me to be called by my own name."

Now, that was definitely *not* an insult, even though Jim wasn't certain of the reasoning behind the request. "Honored, Kasak. Welcome aboard the U.S.S. *Enterprise.* You and your—officers." He had almost said "men," but saw the Klingon female just in time.

He gestured to a small group of seats. "Captain, make yourself comfortable. Your people may sit with us or, if they wish, mingle freely with my crew. We have much to talk about. All of us."

Chapter Nine

Science Specialist Askel sat quietly on the sidelines of what at present was nothing more than an exchange of insincere and inconsequential pleasantries. He had hoped that an argument might develop between the two captains—nothing violent, since that would have been counterproductive, but what the humans liked to call a "frank exchange of opinions." In other words, the sort of mutual criticism that sometimes became brisk enough for either or both parties to let slip things that might best have been left unsaid. To his mild annoyance, however, Kirk and Kasak were both too experienced to indulge in any petty name-calling.

He sipped at his glass of juice, finding it sharp and thin even after two additional pushes of the processor console's sweetness selector. The machine proved stubbornly incapable of synthesizing rich fruit nectars in the Klingon style. Most of the others had settled for double-sweetened juices of one kind or another. Some had not: Dr. Makhoy, the *Enterprise* surgeon specialist, had been most persuasive, and now Force Leader Marag was holding a tall glass in a silver holder and looking at it with all the suspicion he usually reserved only for security matters. The glass was full of crushed ice and sprigs of a green herb whose astringent scent Askel could smell from where he sat. The outside of the glass was so cold that it was frosted with condensation. That made the holder more sensible than elegant; there were few creatures more touchy than a Klingon trying to retain his good manners while his fingers froze.

It was a peculiarity of the humans that they seemed to enjoy their recreational drinks either dangerously hot or ridiculously cold. Even those drinking juice put ice in it; Askel had seen them punching the appropriate button on the selector. He wondered about that for a few seconds, and what relationship it might have with the way that humans were known to behave. Then he shrugged, dismissed the matter, and paid more attention to his surroundings and to those who shared them.

Apart from the humans of the security detachment sent to fetch them here from the shuttle bay, he recognized only Kirk's companions: Makhoy and the Vulcan Spock he knew already, from *Tazhat*'s viewscreen, and Engineering Master Scott from the brief introduction when Kasak's party first came into the recreation hall. Askel knew perfectly well that the official name was "rec deck," but the abbreviation seemed inappropriate for such an enormous two-level vaulted room. He had seen inspirational theaters on planetary installations, never mind spacegoing vessels, that were not so large. And as for the crew members who filled it, they were . . . diverse.

From where he sat he needed only to turn his head to see representatives of a dozen different races in as many shapes and colors. The ubiquitous humans alone had several different skin colors, and the varying shapes that went with each somatotype. Khitar from Communications had struck up a conversation of sorts with one of them, a female as dark as any Klingon who was easily keeping pace with his convoluted specialist vocabulary—despite the speed of its delivery after being lubricated by frequent drafts of black Saurian brandy from the glass in his left hand. Askel made a mental note to discipline him later, not so much for drinking to excess as for having a loose mouth under its influence. Among the humans, talking, laughing, drinking with them, were several other species, all behaving like equals on this human ship instead of like the *kuve* they undoubtedly were—not having insisted on serving aboard ships crewed by their own race. And they were just the *biped* crew.

As one trained in the sciences—Askel knew about the Sulamids and the four races of the Denebian worlds, and even the Janusian living rocks, one of which was shuffling across the floor right now. But that didn't mean he had to *like* them, or the idea of a crew made up of people from twenty different races. Let the Vulcans propound their IDIC theory as much as they pleased. Then show him the extent of their empire and the terror and respect in which it was held. Strength lay in unity, not diversity.

The unity of his common purpose with Kasak sutai-Khornezh was a case in point. If he and I.I. had not supported the captain's scheme, no display of strength would have brought them to where they now sat, in a vessel of the Federation Starfleet, busily engaged in deceiving its most senior officers. It might, thought Askel with a sardonic inner smile, have enabled them to cruise to and fro among its drifting ashes, but the effect would not have been the same.

Kasak's strength had been evident from the first, when he had defied the suspicions of everyone from Thought Admirals and chiefs of security on down to the crew he had chosen himself. At each stage of his gradually revealed scheme he might have been arrested, or just gunned down by one of the interested parties who were following orders or who stood to gain by doing so. Marag, acting for Security, perhaps; or whichever clandestine agent was aboard, also acting for Security; or Askel himself, acting for Imperial Intelligence; or a quiet member of the crew who might act only out of loyalty to the Empire. That Kasak was well on his way to success and glory said something about his luck.

"Setting sunspots to one side, Kirk," Kasak was saying when Askel tuned the content of his speech back in, "it is the belief of my race that the one has only so much luck this side of the Black Fleet. Especially with transporters. Hence the shuttle."

Kai, Kasak, thought Askel. That would reinforce the notion in Kirk's mind, and in the minds of his security people, that to keep hold of these Klingons and thus of their ship, all they had to do was to stay between the visitors and the shuttle bay. It would not matter that sensors surely indicated another three crew members left behind on *Tazhat* and *Hakkarl.* Those three could maintain the life-support and environmental systems and monitor the cruiser's standard orbit, but they were capable of little else.

The Federation officers could not know about the boosted transport hypercarrier wave that could beam safely through even deliberate jamming, nor did they realize that in an emergency the captain could control both ships from his command chair long enough for the scout to escape. *Kahlesste kaase*—Kahless's Hand indeed, except that now a captain had no need to tie his hand to the chair with his sash in order that none might say he fled before his crew.

He listened briefly to Kasak, and his hidden smile grew wider. The captain's deception was perfect. It was almost possible to believe that he really *did* intend to hand himself, his crew, and his secret new ship over to the Federation. Almost, but not quite. There were enough clues visible to the quick mind and the sharp eye. It was just as well that none of the Starfleet officers knew what to look for. . . .

James T. Kirk knew there was something wrong about this whole business, and yet try as he might, he couldn't place it. The Klingons were all being just as nice as pie. Some of them, like the comm officer, had become far too friendly with the hospitality bar and were becoming deadly boring and repetitive as a result. Jim was watching that one almost as closely as the other five put together. He knew that drinking alcohol was as much a part of Klingon culture as it was of human social life, but from past experience on and around Space Station K-7 he also knew what happened when you mixed Klingons, *Enterprise* crew members, and an open bar in the same cubic parsec of space—trouble. At least this time there were no tribbles getting underfoot and trying to eat the buffet. That would have been the last straw, and not just for the Klingons.

Still, all that Kasak had told him so far had been the truth. Starfleet Intelligence could vouch for it. But Jim couldn't shake the sensation that he was being made use of—mocked, teased, toyed with, all those things he hated and had to put up with as a representative of the United Federation of Planets. Except that the mockery of a Klingon was something to be wary of rather than simply to endure. He wished more than anything else right now that the information about Captain Kasak would get here.

The annunciator whistled right then and said "Bridge to Captain Kirk" so pat on cue that Jim almost jumped.

Can't be, he told himself as he made some sort of

excuse to the Klingon captain and tried to hurry from his seat without moving obviously fast.

"Kirk here."

"Lieutenant Knight, sir, acting communications officer. A signal's coming in for you. Shall I transfer it direct or wait until instructed?"

Comms department code words for "How much privacy do you need for this, sir?" *I don't believe it!* thought Jim, even though he wanted to believe it very much indeed. "From Starfleet?"

"Sorry, Captain, not yet. We're still waiting for that one."

A jolt of hurt annoyance that was the mental equivalent of a thumb in the solar plexus ran through Jim, and he glared at the comm grille. Knowing that this wasn't Kim Knight's fault didn't help at all. He wanted to thump the annunciator panel with his fist and say all of the things that had come boiling up inside him—anything to relieve his frustration. But with Kasak and several of his crew carefully not staring in his direction, he absolutely couldn't vent his feelings here.

"All right, Kim," he said at last in a voice that surprised him with its control. "What is it?"

"From Colonel Johnson on the surface, sir. He requested especially that he talk to you. It sounded urgent."

Jim stared at the annunciator in silence for six seconds that felt like six hours. The choice was to put Johnson's message through and risk having him say something out of place, or leave the rec deck and make it plain that he didn't want the Klingons to hear this transmission. Not that doing so was unmannerly, as Kasak would probably admit—the sensor suites on board *Hakkarl* were probably eavesdropping anyway —but it might give the Klingons the idea that things on Dekkanar were worse than their Intelligence reports suggested.

Worse for the Federation, at least; Kasak could make the inverse of that equation all by himself, and perhaps conclude that there was more advantage in staying loyal to the Empire than in accepting asylum. Kasak could simply sit in orbit while the Federation personnel were evacuated and the ships carrying them moved out. Without a request from Councillor Varn or the others to stay and renegotiate their tenure, Kirk would be obliged to conclude the mission as briefed, with a complete withdrawal from the 4725 Cancri system.

Hakkarl, as well as any other Klingon ship claiming access under the Organian Treaty, was so far under no such stricture, and Jim doubted very much that any such would be obeyed, or even issued, if no Starfleet vessels were present to enforce it. With no source of protection other than the weapons of the Klingon battle cruiser hanging in an ominously close orbit right above their heads, the Dekkani would waste no time in asking the Empire to help them sort out their internal differences.

And for the Klingons, sorting out something they had probably started—or at least organized by the usual method of cultivating and arming a group like the PDI—would be simplicity itself.

"Put him through," said Jim, wondering if he looked and sounded as weary as he suddenly felt. "On the main screen. I'll handle it from here." With the rec room's big viewing screen in operation, Johnson would be able to see immediately that there weren't just Starfleet ears listening to him, and he could edit his words accordingly. That, at least, was the theory. He thumbed the channel open.

Little had changed since he had last spoken to

Colonel Johnson. The buildings in the background of the screen image looked a little the worse for wear, and there were dirty smears of smoke around several windows. The colonel and the few men and women who moved in and out of frame behind him were also looking smoke-stained and rather frayed at the edges. Jim was thankful to see that there were no more injuries—at least, none that he could see.

Johnson started to say something, then cut his words short and leaned a little closer to the vision transceiver of his field-comm pack, apparently not convinced that he was getting an accurate picture from the *Enterprise*. *"Good God,"* he said softly.

"No, just Klingons," said Jim. "Captain and part of the crew of IKV *Hakkarl*. They're requesting political asylum."

"Good God," said Todd Johnson again, and shook his head. *"I knew that Klingon captains turned privateer, but I've never heard of one defecting until now."*

Jim winced inwardly at Johnson's use of the word "defect." It was the wince of a diplomat who knew that he'd been getting somewhere in a delicate negotiation, only to see the whole frail house of cards sent tumbling by a single instant's carelessness. And it was the wince, doubled, of someone who knew that after all the nice phrases had been stripped away, it was the right word to use.

"Colonel Johnson, my communications officer told me this was urgent. What's the problem?"

"The PDI have started playing for keeps. Seven of my people have been killed by disrupter fire, Captain Kirk. Ask your . . . your visitors where those weapons came from. I'd be very interested to hear the answer." Johnson shook his head to clear away the mists of whatever pain suppressant his field medics had filled him with, then grinned crookedly. It was the sort of grin that the Klingons probably understood as well as

anyone on board the *Enterprise:* all teeth, no humor. *"But we've got the last of the civilians together and away. No losses there at all. Their shuttle's lifting about now, and—"*

There was a shattering explosion from somewhere outside and above the building in which Johnson had set up his command headquarters. The viewer wailed and flared white for an instant as light and noise overloaded its pickups, then returned slowly to normal through a blizzard of static. By then there were long plumes of dust trailing down from the ceiling, and the image itself had toppled seventy degrees to one side. It came upright again with a jolt as somebody pulled the comm pack clear of the thermoplast rubble that had fallen on it, but for several more of those hour-long seconds there was no sign of Colonel Johnson.

Just as the silent audience on the rec deck started to become seriously concerned, a shadow fell across the screen and Johnson came back into frame. He was limping, and his shoulders were gray-white with dust. *"The PDI's stolen orbiters have atmospheric capability,"* he said, and his mouth was tight with a pain that had no connection with his arm or with his limp. *"We didn't know. None of the Dekkani bothered to tell us. Well, we know now. They took out that last shuttle just after it left the ground, and . . ."* He shrugged; there was nothing else to say that could possibly have any meaning. *"If the Federation ever opens up this embassy again, it's going to need another secretarial section. Because there's nobody left from this one."*

Jim stared at the screen and said nothing. He had heard and seen the same thing far too many times, and every one of those times, mere words had been inadequate.

"Beam-up will be possible in four hours, you said?" Johnson asked.

"Nearer three now."

"Then we'll wait. There are—" Johnson stopped, and his eyes shifted from Jim's face to stare instead over his shoulder at the Klingon officers sitting behind him. Jim was quietly glad that the colonel would be returning to *Sir Richard* or to *Vanguard* rather than to *Enterprise.* Right now he didn't look like the right man for further diplomatic duty. *"Captain, there are things to clean up here. We'll deal with them and then advise for pickup. Johnson out."*

The stillness on Rec Deck One was a shocking contrast to its earlier cheerful hubbub. Someone at the back of the huge room was failing in an effort not to cry, and even the Klingons had contrived to look concerned. Jim doubted very much if there was any more to their concern than worry about their own status. Right now, at any rate, the last thing that he wanted was for any one of them to speak.

His unspoken wish went unheard, for Captain Kasak stood up slowly, put his glass of fruit juice to one side and said, "If the one may prove of some assistance?" He sounded sincere, and for just one second James Kirk hated him for it.

Then the hatred went away abruptly, for a disrupter screeched and its actinic blue bolt went past Jim's ear like the finger of the angel of death. Kasak's discarded glass exploded into sweet steam and flying splinters. *"Straav'! Tokhe straav'!"* There was a voice somewhere, screaming, almost as loud as the disrupter's discharge: "Willing slave!" the foulest insult in all the dialects of the Klingon language and one that only death could cancel out.

Whose death? Jim dropped to the floor and rolled for cover, his mind whirling with confusion, cursing himself for not having carried a phaser and for not having insisted that the Klingons check their duty sidearms with Security. Who was shooting? At whom? Almost everyone, armed or not, had hit the deck at the same moment—everyone except Ingrit Tomson and two of Kasak's officers.

No, three. One of them was the comms specialist who had been boring Uhura and drinking too much. Another burst of energy crackled from the pistol in his wavering grip, and Jim wondered if the alcohol that had somehow provoked the shooting had also affected his aim just enough to save someone's life. His life, maybe, or . . . *whose?*

For all that the human-built chair was awkward for Klingon anatomy, Askel was out of it in the blinking of an eye, and his own disrupter was out of its holster before he was well clear of the seat. *Now we know,* he thought. *But to move here and now!* Khest'n *Imperial Security. . . .*

The brandy had done its work after all, but not by creating drunken aggressiveness. This was both more and less straightforward. Khitar had consumed just enough to make him miss out on Captain Kasak's more subtle kinesic indications of deception. He had assumed that what he saw and heard was real. When Kasak made his masterfully convincing offer of assistance, Khitar had seen not an elegant move in *klin zha,* but mutiny and treason.

Imperial Security had never been renowned for intelligence.

The tall female—Tomson, Kirk's own chief of security—seemed strangely reluctant to open fire, and for an instant Askel wondered if Starfleet Security had a worse vice than single-minded stupidity. Compassion had no place behind a security badge or a security pistol. Then he saw her reset her phaser down to stun, and he remembered the Organians. No matter what he had done or would do yet, Khitar was an officer of the Klingon Empire, and the glowbugs would surely come interfering if he was shot—

A flash of blue-white light carved shadows sharp as glass all across the rec deck, and Askel heard the unmistakable shrilling of a disrupter at its highest setting. Khitar was engulfed in white fire and his screamed insults became a simple scream. It faded swiftly as his body glowed, incandesced, and vanished. Helm Officer Krynn straightened from her aiming crouch, her pistol holstered again before the last echoes of that horrid noise had fully died away, and looked at the scorched place where Khitar's silhouette could still be faintly seen against the wall. *"Ha'DIbaH,"* she said softly, and then to Kasak, *"'utpu', joHwI."*

"jIyaj." The captain saluted her. *"majQa'."*

Captain Kirk and the rest of his crew picked themselves up from the floor. There was some dusting of knees, some adjusting of uniforms, and then Kirk glared at Kasak. "Necessary or not, well done or not," he snapped, "what the hell is going on?"

"Apologies, Captain," said Askel, cutting in smoothly, doing his best to sound calm even though his mind was racing to shape the excuse it had just formed into something that would pass for truth. "That officer is—was—of a line we had all thought dead. Extinct. That line has been at feud with the captain's line, Khornezh, for Keth's years. It would seem that one of them survived and determined to resume what was considered done with and at rest. This one and all of us regret it happened here."

"You *regret!*" Surgeon Specialist Makhoy was blazing with anger, so filled with rage that mere words were inadequate to express it and he was forced to unwilling silence until he had regained his self-control. Askel was careless of mere anger, no matter

204

how intensely felt; all that concerned him was that his words not be questioned. While the Feds were busy being shocked at this demonstration of Klingon frightfulness, they would not take the time to wonder about what *really* lay behind its flaring up just now. But it was starting to occur to him that telling the truth, or at least most of it, about Khitar and Imperial Security might well have been the wiser course.

"Captain Kasak," said Kirk with all the formal outrage he could muster, "I want a full explanation of this incident, and I want it now."

"Kirk," said Kasak, "my executive officer has told you—"

"That's *Admiral* Kirk, mister, and your exec has told me nothing." Askel considered assuming an affronted expression, then discarded the idea as wasted effort. Kirk lacked Makhoy's hot, blind fury, and was in just the mood to take exception to any misplaced word or gesture. "I think that—" Kirk was interrupted once again by the wall communicator and broke off whatever pointless thought had been in his mind, but before he turned to answer it, he gestured to Tomson and to the armored and helmeted security guards who had come rushing in from the corridor at the sound of shots.

Askel looked at the leveled phasers, knowing without being told that they were all set only to stun. And after the stunning, imprisonment. The Federation was weak, it seldom executed prisoners. But it kept them caged until their time of detention was done or until it pleased someone to release them or until the end of life. That thought made him shiver more than any threat of death. And then he shivered again, because Surgeon Specialist Arthag was nowhere to be seen. *So there* were *two of them!* he thought. *One loud, one quiet. Then* kai *Security after all. . . .*

"Bridge, this is the captain," he heard Kirk say,

and the rasp of leashed anger behind the human's voice was plainly audible. "What is it now?"

"Captain, we've picked up a transmission. Definitely Klingon, but a nonstandard frequency. Commander Uhura's autojammer didn't recognize or block it, so . . . What did you say? Confirm that! Excuse me, Captain, one moment please." During that moment, the dark woman with whom Khitar had spoken clenched both her fists and swore. The only other sound was the faint hissing of an open channel from the communicator. Then the voice at the other end came back, sounding agitated. *"We've gotten a confirmed lock on the source of the transmission. Captain, it's coming from Rec Deck One!"*

Jim felt his stomach jolt inside him harder even than when the disrupter bolt had almost taken off his head. "Confirm that, Kim? Rec One?"

"Rec One confirm, rear portside."

All eyes turned to stare at the only place on the Rec Deck where even a Klingon could be assured of privacy from prying or unfriendly eyes. The male rest room. People began to back away as if the place contained a primed bomb, and Jim was not the only one to realize that it might well do just that.

"Captain Kasak," he said, "call your Dr. Arthag and order him to come out peacefully. But before he comes out"—he glanced pointedly at the burn mark where Khitar had been—"you and your crew will immediately surrender all weapons to Commander Tomson. I want him alive and capable of answering questions."

Kasak glowered at him, still managing to convey irritated innocence. "Imperial Security—" the Klingon began to say.

"So they were both security men, eh? I *thought* this was more than just a feud. Tell your medical security man that he has nothing to fear from any of us. *Any* of us, Captain Kasak—Starfleet or Klingon."

The Klingon captain hesitated a moment more, then gave a very human shrug. "If Arthag is truly of Imperial Security, Kirk, I make no promises that he will heed me."

"I've had just about enough of this," said Jim under his breath. Without taking his eyes from Kasak, he held out his right hand, open and palm up. Someone slapped a Type II-B phaser into it, and Jim leveled the weapon's emitter cone at the Klingon's face. "Give it a try, Captain," he suggested, "or we'll get him out our own way."

"Arthag!" shouted Kasak. "Specialist Arthag, this is the sutai-Khornezh."

Arthag leaned suddenly around the corner of the rest room partition and fired twice at his captain before ducking back out of sight in a splatter of stun-level energy flashes from Tomson's security people. Both of Arthag's shots missed their intended target: one of them shattered a screen in the information alcove below the main viewer, and the other slammed a security ensign flat on his back and gouged a smoking crater out of the breastplate of his armor. The man was unhurt and still in sufficient possession of his wits to grab a drink and quench the hot woven ceramic before his chest was seriously blistered.

Of Surgeon Specialist Arthag there was no sign.

Jim flexed his fingers on the grip of his own phaser and checked the weapon's setting. Satisfied, he looked at the group of security personnel. "Ingrit, set your phaser to narrow-beam heavy stun. Mr. Matlock, Mr. Fleming, set to wide-beam. Cover that entrance. First sight you have of anything, hit it."

As the first three settled into aiming position, he turned to the others, deliberately ignoring the remaining Klingons until he was ready to acknowledge their existence. "Mr. Gamble and *tlaza* Rrra'sku, supervise a quick, quiet clearance of Rec One. And Mr. Nakashima, if you're feeling all right . . . ? Good. Then relieve these people of their weapons."

He was quietly grateful to see that Kasak's people neither objected nor resisted being disarmed. Not that it would have done them much good. Jim was too busy thinking about how he could extricate Arthag without any further casualties—and before the Klingon decided to set his disrupter's power pack to overload.

Spock and McCoy appeared at his elbow, easing out of the throng of crew members, all of whom knew they were suddenly no more than targets. Bones was cursing his lack of a medical pouch—not that he had needed one so far—but Spock looked silently at Kirk and seemed, as usual, to know what he was thinking. "I am uncertain of the energy output yielded by this type of sidearm, Jim," he said, hefting one just acquired from Askel, his Klingon counterpart. "However, I presume it is of similar capability to the more recent variants of phaser."

If the information was meant to be comforting, Jim didn't think much of it, and said so. He was uneasily aware that a Starfleet phaser in the same confined-blast situation might blow this section of *Enterprise*'s primary disc clean off the ship. Certainly it would explosively decompress the rec deck and everybody in it.

"Given that presumption," Spock continued, "I feel that we have a method of neutralizing our troublesome visitor close at hand."

"Ah . . ." Jim nodded. "Lieutenant Naraht, could you come here, please?"

The Horta, though basically a horizontal entity, had been hunched up against a table, acting as a makeshift shield for the people making their escape by turbolift two. He slithered down and shuffled rapidly over to

Kirk with that unmistakable sound of granite slabs rubbing together. "Yes, Captain?" his voder said, earnest as ever. For all that Mr. Naraht was still a relative juvenile of his race, he was also the veteran of an intelligence mission that included a covert free-fall descent from orbit onto the surface of the Romulan homeworld—and he was demonstrably resistant to both phaser and disrupter fire. Jim felt no real qualms over what he had in mind.

"Mr. Naraht, you're the only member of the crew who can capture and disarm the Klingon officer in that rest room without inflicting or suffering any harm; at least, you're the only one right now." Despite the gravity of the situation Jim felt a weak grin prickling at the corners of his mouth. Rooting armed enemy agents out of toilets was not one of the strange, new, and interesting parts of the day's work that were mentioned in Starfleet's cadet orientation material. "He has a weapon identical to the one Mr. Spock is holding. And this is just a request, not an order."

Jim was aware that the other Klingons were staring at him with a mixture of distaste and contempt for a captain who would *ask* one of his crew—and a member of an "inferior" race at that—to do something. That, thought Jim, was *their* problem.

Naraht shuffled his fringe and made the bizarre crackling sound that was analogous to laughter. "Thank you for that courtesy, sir," he said. Various glittery crystals on his carapace surveyed the Klingon disrupter in a gesture that might not have had true visual connotations but at least looked as if he was giving it a once-over. "If that's all he's got, I won't feel a thing. And neither will he. At least, he won't remember feeling it."

"Dr. McCoy," said Spock as Naraht rumbled off about his mission, "I think that young officer is picking up your patterns of speech."

"The boy's got style," said Bones, and wouldn't be drawn further.

The annunciator called Jim's name again, and he muttered something under his breath. He was rapidly becoming as tired of the annunciator's three-note whistle as he was of the red-alert sirens, but this time Lieutenant Knight didn't even wait for him to respond. *"Captain, that earlier transmission has just been acknowledged—from out of system. Same frequency, same code groups, but Signal strength and repeater fluctuation indicate three-plus heavy cruisers."*

Damn! "Any indication of speed or heading?"

"Yes, sir, I'm afraid so. The way their signal broke up matched interference from an acceleration to warp speed, and before we lost them they were heading straight for—"

The rest of what Knight had to say was lost in the sound of a disrupter firing within an enclosed space. Naraht was still well clear of the rest room, although he was hurrying toward it now with the startling speed a Horta could produce when pressed, but the brevity of the pistol's discharge suggested to Jim and to everyone else that there was no longer any need to rush.

Naraht came out a moment later, moving much more slowly, and all suspicions were confirmed even before he spoke. "The Klingon shot himself, Captain," Naraht confirmed grimly. "He's quite dead."

"Are you certain?" said McCoy, starting forward.

"Quite certain." Naraht sounded annoyed. He probably felt that he hadn't moved fast enough to prevent what had happened. "He was obliging enough to set his disrupter low enough to leave most of a body, but the setting was sufficiently high to leave my diagnosis in no doubt."

"Captain Kasak," Jim said, swinging around on the

Klingon commander, "what do you know about this?"

"Imperial Security would scarcely approve of what I have attempted," said Kasak evenly. "The one tried to stop me and failed. It seems that he was less alone than either of us thought. These new ships are moving to prevent the theft of imperial military property; they have probably been following *Hakkarl* at a discreet distance since he left drydock."

If Science Specialist Askel had an opinion about that, he said nothing.

Jim looked up and down the line of Klingons and couldn't decide what angered him more—what they had done or how little they seemed troubled by the consequences. "It would appear, Captain Kasak, that whether accidentally or through deliberate malice, you have engineered a way in which several Klingon ships can legally"—Jim spat the word as if it tasted bad—"enter a restricted and already sensitive sector of Federation-protected space. You must realize, of course, that your request for asylum is null and void, but you will remain on *Enterprise* under close arrest."

Kasak smiled venomously. *"jol yIchu,"* he said to the empty air, and the LED telltale on his communicator that indicated a transporter lock began glowing red.

Jim remembered then what he had forgotten during the years behind a desk: that Klingon communicators could and did run in a standby mode, without lights or beacons to betray the fact. But a transporter, with 4725 Cancri still three hours away from being safe? He didn't waste time thinking about it, but stepped sharply out of the way and snapped "Fire!"

The security phasers flared uselessly almost a meter from their targets as, in total silence, golden light enveloped the four remaining Klingons. "Arrest, Captain Kirk?" said Kasak's mocking voice. "I think not.

Katta, *ghojol.*" The light flickered, faded, and they were gone.

Jim stared for half a second at the empty area of deck while thoughts and words and actions roiled and fought for precedence inside his head. He turned away from the embarrassing emptiness, walked to the wall communicator, and with an ironic little smile punched in the command code that gave him all-call. *"Enterprise,* this is the captain." He paused, took a deep breath, and thought, *Here we go. Again.* "Go to condition one. This is a red alert. I say again, red alert. All departments to battle stations. Kirk out."

Then he squared his shoulders, unhooked the wrap-around of his tunic, brushed a trace of lint from the rank pin on his sleeve, and headed for the bridge.

Chapter Ten

"IT IS MY BELIEF," Spock said as the turbolift got under way, "that they were employing some form of enhanced or boosted carrier wave. It is essentially the same kind of signal repeater as that which creates noise in the Starfleet standard transporter. However, being Klingons—"

"They've gone for the military application rather than the safety aspect," said McCoy with an edge of disapproval in his voice. "It's nice to know they're following form, at least."

"Quite so, Doctor. I doubt that you would like Klingon transporters. Everything that you believe about the equipment aboard *Enterprise* is true of theirs. So much so that high-ranking officers have personal transport controllers responsible for their safety."

"Huh," said Bones noncommittally. It was impossible to tell whether he thought the idea good, bad, or typically Klingon in that there was someone to take the rap for a mistake.

Jim hadn't become involved in the discussion; he spent the short trip leaning against the back wall of the turbolift car with his arms folded, waiting until he reached the bridge, where he would find out what else the universe had up its sleeve to throw at him. One element of Spock's theory disturbed him, though. "What about the power consumption?" he said. "It's got to be ridiculously large."

"The sensor scans give every indication that this particular Klingon cruiser has a power-production curve well able to match the most extravagant demands," said Spock. Jim didn't like the sound of what Spock was saying, and liked the sound of what he didn't say still less: *Anything they want, it can do—with power to spare.*

The turbolift slid to a halt and opened onto the bridge. Jim walked into a scene of controlled scurrying as department heads took over from their deputies. He realized that he had become more accustomed to seeing the place in red-alert lighting than in standard white. The superimposed tactical plot on the main screen was one of the least encouraging pieces of graphic design that he had seen for a very long time; there were altogether too many contacts whose only ID symbology was an assigned DK registry and the words Unknown/Hostile.

Six new blips—the armed vessels stolen by the PDF terrorists were rising steadily toward orbit. There were none of the massive infrared traces that had characterized the previous booster-assisted launches. That meant there was no chance they might be a flight of missiles, but it also indicated that these orbiters were of a more advanced type than the old space shuttles the Dekkani had used for their earlier harassment. The effectiveness of *their* armament had already been conclusively demonstrated.

Nearest of all, the image not quite hidden beneath the tactical overlay, was KL 1017 *Hakkarl*. The battle cruiser was winding up from orbital shutdown to active status, and the data readouts beside the crank-winged silhouette that was the standard tactical symbol for a Klingon vessel were changing too quickly for the eye to follow.

"What a wonderful view we're having today," said Bones.

Spock lifted an eyebrow at him. "Stimulating, certainly," he said. "And full of useful information."

"Bridge to Engineering," said Jim, not taking his eyes from the screen as he thumbed the seat communicator. "How are we doing down there?"

"Ye can have power for shields or weapons or maneuverin', but not for all of them jist yet," said Mr. Scott. *"The intermix is readin' green, but since we've had the mains off line we'll not be up an' runnin' for another twenty seconds."*

Jim clenched a fist and swore softly under his breath. Scotty hadn't sounded accusing, bless him, but *Enterprise* had still been shut down on the order of her captain and nobody else. *That'll teach you to assume things about Klingons,* thought Jim. It didn't help that *Vanguard* and *Sir Richard* were in the same situation and for the same reason; spreading a mistake around didn't help change wrong to right. "Divert all available power to the shields, and Scotty . . . ?"

"Aye, sir?"

"Quick as you can."

"Aye, sir!"

Hakkarl's data began to flash green on the viewscreen as the battle cruiser achieved nominal power output, but the figures continued to change. "They're raising shields, Captain," said Spock.

"Raise ours: shields two and three full power, full deflection; one and four, maintenance only—but watch out for any change in firing arc."

"Shield setting confirmed, aye," said Chekov. "Shall I set up a precautionary weapons lock, Keptin?"

Jim hesitated for a moment. He didn't want to start an escalating spiral of threat and counterthreat, but bending the rules didn't seem to work where Captain Kasak was concerned. The safest refuge was in doing things exactly by the book. "Yes, Mr. Chekov. Do it—but nothing else without my direct command. We don't have any power to spare."

"You do now, Captain," said Spock, swinging around from his monitors. "The mains are back on line; we have full power."

"Good timing, Scotty," Jim said to the bridge in general. "Mr. Chekov, boost the other shields up to defense standard. Mr. Sulu, stand by to put some distance between us and the Klingons. One-third impulse power, on my mark. . . ."

Jim never gave that order, for the screen had developed some sort of a glitch and strange things were happening. The data display for *Hakkarl* had started to flicker between a single and a double image, both readouts showed different instead of duplicated information, and both were flashing green. Spock moved controls on the sensor suite and the displays stabilized. It wasn't a glitch after all, but the information from two separate ships—even though they weren't separate just yet.

"Reset that phaser lock, Chekov," said Jim. "It looks as if things are going to get busy around here." The tactical projection broke up just then, and when it reformed with updated information just a moment later, Jim realized that he hadn't guessed the half of it.

The six PDI shuttles had achieved orbit a few seconds previously, and now they were assuming a standard small-ship attack formation. It was all too likely that they intended to do more than simply fly dangerously close. As if that wasn't enough, the eight original orbiters that had been such a bloody nuisance at the start of the mission had broken out of their polar holding orbits, and were now sliding up toward where the Federation ships were held immobile by the requirements of a geosynch parking position.

And *that* wasn't enough either.

"Visual," said Spock abruptly, clearing the screen of its tangle of plots and vectors. "All recording systems are enabled and set to automatic."

"Ship separation, Mr. Spock?"

"Imminent, if I read these power curves correctly. A violently evasive maneuver seems most probable in the . . ." Spock's voice trailed to silence, and he shifted his attention to the main viewer with a little intake of breath that Bones and Jim recognized as annoyance. "Or perhaps not," he finished.

Spock was not the only person on the bridge who had expected a dramatic full-power breakaway. What actually happened came as something of an anticlimax. The Bird of Prey *Tazhat* lifted clear of its parent vessel as slowly and as cautiously as a newly qualified pilot taking up a hover-flier for the first time.

Tazhat's upward motion ceased, and it hung bare tens of meters over the dorsal surface of *Hakkarl's* main hull. With equal slowness, both ships rotated until they were facing in opposite directions, presenting starboard and port elevations to *Enterprise*—like the ID profiles in the library computer. It was almost as if Captain Kasak was deliberately flaunting the size and power of his command to the man who had hoped to seize it. Indeed, he seemed to be daring Kirk to fire point-blank at this target, render it immobile, and claim it as his prize.

"Captain," said Spock urgently, cutting off that dangerous line of thought before it grew any more attractive, "long-range scans are picking up multiple contacts dropping out of warp. All of them are Klingon."

The scout and the cruiser went transparent, shimmered, faded, and were gone.

"Hell and damnation!" The words were relatively mild, but they were spoken in a voice so loaded with vicious sincerity that heads turned all over the bridge to where Captain James Kirk cleared his throat and went slightly pink. Only Mr. Spock pretended not to have noticed anything.

"Feel better now?" said Bones, leaning over the back of the center seat.

Jim nodded, and smiled crookedly at his chief medical officer. "Somewhat. But I should have suspected a cloaking device."

"Suspect away. It wouldn't have helped even if Kasak had told you about it himself. What could you have done about it—opened fire?"

"And blown all their engines into scrap, yes. I was so tempted, Bones. They were just sitting there, begging for it."

"I suspect the Klingon captain hoped you'd do just that, Jim," said Spock. "Hoped he could provoke you into acting rashly and thus placing yourself and the Federation in violation of the Organian Treaty. If the behavior of those covert Imperial security agents means what I believe, Kasak and his ships are here without official orders and without the knowledge of his government and his superiors. If necessary the Empire can repudiate his actions and refuse to be responsible for the actions of a mutinous privateer—unless of course the Empire stands to gain something. If so, the Klingons will claim that Kasak was acting under orders all the time."

"Spock," said Bones, "it's been a long day and I'm probably getting a bit slow, but—what can the Klingon Empire hope to gain from this?"

"This planet," said Spock simply. "Ceded to the

Klingon Empire under the terms of the Organian Treaty."

"I worked that one out for myself down in Rec One," said Jim. "But the way I saw it, all Kasak has to do is wait until we've gone and then 'persuade' the Dekkan Council to request Imperial protection. Why drag the Organians into it?"

"As for that, Captain, I must confess to ignorance based on a lack of information. When Starfleet Intelligence answers your questions about Kasak sutai-Khornezh, his reasoning may become a little clearer. In the meantime there is a Klingon battle group of nine more K't'inga class cruisers entering this system, and their squadron leader wants to speak with you on a matter of some urgency."

"Does he indeed?" said Jim, and swung his chair around to face the main viewer. "Then let's find out just how urgent it can be."

"I am Korzhan epetai-Kenek," the Klingon said, his speech heavily formal. *"You are Admiral Kirk of the Federation Starfleet. You have possession of a stolen thing that is not yours. I want it back."* Although his title for this duty was squadron leader, the rank insignia at his collar was that of an admiral. It indicated several things about the importance of this mission, and about the importance of the ship that Captain Kasak had stolen.

Since the battle cruiser *Hakkarl* was nowhere in sight, and since the Dekkan shuttles were the only other ships in the area besides the Klingon and Starfleet vessels, Jim wondered how Korzhan had reached his conclusion. He realized, moments later, that the Klingon admiral thought the other ships had been put into cloak by a prize crew from the *Enterprise.*

Korzhan was in no mood for explanations. *"This one has recorded information concerning the mutineer Kasak sutai-Khornezh,"* he said. *"Information that was transmitted from your own ship. It is proof of treason against the Qomerex Tlhingan, and proof of your collusion."*

Jim listened to the Klingon, but most of his attention was focused on the tracking display that had been keeping an electronic eye on all the Dekkan shuttles. It was only when they had moved out of the immediate vicinity that he gave his full attention to Korzhan.

"Squadron Leader," he said, "neither I nor the other captains of this force had anything to do with the matter you refer to. Captain Kasak, on the other hand—"

"Requested political asylum so as to evade punishment. He secured your cooperation by offering you the secrets of his ship!"

"Your information is not accurate," Kirk said. "His request for asylum was part of whatever game Kasak is playing. I know neither the rules of that game nor its ultimate goal." *Unlike you, Korzhan. You know all about it.* Jim shifted in his seat and realized that the Klingon might even know why Kasak was trying to draw fire down on himself. If only the Intelligence data had arrived before Korzhan's squadron, or before Kasak's escape or . . .

The communications console beeped. Uhura tapped switches, looked at her repeater screen, and smiled. "Captain, here's that information you requested," she said.

Jim released the breath he hadn't known that he was holding. *Better late than too late,* he thought. "Leave it on your screen please, Uhura. And run a hard copy." He turned back to Squadron Leader Korzhan on the main viewscreen, inclined his head in

220

the sort of curt nod that would never grow up to be a bow, and got to his feet. "You will excuse me, of course," he said. "Starfleet business."

A few minutes later, everything had become a great deal easier to understand.

"Squadron Leader," said Jim, "I may have the answer to our mutual dilemma." Korzhan looked puzzled and said nothing. "Is there an access to personnel files from your flagship's main library computer?"

"What bearing has this?"

"More than you might think. Have your science specialist pull Captain Kasak's file and cross-check with"—Jim read through the data on the screen again, knowing that mistakes and consequent delays were something he didn't need—"Captain Koloth vestai-Lasshar; Space Station K-Seven; the reams of information you must have on me and on the U.S.S. *Enterprise;* and, uh, tribbles."

Korzhan looked at him as if uncertain whether this Federation captain was insulting him or had simply taken leave of his senses. Then he shrugged, turned away from the screen, and started giving orders.

Bones looked again at the Kasak file. "Now, that makes a whole lot of things a whole lot clearer. The crafty, sneaky little son of a bitch."

"It is probably as well that the sutai-Khornezh preferred subtlety over a more direct approach," Spock told McCoy. "He had ample opportunity while he was aboard the *Enterprise* to leave Jim in a state not even you could put back together."

McCoy straightened up and looked at the Vulcan in surprise. "Why, Spock, did I just hear a compliment?"

"If a compliment is the recognition of abilities it would be illogical to ignore, Doctor, then, yes, you did."

"Gentlemen," said Jim, "the admiral is back."

Korzhan looked confused. *"Kirk,"* he said, *"how much of this is true?"*

"All of it. Squadron Leader, what you have read was presumably drawn from your own intelligence reports. If you question them, then I can't help you."

"And where is Hakkarl?"

"Cloaked, but I believe still somewhere in this system."

"Message from *Vanguard,* Captain," Uhura interrupted, sounding angry. "The PDI-held shuttles have opened fire on them. No damage done, but Captain Farey recommends caution."

"Damn them! Why now?" muttered Jim. "Engineering."

"Scott here, Captain. We're shovelin' as fast as we can."

"Scotty, get some of your stokers up to the tractor installations. I think we're about to have company."

"You mean apart from Klingons? Captain, I canna thank ye enough."

"Don't try. Just get those tractors manned."

"Tractors, Kirk?" scoffed Squadron Leader Korzhan. *"Can the Federation no longer afford to fit phasers to its ships?"*

"The Federation doesn't use phasers on people it is protecting."

"Those same people have ordered the Federation off their planet and out of their star system. What reason remains for protection?"

The answers to that one were various, but since most were insulting to Korzhan, his race, and his presence here, Jim didn't bother to answer.

"Here they come," said Sulu, saving Jim from further questions. With the ship already at condition one, there were no raucous sirens when the sensors picked up the approaching shuttles. Instead they were announced by a decorous chime and a tactical plot superimposed in three colors on Squadron Leader Korzhan's face.

Jim, for one, found it an improvement, but was too tactful to say so.

"The epetai-Kenek will pardon me," he said, "but this one has a matter of imminent importance requiring all his attention. Kirk out."

The Klingon face broke up in sparkle and became a double-V formation of spacecraft rising above the curve of Dekkanar's horizon. They looked more rakish—and more dangerous—than the cumbersome orbiters that the Dekkani had first sent up, and they moved with a good deal more purpose.

"Weapons, Spock?"

"Scanning." The Vulcan stared down his hooded viewer for several minutes, then punched its download controls and sat back. "No energy weapons," he said with more relief than he allowed to show on his face. "They have a crude radar-based target-acquisition system, and they are armed with active-homing solid fuel missiles."

"Primitive," said Jim. "But are they dangerous? Are the missiles nuclear-tipped?"

"I doubt it, Captain. The one they used to shoot down *Sir Richard*'s shuttlecraft was a conventional warhead."

"Bridge to Engineering."

"Aye, Captain?"

"Scotty, are the tractors ready on standby?"

"They are that. Jis say the word."

"The word is 'careful.' I'm authorizing free fire at operator's discretion. Just don't pull the shuttles into each other, or us, or anything else—and that includes the Klingon ships."

"Och, Captain." The sigh of resignation was heartfelt, and Jim still didn't know how much of Scotty's

223

attitude was a put-on. *"Aye, well, all right, sir. Then I reckon it does."*

"You reckon right. Kirk out." Jim stared at the incoming orbiters and wondered which one of them had shot down that last shuttlecraft as it lifted from the Federation consulate. Did the person who had done it care that he had killed eight people, or would there be an impassioned freedom fighters' argument to explain why such things had to happen, to benefit the Movement? He didn't really want to know, in case the temptation to forget about the tractors and instead issue that free-fire order to Chekov and his phaser banks became too strong.

One of Defense's threat receptors beeped as a target-acquisition sensor swept over them, then warbled an alert as it locked on. The orbiters carried their missiles inboard on a rotary ventral tray. The first of them was plainly visible as it streaked from its launching rail in a flare of light and heat toward *Enterprise*.

"What do you think they're trying to prove?" said Jim. "Pigheadedness or suicidal tendencies?"

"They'd call it stubborn courage in the face of odds," said Bones, "and what does Scott think that he's doing, waiting all this—"

The missile jerked violently sideways in a ninety-degree change of course that didn't merely break the homing lock but broke the missile too. The massive stress was too much for its structural integrity, and though the long, slim body tried to flex, it snapped in half like a stick of celery. Propellant and warhead went up together in a vivid puff of flame; but by that time Scotty's people were attending to the next one.

They dealt with the shuttles, too, flipping them one by one and two by two around the *Enterprise* in parabolic curves so wild and whirling that neither the pilots nor their electronics had a chance to lock on long enough to do the starship any harm.

224

Jim's chair-arm communicator whistled, and when he switched it on, Admiral Korzhan was laughing at him. Spock half turned to look toward the sound, then raised his eyebrow to an angle that spoke volumes. "I have noticed this before," he said. "Repeated encounters tend to confirm the theory that Klingons are easily amused."

"*Kirk,*" said Korzhan, recovering his self-control with elaborate difficulty, "*I now believe your claim of innocence in the theft of* Hakkarl. *Nobody who lacks the nerve to defend his own ship, as a ship should be defended, would have enough blood in his liver to try to steal from the Klingon Empire.*"

"I'm glad that you find all of this so humorous, Squadron Leader," Jim said dryly. "At least something's managed to convince you."

The Klingon-accented chuckling stopped abruptly; there was no point in a joke if the butt of it refused to recognize the humor. "*You are innocent by default, Kirk,*" rasped Korzhan. His voice had gone cold and angry, and Jim fancied he didn't like being so thoroughly shot down in front of his own bridge crew. "*But it is my intention to remain here until I discover where guilt is to be found.*"

"Only if you're asked to stay, Korzhan. Remember the treaty terms. If the Dekkani don't want you in their sky, you can't stay."

"*And who will make me leave? You and your three ships, Kirk? They will be long gone once this evacuation is concluded. And as for these gadfly shuttles, they would never dare make any move against my squadron.*"

The angle of view on *Enterprise*'s screen was changing, tracking around to follow the PDI shuttles as they regained a semblance of formation after their mauling by the tractors. Jim looked at it, then looked again, harder. "Mr. Sulu, magnification level five, please."

What the lower setting had only suggested was revealed now to be completely true: the terrorists were starting an attack run on Korzhan's squadron.

Bones stared, not believing that any sentient being could be so crazy. "Jim, you were right when you mentioned suicidal tendencies. They'll be cut to pieces." He watched silently for a few more seconds, then said, "Warn the squadron leader. Ask him not to return fire."

For a moment, Jim saw not the screen and his chief medical officer, but a Starfleet shuttlecraft exploding as finally as that missile had done, spilling out dead people instead of electronic guidance chips. *Let the terrorists get what's coming to them,* he thought. *We can't do it—we're the good guys—but the Klingons will oblige.* He shivered at letting such a thought inside his head, then reopened his link to the Klingon flagship and to Korzhan.

It was very quiet on *Tazhat*'s bridge. The killings, the confusion, and the narrow escape had served to sober all of them. "Report status," said Kasak. His first rage at the intruding squadron had died down by now, but it was only the difference between an oil-soaked blaze and a raked, banked, slow-burning fire of coals.

"We are cloaked," said Askel. "*Hakkarl* is cloaked also. His power output is constant full. All weapons are charged." He touched controls, put a tactical display on the screen. "Relative positions give free crossfire in five directions, as I now show. And we may escape—"

"Escape?" There was threat in the way Kasak said it.

"Execute withdrawal," Askel corrected, "through this quadrant. Shown." He operated the controls

226

again and cleared the screen of all but its visual image. "Awaiting orders."

"Viewer track right, show mag four, hold."

They watched as the orbiters attempted to press home an attack on *Enterprise,* and laughed quietly as the starship employed tractors to fling the little ships aside. Kirk showed a fine contempt for *kuve* opponents, worthy of a Klingon; it would make bringing dishonor to his name that much the sweeter. But then they saw how the orbiters regrouped and continued their assault on the next ships in their path, regardless of the fact that those were the nine K't'inga cruisers of Korzhan's squadron.

"Are they brave or stupid?" said Force Leader Marag in wonderment.

Weapons Specialist Katta leaned over her console for a moment, comparing her readouts with those scanned from the squadron. "Both. Then dead."

Invisible to eyes and sensors alike, they settled back in comfort to watch the sport until Captain Kasak said "Stations" in the deadly tone of one who had not yet given any order to relax. He studied them well from where he sat in the command chair, then glanced at the foot repeaters and said, "Weapons, precision fire."

"Targeting which shuttle, sir?" said Katta, tracking prelock triangles from one to the other until ordered where to stop and fire.

"No shuttle. Target the battle cruiser nearest to them."

If the bridge had been quiet before, it was stunned now into utter silence. No head turned or lifted from monitor or station, but eyes slid sideways to meet other eyes and to wonder what the captain was planning now. There was no outcry of protest as there might have been before: the sutai-Khornezh had requested too many strange things on this first flight, things that had later proved to be wise, or cunning, and always the proper thing to do.

Kasak took note of it and struck his hands together. "Good!" he said. "You have learned at last. Now: target starboard engine, disabling only, affirm action."

"Acting."

"Lock on."

"Affirm."

"Fire!"

It was the viewing angle, nothing more deliberate, that put the Klingon battle cruiser *Tarkan* square in the middle of the viewscreen at the moment when his starboard engine and part of the supporting wing were chopped away. Because of that accident of position, only the bridge crew of the *Enterprise* and that ship's visual flight recorder log saw that the explosion had not been caused by any sort of missile. The actinic blue track of a shipboard disrupter had been brief, but all too plain. And the most appalling part was that the firing ship hadn't needed to decloak. . . .

Admiral Korzhan's response was typically Klingon: his flagship locked every disrupter battery that could be brought to bear onto the approaching targets and, without issuing further warnings, opened fire. The leading Dekkan orbiter instantly became an expanding cloud of debris—and Jim's hailing frequency broke up, swamped by the raw energy of the weapon discharge. Whatever he might have said to Korzhan was lost in a screech of static.

The main viewscreen's tactical overlay showed the other eight shuttles already within easy range, and the Klingons weren't likely to waste time scanning them when achieving a disrupter lock was just as easy. Another orbiter flared up, then collapsed into a spitting globe of irradiated scrap, and made the Klingons' intentions for every other potentially hostile target only too clear.

Terrorists or not, the people on those orbiters were under Federation protection. Until Uhura managed to filter the channel back down to something that could be used for communication, there were only two things Jim could do to prevent a massacre: move *Enterprise* between the Dekkani shuttles and the massed firepower of Korzhan's squadron . . .

Or order Chekov to open fire.

His stomach cramped into a knot as he thought of the consequences of either decision. Federation starships were well shielded, but not well enough to survive the punishment that nine K't'inga class battle cruisers could hand out if the Organians weren't around to stop them. He could get himself and his entire crew killed, and his ship destroyed, to protect a bunch of terrorists who probably couldn't care less about them. And the other alternative was worse.

If the Organians regarded this sector as part of the Treaty Zone, and *didn't* regard Jim's action as correct and necessary, they would immobilize *Enterprise*'s phasers, so that the Dekkani would be butchered anyway. The Organians would also be completely within their rights to hand Dekkanar over to the Klingon Empire as a penalty for the violation of firing unprovoked on a cosignatory. Just as Captain Kasak had intended all along.

A third armed orbiter exploded, and Jim realized that, right or wrong, he had to do something before any more of these stupid, malicious—and plainly helpless—civilian terrorists were killed. Those who had committed murder were probably already dead, and as for the remainder, their only crime was to have made bloody nuisances of themselves. It wasn't enough to die for.

"Sulu, one-half impulse power. Get *Enterprise* into

the line of fire before Korzhan's entire squadron opens up." He was aware of shocked stares from all over the bridge, and equally aware that his own voice was far steadier than it had any reason to be as he fitted a sort of weak grin onto his face. "Maybe they'll be so surprised they'll hold their fire."

And then the hailing frequency came back on line.

The bridge crew of the *Enterprise* had probably never been so happy to see a Klingon's ugly face as they were to see Admiral Korzhan now. Jim Kirk talked fast, as fast as he had ever done in such a situation—and to such effect that the Klingon admiral glowered doubtfully for no more than a second before calling a general cease-fire. On the tactical display that overlaid Korzhan's face, Jim watched as the surviving orbiters and their unarmed companions fled over the horizon and out of the line of fire before making a very fast unscheduled reentry and descent down to the planet's surface. Only when they were safely gone did he breathe a bit more easily. Jim delicately wiped the perspiration from his palms and brow and upper lip, drew another easy breath, and began explaining facts and theories to Korzhan epetai-Kenek. At a speed rather more appropriate to comfort and to the dignity of their rank.

"So that was Kasak's intention," said Korzhan grimly. *"To provoke you by provoking me. He knew that the Organian glowbugs would not be troubled by an internal quarrel among Klingons. Such disagreements are . . . not uncommon. It was a good plan—unless it worked against the Empire, as it might have done had you persisted in this madness of making your starship a shield for those Dekkan fools."*

He had watched the relevant part of the flight recorder data, had heard statements from Sulu, Chekov, and several others, and had been convinced

—eventually. Jim was surprised by that; pragmatism was not a trait he had encountered much in Klingons. This squadron leader had evidently been selected for good sense and restraint rather than aggressiveness, in an attempt to put a stop to all those instances along the borders of the Organian Treaty Zones where overhasty Klingon captains had burned their fingers and the Empire's. It was a fortunate choice for all concerned; the present situation had enough of a hair trigger already.

The admiral smiled, no more than a stretching of lips back from teeth. *"Kasak might have caused us to forfeit an imperial world instead of gaining one. This will not be forgotten. I will speak with you again, Kirk,"* said Korzhan, and broke off the connection.

"Captain," said Uhura, "Chief Councillor Varn is requesting you speak with him. He's somewhat agitated and got more so when I told him whom you were talking to. Shall I put him up on the screen?"

"Yes, Uhura. Thank you." Talking to the wily Varn would be a holiday after Korzhan epetai-Kenek, and Jim was no longer disposed, or required, to put up with any of the old man's bluster. The chief councillor would use language appropriate to a diplomatic exchange or Jim wouldn't listen to what he had to say."

In the event, Varn spoke like someone calling the police to come and prevent his house from being burgled. *That was appropriate enough,* thought Jim, *if a little late.* Planetside, it seemed things had gone a little crazy. The realization that an entire Klingon battle squadron had somehow been invited into orbit, and that as a result the Federation ships present were heavily outnumbered, had thrown what presently passed for the Dekkan government into a panic.

They had ordered the Federation representatives off-planet, but failed to negotiate any military or diplomatic protection to fill the gap. The instant the

Klingon squadron arrived, the Dekkani realized that their world and their culture were wide open, not for development but for exploitation. And they knew that so far as the Empire was concerned, the PDI terrorists in their little ships were likely to start something that only the Klingons would finish.

It all came out in a tumble of words that little time for breath and none whatsoever for the haughtiness Jim had heard before. "Councillor Varn," he said during his first chance to get a word in, "this is not a matter for me to decide. There are Federation diplomats on the other two ships of this force. As you should well know. Address your problems to them. And, Councillor?"

"What is it, Kirk Admiral?"

"Remember the alternative. Kirk out."

Klingons were hunting Klingons. Korzhan's squadron was moving against the renegade Kasak, outraged that this passed-over failure had succeeded in making them all look like fools. All on board the *Enterprise* were aware of their new allies by now, and the general feeling was one of relief tinged with grimly ironic amusement.

James Kirk was not quite so relieved. The Klingons' assistance was welcome in tracking down *Hakkarl* and *Tazhat,* but it made the change in situation all too clear. If Kasak's cloaked ship was still in the sector and if Kasak had been monitoring the frequencies as a sensible defector should, he would know he could no longer claim association with the Empire—but he would also know that the political restraints on his actions were gone now, and for the same reason.

Spock, hands clasped behind his back, stood quietly beside the center seat. "Kasak is now a criminal, Captain. And any attack he might make on the *Enterprise* or on you would be in the nature of personal rather than political aggression. Even assuming that the Organians would intervene in this system, there is a considerable doubt that they would do so in such a circumstance. It would be outside the restrictions laid down in the treaty."

"What you're saying, Spock," said Bones, "is that Kasak's still got a state-of-the-art ship that we can't even see, and once he works all this out for himself, he'll try using it?"

"Laudably succinct, Doctor. It seems—"

And then *Enterprise* jolted, vibrating like a tuning fork as raw energy splattered against her shields and leaked through to the gravity and guidance systems. The main viewscreen went black. Bones grabbed the bridge handrail, but even then almost fell as a sine wave of grav fluctuations rippled through the ship. Her durasteel hull members groaned with the intolerable anguish of the stresses surging through them before shuddering back down to stillness again. But not silence; for the sirens were whooping again.

"It seems you were right, Mr. Spock," finished Jim, his voice deadly calm. "Have we got visual back yet?"

"Yes, sir." The screen came back to life with an astonishing image: nine Klingon battle cruisers were concentrating their fire on a single point, the source of that last shot, so that they formed the base of a distorted pyramid whose sides were a mesh of blue fire. Its apex flared intolerably bright: all that energy was splashing back from shields so powerful that they were radiating out into the ultraviolet.

Suddenly the firing ceased, and *Hakkarl* was back in view. Jim didn't know whether its cloaking device was damaged, overloaded, or merely bleeding off too much power now that it was involved in full-scale combat rather than the hit-and-run raids for which it was designed. All that mattered was that it could be seen and destroyed, and he waited for the other Klingon warships to close in for the kill.

Nothing happened. Instead of pressing home their attack until *Hakkarl* was no more than a swirl of irradiated particles, the ships of Korzhan's squadron fell back, withholding their final salvo. Then Communications chirped the presence of an incoming signal. At a nod from Jim, Uhura transferred it to the screen.

Squadron Leader Admiral Korzhan epetai-Kenek gazed levelly at Admiral James T. Kirk. He said nothing for several moments, merely looked long and hard, as if impressing Jim's face onto his mind. *"There is your enemy, Kirk,"* he said at last. *"And your battle, if he has power enough remaining to make a fight of it. Not mine."*

The screen went dead.

"They have given him to me," said Kasak softly. He had replayed the monitored transmission back three times before he spoke a single word. "Kirk and his ship are mine to destroy."

"This was not why we supported you," said Krynn. "Where is all the glory that the one promised in the winning of a planet for the Empire?"

"That is past," said Kasak. He was growing impatient with this pedantic insistence on less important matters while the *Enterprise* and Kirk were waiting to be killed. "Stations."

They did not move. Kasak stared at them, unbelieving for an instant, then grabbed for his pistol. Marag's huge hand came down on top of his and forced the disrupter back into its holster. "This is mutiny!" snarled Kasak, his teeth bared to the gums.

"No, Captain, it is wisdom. *Hakkarl's* cloak is destroyed, and you do not yet know what other damage has been done." Askel leaned forward, pulled the pistol's charge slide out and tucked the weapon behind his belt. "Imperial Intelligence was willing to defend even the wildest schemes of the sutai-Khornezh who was full of skill and brilliance." He was fully aware of the shocked way in which the others were all looking at him, and ignored it. "But not the one who is *bortaS straav.*'"

"What did you say?" Kasak's voice had dropped to no more than an exhalation of air; none present had ever heard him made so angry.

"Only the truth. A captain may not lead his ship and serve the Empire and yet be a slave to revenge. Something must lose. I"—he looked from side to side and nodded at the agreement he saw there—*"we* do not like to lose."

"Then go. Get off my ship."

"It is not your ship but the Empire's." Askel looked as though he might have said more, but the words remained unspoken. "But we will leave it, just the same. And leave it for you to hold as best you can."

Kasak stared at him for several seconds, then showed his teeth. "Better than you think, mutineer. Say what you will, this ship is mine, and *Hakkarl* is mine." He swung back the padding on one arm of the command chair and unlocked the security lid that covered a key pad beneath it.

"Mine to command," he said, touching keys in a coded sequence that brought different readouts to the data screens around the chair's base. Kasak entered a last command series, closed cover and padding, and pressed the switch that normally opened the intercom circuit. This time it caused changes in the very structure of the chair as panels slid back and additional equipment swung up, locking in place with small, solid sounds: thrust levers, a sidestick controller, a sensors board, a weapons status display—all devices more appropriate to a single-seat fighter. Kasak looked at them, then at his crew. "Mine to control," he said, and dismissed them by turning his back.

Askel shook his head at this stubbornness and made to follow the others from the bridge to the transporter room and thence to the flagship of Admiral Korzhan. But he paused at the door of the turbolift and glanced over one shoulder at this captain who had been his friend. "Success, sutai-Khornezh," he said. "Whatever has passed, you will be remembered with honor."

Askel entered the lift car and did not look back again. Its door closed, and he was gone.

"Full sensor scan completed, Captain." Spock studied the data for a few seconds. "Energy readings are residual, decaying fast, and more a result of irradiation during the bombardment than of activity on board the cruiser. I would say that *Hakkarl* is dead in space, except—"

"Except that it looked the same way last time," growled Bones.

"Precisely, Doctor."

"It sounds to me as if you don't trust your own instruments, Spock," said Jim, swinging his seat halfway around to study this phenomenon.

"The instruments are accurate. But I do not trust that Klingon ship. That machine. Without a living crew, it has no need for any power stages except on and off. That makes every deactivation a potential ambush."

They looked more closely at the battle cruiser, now hanging nose-down, slanted across the screen in an attitude that made it look totally derelict. Admiral Korzhan had given this enemy to them. It was unlikely he meant it as a gift or that his un-Klingon tolerance would outlast any effort to capture it. He had presented it as a target, whether in battle or as a hulk on a live-firing range. And there was no one on board anyway. . . .

Jim reached his decision. "Mr. Stewart, man the weapons console, arm photon torpedoes. Mr. Chekov, lock phasers on target; stand by on phasers and photon torpedoes. On my—"

"Captain! Power surge! Shields are—"

"Fire!"

The photon torpedoes spat from both tubes in a left-right-left-right ripple that for all its speed was not quite fast enough. In the bare seconds between the torpedoes' launch and their impact, the Klingon cruiser had raised full forward shields and at the same instant had begun the first phase of an impulse-powered evasion sequence. It vanished for a moment behind four blooms of white fire, an incandescent daisy chain of destruction two hundred kilometers long as the torpedoes altered course to track their suddenly moving target, and for that moment the watchers on the *Enterprise* shared a sickening feeling that it had gone back into cloak. Spock was the only person on the bridge who did not release an audible sigh of relief when the battle cruiser came back into view, and that only because his sensors had told him an instant before everyone else. The relief was short-lived, for *Hakkarl* was lined up on an attack course.

"Sulu, evasive," said Jim, and saw the Klingon ship heel wildly across the screen as *Enterprise* hit a savage combination break of yaw and roll and pitch all at the same time. He gulped as his stomach tried to keep pace with what his eyes said he should be feeling, despite insistence from his inner ear and the gravity field beneath him that nothing was wrong. Sulu wasn't using the automaneuvering protocols, that much was obvious: anybody trying to program that sort of behavior into a starship's guidance systems would be certified.

But it worked. *Hakkarl's* incoming fire seared under them and through where they had been with satisfying impotence, ionization and hard radiation sleeting off in its wake as the massive energy yield dissipated in atmosphere.

But any satisfaction generated by that evasion was squashed by the way the Klingon snapped around in pursuit. It was a maneuver that would have drawn shrieks of protest from Scotty and the pylon-stress monitors if Sulu had tried it with *Enterprise;* more than that, if the inertial compensators so much as flickered during such a wrenching turn, pulling forty-plus G at rock-bottom minimum, the entire crew would be smeared into paste.

But *Hakkarl* of course had no crew, and no energy drained off to maintain their good health, for that matter. Jim understood the thinking behind that very clearly now, because that spare power, and there seemed to be plenty for every demand, be it thrusters or weapons or shields, was now being channeled through the disrupters—and threatening *Enterprise* shields five and six with an imminent overload, warp-boosting or not.

It kept happening with a frightening inevitability: whatever impossible maneuver Sulu attempted, *Hakkarl* matched and exceeded, a little tighter, a little faster, much less concerned about structural violations.

Spock looked up from a monitor, his expression grave. "Captain," he said, "sensors indicate an overall reduction of shield efficiency to fifty-three percent of standard. Critical overload and total failure will occur in fifty-seven seconds unless we are given some respite from this constant battering."

In other words, do something or we're dead.

But what? Against a computer-crewed ship that could outmaneuver and outgun them a dozen times over, what could be done? Jim suspected that *Hakkarl*, unlike M5 or Nomad, would not be talked into its own destruction, nor could they simply pull the plug on it. . . .

Or could they?

Jim smiled tightly—a smile that, a few seconds later, the rest of the bridge crew was sharing, Mr. Spock, of course, being the sole exception. Now if it would work . . .

"We're in your hands, Mr. Sulu," said Jim softly. "Do your best."

"Sir," said the helmsman, his acknowledgment coming as if from very far away. Sulu leaned over the helm console, checking readouts and tapping controls, then straightened up, his hands poised. "Chekov, set prelocks dead ahead and stand by; I'll only be able to get away with this the first time, but you ought to have a target in three, two, one—"

Both hands came down, fingers spread, on the reaction-thruster controls. It was as if the rearmost shield had given way and let something through to the hull. *Enterprise* shook, then rattled, as she simultaneously dumped velocity and was shoved sideways out of her line of flight.

Taken unaware, *Hakkarl* went streaking past—straight into the prelock zone. Two photon torpedoes and the output from all of the forward phasers hit square and punched through to the primary hull, detonating on that section of plating where the scout ship *Tazhat* was carried, and where remote command transmissions were received. . . .

The battle cruiser reeled more violently than seemed justified even by four clean hits. It wobbled in space for what seemed like several minutes. Then all at once it regained its equilibrium and swung toward them again.

And kept on turning as *Hakkarl* swung by them

and toward an area of space between Korzhan's squadron and the other Federation ships. It was an area where there was nothing out of the ordinary to be seen, even with full sensor assistance; and that was, of course, the intended effect of a cloaking device.

Hakkarl, brain-damaged and blind, as Jim had intended, and lethal, was homing on the source of its own command signals—a circumstance he had *not* foreseen.

"Weapons are locking on, Captain," said Spock. On the viewer there was still nothing for them to lock onto. "Firing." Or to fire at. "Firing again."

Tazhat shivered out of cloak, pitching up and back on its plane axis like an animal acknowledging defeat by displaying an unprotected throat and belly. According to the screen readouts, the display had no effect on *Hakkarl*.

"Cruiser is firing for a third time." Spock glanced at a scrolling schematic and then returned his attention to the main viewer. "The Bird of Prey's shields are failing. Have failed. It is defenseless."

"Why has *Hakkarl* ceased firing?" wondered Chekov.

"It was programmed by Klingons," said Jim. "They take prizes for profit. Someone must have included surrender-recognition parameters, like dropping shields."

"Maybe they've stopped talking to each other," said Bones. The statement was less facetious than it sounded: *Tazhat*'s transmissions would have been combat maneuvers or weapon-firing instructions, and by the look of its behavior, continuing to follow such orders even when they became inappropriate, *Hakkarl* had an unfortunately large resident memory buffer.

And then the message from *Tazhat* came through.

Captain Kasak sutai-Khornezh sat as Jim had first seen him, on his bridge in his command chair, but this time it was smoke rather than atmosphere-moisture clouding the scene. Kasak wore no respirator mask, but was breathing the unfiltered fumes; he was already dying, from that as much as from the wound that had mangled his body. Fire stained the murk a dirty orange, and it was shot through with the sparks that spat from shattered consoles.

"Kirk . . . I see you have survived again." Kasak could have seen nothing of the sort. Splinters of screen from an exploding monitor had made certain of that. *"Be assured, this cannot last. You have made too many enemies during your years, and luck is a finite commodity. Somewhere out among the stars there will be another enemy waiting for you, one more fortunate than I. One day you will know the bitter flavor of the coldest dish, and in the Black Fleet I will know, and laugh."*

He laughed now, painfully, and blood shone on his teeth. *"So Hakkarl, too, is taken from me,"* Kasak said. *"There will be no more. Tazhat I keep."* Moving slowly, he stripped off his officer's sash and used it to tie his free hand to the command chair. "Kasakte kaase," he said. *"Witness it, Kirk. It would be good if you did not forget."* He touched a control, then sat back and made himself comfortable.

"Hakkarl has resumed its attack run," said Spock.

Jim did not reply. He was staring across a gulf that was more than simply empty space, looking at what might have been himself, and wondering how and when that gulf could be bridged so that a Klingon could stand aboard the *Enterprise* without suspicions of some ulterior motive. He was still wondering, still watching that figure, all alone in the chair and tied there by tradition far stronger than the mere fabric of a sash, when Spock said, very softly, "Firing." The image on the screen flared white, then black, and broke up in static.

The battle cruiser's firing pass lasted no more than a second, and when it was over Jim sat in silence, looking at the crackling interference on the viewer that nobody right now would switch off without orders. Finally he got to his feet. "Screen to exterior visual," he said.

Hakkarl hung there, truly dead in space now, as dead as anything that had blown out its own brains. Nothing but scrap. "Destroy that," Jim said. "Completely."

He didn't stay to watch his orders carried out, but turned his back on the bridge and went to his quarters and was alone with his thoughts and the darkness.

"The Klingon battle group is leaving orbit, Captain," said Uhura, "and their admiral wants to speak to you. I told him you were taking your first rest period after a long time on duty, and shouldn't be disturbed, but he was very, er, persuasive."

"Leaving orbit?" Jim was suddenly very much awake. "Put him on, Uhura—and thanks for being persuaded."

Korzhan epetai-Kenek gazed at him from the screen, and though Jim didn't know much about Klingon facial expressions, it struck him that this particular Klingon was at ease with his world. He was soon to learn the reason why.

"So you have seen our Great Experiment, Kirk," Korzhan said. *"As have we all. No one asked for or agreed with my opinion of it, but all have witnessed my vindication."* The image on the viewer drew itself up much straighter, and it gave Jim a small shock to suddenly realize just how very old, and therefore highly placed, the squadron leader had to be to get this particularly satisfying command. Vindication in-

deed, and satisfaction by the personal and political bushel.

"Know this, as they will know when I return: Klingons need no machines to do their fighting for them. Stand your force down from its battle stations, Kirk. There will be no more fighting done today, either by machines or by flesh and blood. Maybe we will meet again when both of us have different orders and no interfering Organian light bulbs to prevent a warrior from seeking glory. Until then, or until the Black Fleet, I salute you. Kai kassai, Enterprise. Kai kassai, Kirk."

The picture changed from an elderly Imperial race Klingon in a Navy uniform to nine bright specks accelerating out of the 4725 Cancri system, and James Kirk lay back on his bed and breathed easily for the first time in days.

The Klingon withdrawal had been the only item missing from a small catalog of good things that had quietly accumulated over the past four hours. Bones had repaired Todd Johnson's elbow, replacing the smashed original joint with a pattern-linked implant that was quite literally as good as new. The colonel was back with his people on the surface again, heading a peacekeeping police force that needed no weapons, no armor, and indeed had very little to do except sit in the sun—until the new, and by the sound of them, very easy negotiations for Federation tenancy began. *Vanguard* and *Sir Richard* had already returned to normal duties.

And *Enterprise* had been cleared to leave Dekkan space and head for Star Base 12.

The news of that was probably all over the ship by now, and Jim decided he might as well put sleeping back on hold until he had gone back to the bridge and made it all official. As soon as he checked on readiness with the department heads, they could actually get out of here. He began to close his eyes for just five more lazy minutes—and then opened them again, very wide, when the ceiling somehow grew a . . . glowbug.

Jim sat up very straight and very fast, and stared as the globe of pure energy drifted down to eye level. "Ayelborne?" he hazarded, pulling the name up through a dozen years of memory.

Claymare, corrected the voice in his head, without rancor for the mistake.

Organians, thought Jim, were probably a sufficiently advanced race to know that their energy forms were difficult to tell apart. Pity about their sense of timing, though.

There was no need, said Claymore, making Jim glad he hadn't thought anything more insulting. *We merely observed. It is pleasing that our intervention was not required.*

All the questions about that decision shot through Jim's brain, and he hoped the Organian was not so advanced that it couldn't recognize outrage when it heard some. However, since all the answers to those questions inevitably accompanied them, Claymare was saved the trouble of accounting for each one. *The conflicts of personal enemies, while regrettable, are not a part of the treaty,* it said, *and do not warrant intervention regardless of which party an individual might claim to represent. The late Captain Kasak acted throughout on a most erroneous assumption of our response.*

Jim considered all of the ways that he might have resolved the situation, ways he had discarded as being provocative but which evidently hadn't been anything of the kind, and slapped one hand against his forehead. He groaned softly; for some emotions, words were notoriously inadequate.

Kasak aside, said the Organian soothingly, *the reactions of both sides were most laudable. We are extremely pleased by this, and await further develop-*

ments with interest. Claymare's glowing light shrank and began to fade. *Captain James Kirk, we salute you. . . .*

Jim gazed across the empty room and blinked a couple of times to remove the purple afterimages from his vision. He reached for the communicator panel, then hesitated and decided that since no intruder alert had been sounded, he would save news of the Organian's visit for a more appropriate moment. Jim made a brief official note of the incident in his personal log. That would do for now. Then he pulled on his boots, shrugged into his tunic and made for the bridge.

From the looks he got as he stepped from the lift, Jim knew that his crew knew what had ended his off-shift so early. *Shipboard gossip strikes again,* he thought, and wondered what the grapevine would make of the visitor—once he got round to officially transferring the log entry. Right now there were more urgent matters needing attention.

Such as shore leave.

"Shore leave?" he heard Chekov mutter in a tone of studied incredulity. "But my calendar says that this *was* shore leave!"

"Oh, no, Mr. Chekov," said Jim, grinning. "This was just practice. Now you get to survive the real thing. Lay in a course for Star Base Twelve, if you please. Mr. Sulu, take us out of orbit. One-half impulse power till we're at the perimeter, then warp factor six."

They turned from the planet and returned to the stars.

THE STAR TREK PHENOMENON

____ ABODE OF LIFE
70596/$4.50

____ BATTLESTATIONS!
70183/$4.50

____ BLACK FIRE
70548/$4.50

____ BLOODTHIRST
70876/$4.50

____ CORONA
66341/$3.95

____ CHAIN OF ATTACK
66658/$3.95

____ THE COVENANT OF
THE CROWN
67072/$3.95

____ CRISIS ON CENTAURUS
65753/$3.95

____ DEEP DOMAIN
70549/$4.50

____ DEMONS
70877/$4.50

____ DOUBLE, DOUBLE
66130/$3.95

____ DREADNOUGHT
66500/$3.95

____ DREAMS OF THE RAVEN
70281/$4.50

____ DWELLERS IN THE
CRUCIBLE
66088/$3.95

____ ENTERPRISE
65912/$4.50

____ ENTROPY EFFECT
66499/$3.95

____ FINAL FRONTIER
69655/$4.95

____ THE FINAL REFLECTION
70764/$4.50

____ HOW MUCH FOR JUST
THE PLANET?
62998/$3.95

____ IDIC EPIDEMIC
70768/$4.50

____ ISHMAEL
66089/$3.95

____ KILLING TIME
70597/$4.50

____ KLINGON GAMBIT
70767/$4.50

____ THE KOBAYASHI MARU
65817/$4.50

____ MEMORY PRIME
70550/$4.50

____ MINDSHADOW
70420/$4.50

____ MUTINY ON
THE ENTERPRISE
67073/$3.95

____ MY ENEMY, MY ALLY
70421/$4.50

____ PAWNS AND SYMBOLS
66497/$3.95

____ PROMETHEUS DESIGN
67435/$3.95

____ ROMULAN WAY
70169/$4.50

____ RULES OF ENGAGEMENT
66129/$4.50

____ SHADOW LORD
66087/$3.95

____ SPOCK'S WORLD
66773/$4.95

____ STRANGERS FROM
THE SKY
65913/$4.50

____ THE TEARS OF THE
SINGERS
69654/$4.50

____ TIME FOR YESTERDAY
70094/$4.50

____ THE TRELLISANE
CONFRONTATION
70095/$4.50

____ TRIANGLE
66251/$3.95

____ UHURA'S SONG
65227/$3.95

more on next page...

THE

STAR TREK

PHENOMENON

_____ **VULCAN ACADEMY MURDERS**
64744/$3.95

_____ **VULCAN'S GLORY**
65667/$3.95

_____ **WEB OF THE ROMULANS**
70093/$4.50

_____ **WOUNDED SKY**
66735/$3.95

_____ **YESTERDAY'S SON**
66110/$3.95

• •

_____ **STAR TREK– THE MOTION PICTURE**
67795/$3.95

_____ **STAR TREK II– THE WRATH OF KHAN**
67426/$3.95

_____ **STAR TREK III–THE SEARCH FOR SPOCK**
67198/$3.95

_____ **STAR TREK IV– THE VOYAGE HOME**
70283/$4.50

_____ **STAR TREK V– THE FINAL FRONTIER**
68008/$4.50

_____ **STAR TREK: THE KLINGON DICTIONARY**
66648/$4.95

_____ **STAR TREK COMPENDIUM REVISED**
62726/$9.95

_____ **MR. SCOTT'S GUIDE TO THE ENTERPRISE**
70498/$12.95

_____ **THE STAR TREK INTERVIEW BOOK**
61794/$7.95

POCKET
B O O K S

Simon & Schuster Mail Order Dept. STP
200 Old Tappan Rd., Old Tappan, N.J. 07675

Please send me the books I have checked above. I am enclosing $_____ (please add 75¢ to cover
postage and handling for each order. N.Y.S. and N.Y.C. residents please add appropriate sales tax). Send
check or money order–no cash or C.O.D.'s please. Allow up to six weeks for delivery. For purchases over
$10.00 you may use VISA: card number, expiration date and customer signature must be included.

Name_____

Address_____

City_____ State/Zip_____

VISA Card No._____ Exp. Date_____

Signature _____ 118-25